Civil Hearts

A Haunted Romance

Claire Gem

I dedicate this book, as I do all my writing accomplishments, to Clark. He has been my inspiration & my muse for over 47 years on this earth, and will continue in that role from 2025 forward... from Heaven.

Chapter One

Liv

"If you want authentic Greek Revival, this is as close as you're gonna get. The last coat of paint on those columns was barely dry when the newlyweds moved in. In . . . " he paused, checking the papers stuck in his clipboard, "April, 1861. Only five days before our boys in gray attacked Fort Sumter."

Thomas Edwards fit the profile of a used car salesman, not a real estate agent. Even his name rang of "alias." No matter. Camellia, a town that barely deserved its own miniscule dot on my GPS screen, boasted only one realtor. Edwards was it.

I felt guilty standing on the sparse grass. The pale blades were obviously having a hard-enough time hanging on in the sand, starved of sunlight by the massive live oaks above. They're a little like me, I mused. Living in the shadow of all that came before. Uncertain if their roots would hold them fast. Anywhere.

Edwards plucked a reed and stuck it between his teeth. He studied me for a long, silent moment with a furrowed brow. His next words were softer, trying to disguise his curiosity with shallow sympathy.

"What on earth is a sophisticated city lady like you going to do in a big, old antebellum house?" He turned, sweeping an arm toward the grove of ancient oaks flanking the house, the acres of open pasture behind it. "Here. In the middle of nowhere?"

I folded my arms across my chest and turned to face him

square on. "Start over, Mr. Edwards. Start my entire life over, in a completely different fashion."

Edwards pulled off his battered golf cap and scratched a balding head. "Did you want to take a look inside?"

I studied the regal exterior of the two-story house. It was a mansion. At least, it had been at one time. A wedding gift to a wealthy plantation owner's daughter, Edwards told me. A bride who ended up a widow by the time the last Civil War cannon fired in 1865. The list of deed owners, over the last 150 years, was short, with big gaps in between.

The once-white paint was yellowed now, peeling around the casements. One of the windows on the second-floor balcony sported plywood like a lopsided bandage. Dead leaves and untethered Spanish moss choked the corners of both porches, above and below. The house looked tired, weatherworn. Sad. Lonely.

We had some things in common, this house and me.

Peeking around the side of the building was the barn Edwards had told me about. Its exterior boards had mellowed to a silvery grey. The top half of a Dutch door hung open and askew.

"I'd like to see the barn first," I said, though I wasn't sure why. A gut feeling? Curiosity?

I'd grown up in a suburb of Boston, then moved to Manhattan when I married at nineteen. Never spent any time on a farm. Never even owned a dog. Yet as we made our way through the wispy grass in that direction, I could almost envision a horse pricking curious ears from over the Dutch door.

I'd never owned a horse, either. A childhood dream, one never consummated. The longing had faded with the onset of puberty.

Well, I was following a fantasy, so I might as well go all

the way.

The aroma of freshly cut pine engulfed my senses as we stepped inside. Three new, roomy box stalls lined the front wall, each with its own Dutch door leading to a community paddock. Edwards explained the previous buyer had fancied keeping his daughter's horses here. He'd completed the reconstruction on the barn before they'd even moved in.

They never had. When I asked why, the realtor turned away from me, shaking his head.

"Not really sure, Ms. Larson. I just got the word one day that the family had changed their minds. Wanted the place relisted."

"How long ago?" I asked.

He sighed. "Almost three years ago. Went into foreclosure within a year after they quit paying the mortgage."

I knew the house was bank-owned, and had been empty for a long time. No renovation had been done on the house itself, just the barn. It was actually one of the details about the place that appealed to me. A project, I thought. A blank canvas I could redesign to suit me. The new me.

Whoever the hell that was.

"Why Alabama?" My best friend, Delphine, wrinkled her nose and squealed the state's name like it soured her mouth. "Do you have family there or something?"

I raised an eyebrow and glared at her. "You know I have no family, Del. Josh was all the family I had." I lifted my wine glass and sipped, but my usual favorite chardonnay's delicate tones of lime and citrus puckered my tongue like vinegar. I looked away, vowing not to give in to another bout of choking emotion.

"What about Josh's parents?" she asked.

I sucked in a deep breath and pushed the air past the tightness in my throat. "You know they never cared for me that much. It's been almost two years since the funeral. We've spoken on the phone twice, maybe three times. We don't have anything left to say."

The classy Soho eatery, usually our favorite spot for lunch, felt foreign and cold to me now. Nothing about my life was the same. I wasn't the same.

Del laid her elegantly manicured hand over mine on the tablecloth. "You've still got me, Liv. Me and Bill. And Laura and Nick. Sarah and Pierre. And—"

"Yeah. All the couples who Josh and I hung out with. Our close-knit, social unit." I levelled my gaze on the one of our group whom I considered to be my closest confidante. It was obvious by her perplexed expression—she had no clue what I was getting at.

"All couples, Del. I'm a lonesome dove now. Doves mate for life, you know. I'm a mourning dove. I don't belong here anymore. The problem is, I'm not completely sure I ever belonged here at all."

I moved into what the locals called the Belle Bride House the day after Confederate Memorial Day, on April 28. I hadn't planned it that way. It took six weeks of back-and-forth contracts and deed searches and whatever the hell else the realtors and attorneys had to go through to close the deal. This perplexed me: I was paying in cash. Seemed it should have been simpler.

There wasn't much to the actual moving process, either. I quickly realized the trendy, modern furnishings of my husband's and my Soho condo wouldn't suit a country home built a century and a half ago.

My *late* husband. The brilliant corporate lawyer who'd

been reduced to a glassy-eyed, drooling zombie within six short months. Brain cancer—particularly a glioblastoma, the most aggressive form—has no mercy. Josh had joked when his doctor broke the news that he had something in common with Senator John McCain after all.

McCain outlived him. The senator was lucky. His tumor had been discovered in time.

I also quickly realized Josh's shiny white Tesla would not be the most practical vehicle to go bumping around the backroads of the Alabama countryside. Instead, I drove into the tiny main street of Camellia that sunny April morning in a sensible, four-door Toyota Tacoma. I'd need a pickup truck, surely, to tackle the logistics of what lay ahead of me.

Not that I intended to wield a hammer or jigsaw. I'd hired, remotely, a number of local handymen to get the building back into a livable state over the six weeks since I first saw the place. An attentive realtor, Thomas Edwards had kept me abreast of the progress, complete with digital photographs emailed on a weekly basis. He assured me when I arrived the house would be pest-free, buttoned up against the elements, and clean enough to move right in.

Except . . . I had no furniture. In the back seat of my Tacoma, I'd stacked my luggage, packed with every casual piece of clothing I owned. No need for the cocktail dresses or business suits. Knowing I'd insult my old circle of friends for even offering them the goods, I simply boxed them up and called Salvation Army to cart them away. In addition to the clothing, I had my iPhone, my laptop, and my iPad. A Bose Wave wireless music system, three boxes of original Nora Roberts hardcovers I couldn't bear to part with, and a small security box with important papers rounded out the inventory.

I hadn't even had to use the bed of the truck at all. Until I stopped at a Wal-Mart in Birmingham to pick up an air mattress, some new pillows, and a bed-in-a-bag sheet and comforter set. It didn't look like rain, and I was out of room in the cab anyway. I tossed the mattress box and the bags of soft goods in the back and set out to cover the last sixty miles to my destination.

My new home. The Belle Bride Plantation Home in Camellia, Alabama.

Edwards was waiting for me, sitting on the freshly painted front steps of a house that looked a sight better than the last time I'd been here. The upstairs window no longer wore a plywood bandage. The columns gleamed slick and shiny with a fresh coat of white. Even the straggly weeds around the foundation had been trimmed.

As I climbed out of the truck, I watched Edwards wince as he peeled his trousers off the apparently, still sticky paint. He was examining his backside when I walked up.

"Am I going to have your butt-print on my front stoop as a reminder you sold me the home?" I asked, grinning.

He regarded me with lips pressed into a thin line. "No, paint's dry. Just felt a little tacky with the morning dew. Got a wet butt, 's all." He thrust a thick manila envelope toward me. "Here's copies of all your paperwork, two sets of keys for the front and back doors, and receipts for all the work you've had done on the place. If you have any problem with any of it, there's contact information on every invoice."

"I'm sure it will be fine." I took the bundle and stuck it under one arm without opening it. "You said there was heat, but no central air conditioning, right?"

"No ma'am. It won't get too hot for a few months in these parts, though. The same HVAC man who updated your heating system can install a new unit, if you like."

I watched as the branches overhead swayed in a still cool morning breeze, fluttering the Spanish moss like green-grey pinwheels. "I should be fine. For a while, anyway."

"Walk-through?" he asked.

"No. You took me through before. If I have any questions as to what's been done, I'll contact the handymen directly."

Edwards looked past me, out toward the road. "Your furniture be arriving soon?"

I shook my head. "I don't have any. Came with just what's in my truck there. I sold my place in New York furnished."

His eyebrows lifted, folding his forehead into an oddly-displaced six-pack. He was silent for a moment, then dropped his gaze to the ground and kicked at a bare patch of sand. "You weren't kidding when you said you were starting over. Were you?"

"No sir, I was not. But I will be needing furniture at some point. Any suggestions locally? Or will I have to trek back to Birmingham to go shopping?"

Clearing his throat, he studied my face. "Birmingham's your best bet if you want a big selection. Depending on your style, that is. There is a furniture shop here in town. Mostly antiques. Run by a real nice fella. Heath's Heirlooms. It's right on Main Street. You can't miss it."

"I'll check it out," I said distantly, shifting from one foot to the other. I was ready for this meet and greet to be over. I was anxious to be alone. Anxious to get a feeling for the place. Anxious to reset my life's barometer.

It would take a bit of doing for this major a change, I was certain.

Edwards took the hint. "Okay, then," he said. He shook my hand before turning toward his battered Jeep. "Good luck, Ms. Larson. You know my number if you need anything."

It wasn't until he'd climbed into his vehicle that I spotted the movement near the old barn. A flash of white at the base of one of the Dutch doors, inside the paddock. I took a step to one side and caught sight of the dog.

A hound of some kind, the dog was medium sized but rangy, thin. His lowered head and curved backbone spoke of hard times and fear. Worry wound a fist in my chest.

I'd never owned a dog. What if this one was aggressive? And whose dog was he, anyway?

I turned to wave at my realtor to ask those very questions, but Edwards had his windows rolled up tight. The clatter of his engine shattered the morning quiet, and his radio's mournful country music vibrated even over the din.

He mistook my wave for a farewell, shoved the Jeep in gear, and spun out of the driveway with dust and leaves floating in his wake.

I halfway considered ringing his cellphone to bring him back. Then I chastised myself. Here I hadn't been an Alabamian for more than twenty minutes, and I was sporting yellow streaks on my back as wide as the ones on the winding road I'd driven in on.

Hugging the manila package to my chest, I turned and took a step toward the barn. Might as well introduce myself to my new neighbor right here, right now.

After circling the barn, walking through its cool, dim interior, and scanning the corners of every one of the three horse stalls, I came up empty. The dog was gone.

Although the air was steadily warming as the sun rose higher toward noon, I felt a chill slither down my back. Maybe it was just a trickle of sweat. The animal I'd seen was so white he'd almost glowed. Yet he looked lost and half-starved. The disparity of those two conditions haunted me.

Perhaps I had imagined him.

Heath

Tuesday was the shop's slowest day of the week, so Heath was never in a hurry to open. It was nearly eleven o'clock by the time he arrived at the glass-fronted doors of Heath's Heirlooms. Shoving the local paper under his arm, he fumbled in his jeans pocket for the keys. He yawned.

Should have picked up a coffee from Nan's Diner on his way through.

He hadn't rolled in from Birmingham until nearly midnight last night, and then he was so wired he couldn't even think about sleep until nearly three. The one cup he'd brewed at home this morning had gone cold on the bathroom counter while he shaved and showered.

Heath Barrow was not a fan of cold coffee.

He would have bet his mother's china on the fact that it was *iced* coffee clutched in the fist of his first customer of the day. Immediately, he didn't like her.

Tall and willowy, he knew just by the way the blonde carried herself she was a city gal. Oh, she'd made an effort to fit in. She wore the casual, Southern uniform of jeans, tee shirt, and sneakers. Except the jeans sported a razor-sharp crease down the front. The sneakers, with their floral-printed laces and shiny metallic stripes, didn't come from Wal-Mart. And the cup in her hand—clear plastic, with a straw and jiggling ice cubes—featured the logo of the fancy new cafe out near the highway.

Cold coffee. What was it they called it? Iced something or other . . .

He watched her wander along the display at the front of the shop, pausing to run slender fingers down the cut glass shade of an Astral Oil Lamp, one whose brass base had been re-worked to hold electrical wiring instead of its original power source. She flipped the dangling glass pendants with one finger and they made a tinkling noise, making her smile.

Something warmed inside Heath's chest, though he wrote it off to the slice of cold pizza he'd eaten on his way in. He pushed himself away from the computer desk at the back of the shop, rising to lean on the display counter.

"Help you, ma'am?"

Her head snapped around, sending her golden ponytail to swing wildly over one shoulder.

She pressed one hand to her throat and chuckled nervously. "I'm sorry. I didn't see you back there." She pressed the dewy side of her drink cup to her cheek.

Guess he'd startled her. Oh well. Did she think the local yokels in a small town left their businesses unattended while they ran errands?

Heath cleared his throat. "Looking for anything in particular? Or just browsing?"

Wasting time, he thought wryly. Hers *and* mine.

The passers-through in this part of the South were usually just that—passing through. Camellia didn't have any well-known tourist attractions, other than a few marked Civil War battlefields and a couple of dilapidated plantation homes. They didn't even have a chain hotel.

His interior bitch session screeched to a halt with her next four words.

"I'm new in town."

Heath blinked. He knew just about everybody in this small burg, and surely would have heard if—

"I bought the old Belle plantation home. The Bride Belle, I think they call it?" she said. She was walking toward him now, and he couldn't help his gaze from straying down. The thin cotton of her shirt didn't do much to disguise the generous, peaked mounds beneath them.

Probably plastic too, he thought.

He cleared his throat again, and felt sweat prickle the back of his neck. "You did? Wow, how did I miss that bit of town gossip?"

Her eyes narrowed, pink lips pressing tight.

What the hell was wrong with him? He scooted around the counter. "I mean, well . . . congratulations. The place is in need of some TLC. I drive by there now and again, and hated to see it standing empty."

She was studying him now with a critical gaze. Pale, grey eyes. Or were they blue? Hard to tell in this light. Big, wide-set, pretty eyes.

Then suddenly, she was laughing. Embarrassment flushed her cheeks and she covered her mouth with her free hand. "I know this is going to sound ridiculous. Impossible, even. But I bought a gigantic old plantation house, and I don't own a stick of furniture."

Her giggling sent a warm flush through him, and he smiled back. "Well, you've come to the right place. Welcome to Heath's Heirlooms." He stuck out his hand. "Heath Barrow."

She hesitated only a moment before grasping his hand with her soft, smooth one. Her grip was confident and strong. Meeting his eyes, she said, "I'm Olivia. Olivia Larson. Nice to meet you."

And it was.

An hour later, Heath had completely forgotten how tired he was. He also hadn't sold a single piece of furniture. Not even a knick-knack. But hell, he reminded himself—she didn't have any tables or shelving to put any knick-knacks *on*.

He'd given her a tour of his shop, along with a rudimentary education on plantation-style interior design. She'd listened raptly, asking questions like, "A Rice Bed? What on earth is that?" and "I didn't see any chandeliers at the Belle house . . . *my* house. I guess maybe I should think about getting one."

"If you'd like, I could come out and see what the floor plan of the Belle looks like. Maybe give you some ideas on what styles might fit."

Did the gesture seem forward? He usually didn't make house calls. He usually just sold antiques.

The smell of her was making him light-headed. She was leaning close to him, studying the image of a Rice Bed he'd pulled up on his computer screen. Not perfume, but something earthy and clean. Her shampoo, maybe? The fan over his desk blew a loose strand of her hair to tickle his cheek. He shifted in his chair, making it creak.

Damn his errant hormones.

"It reminds me of a canopy bed, only without the canopy," she said. "I like that look. Why 'rice'? The designer's name?"

Heath shook his head, zooming in on the image and pointing. "The wood's carved. They say the designs are supposed to look like rice. Sometimes tobacco leaves." He wheeled his chair to the side and turned to face her. To put a little distance between them. His jeans were rapidly snugging up in the crotch. "I think I might have one . . . a Rice Bed. But it's not here. It's in my warehouse in Birmingham."

"Oh," she said, disappointment puckering the pale skin between her eyebrows. She sighed. "I guess I need to decide on a style before I buy any one piece anyway. When can you come out and take a look at my house?"

How about right now? That was the thought running through his brain. He glanced at the grandfather clock standing in the rear corner of his office area. Not yet one o'clock.

Shit and damn.

"Will you be available this evening? I have a delivery coming this afternoon, but I can come by when I close up. About five-thirty."

She was nodding before he even finished the sentence, sipping from the melted ice in her cup. "I just arrived this morning and haven't even unloaded my truck yet." Tucking the loose wisp of hair behind her ear, she blinked rapidly and took a breath. "I don't have any food in the house, either." She pressed fingers to her forehead. "I don't even have a refrigerator yet. The one I ordered in Birmingham won't be here until tomorrow."

Heath stood. Okay, this situation was starting to sound a bit suspicious.

"Hey," he said, tentatively laying a hand on one of her shoulders. "Are you . . . running from something? Somebody? Where are you from, anyway?"

Instead of guilt or shame, her guileless eyes widened. "No. It's not what you think. I mean, I *am* running from something . . . my old life. But I'm not a criminal, and there's nobody looking for me. I was living in Manhattan. Alone."

Heath tilted his head. "Are you . . . from the South? Family here?"

"No. I have nobody. Not anymore."

Running his fingers through his cap of curls, Heath stifled the temptation to probe further. He sensed pain, saw it flash in those oddly silvery-blue eyes, but realized she was trying hard to keep it hidden.

Time. He had time to get to know her better. Find out what her story was.

"How about this?" he began. "I'll run by Nan's and get her to pack up a box of her special-recipe fried chicken. Some biscuits. Be by your place around six. That work?" He hesitated. "You're not a vegetarian or anything, are you? Nan also makes a pretty decent—"

"I eat chicken," she said. Then she smiled. "What kind of beer do you drink? I'll pick some up and refill my cooler."

"How do you know I drink beer?" he asked, unable to suppress the grin.

"I don't. But it goes pretty well with fried chicken, right?" She lifted an eyebrow. "Or are you a sweet tea kind of guy?"

"Bud Light."

She wrapped those delicious looking pink lips around the straw and drained the cup noisily. Then she said, "Bud Light it is. See you around six." The cup landed with a whoosh in the trash can beside his desk, and she turned to leave.

"Hey, Olivia?" he called after her.

She did an about-face.

"I think I can forgive you, you know."

Her shoulders lifted. "For what?"

"For drinking cold coffee."

She snorted and turned on her heel. "Gee, thanks. And you can call me Liv."

Chapter Two

Liv

The empty feeling of strangeness and loneliness lifted somewhat on the three-mile drive back to the Belle Bride house from my downtown run. I wouldn't have to spend my first night here alone. Bottles of water and Bud Light lay buried under twenty pounds of fresh ice in my cooler. I'd also picked up a blister pack of mini-cupcakes for dessert, and a bunch of only slightly wilted fresh flowers. Might as well start to make my new house feel like a home.

I was having company tonight. I had made a friend. Already.

Sort of.

Dust billowed around my truck as I pulled up beside the house. I shut the engine and sat there for a long moment, studying its regal facade. Silently, it studied me back.

The front porch, swept free of last autumn's—probably the last *three* autumns'—dead leaves, beckoned to me. The wide oak boards shone with fresh polyurethane. The crew I'd hired had fixed the few broken spindles on the railing, and they glistened shiny white, linking the regal columns like an elegant necklace.

For a moment, I experienced a flash of deja vu, as though I'd been plummeted back through time, and was about to climb out of a horse-drawn carriage instead of a Tacoma pickup truck. The sensation was strange, yet familiar. Comforting, almost.

It took me several minutes to fit the old-fashioned, skeleton-like key into the lock on the front door. This, I decided, would need to be replaced. Something more modern, more secure. With a deadbolt, for sure. Although I'd been assured Camellia had the lowest crime rate in the entire state of Alabama, I would still be living here alone. And I'd lived too long in big cities to ignore the possibility of unwelcome intruders.

The door sighed open, and instead of the musty, stale odor I'd encountered on my first visit, the air now smelled clean and new. The hardwood floors in the entry hall gleamed, and someone had put down a used but functional doormat just inside the threshold. The hallway ran all the way through the house, straight back to the parlor, passing under several curved archways on its journey. Long bands of sunlight streamed through the distant windows. Swaying branches in the backyard tossed the rays into a dancing pattern on the floor.

The dust, the cobwebs, the neglect of God-only-knew how many years had been swept away. The walls, once faded and peeling, were now sporting a fresh coat of ivory. The house had been thoroughly cleaned, and the faint scent of disinfectant and paint still hung on the air. Even so, there was still plenty of work yet to do.

I noticed now some previous owner had decided to strip the place of most of its light fixtures. Guess if they were genuine period, they must have been worth some money. Little wonder I hadn't remembered seeing a chandelier.

The Belle Bride had been brought back to livable, yet reduced to a clean slate. I was free to make the house mine, choosing my own palette for the walls and ceilings. My style for the furniture and accessories. My own chandelier.

I carried the bag with the cupcakes, along with some paper plates and picnic utensils, back to the kitchen. Laying them down on the newly polished granite countertop, I glanced at the pathetic looking bunch of flowers I'd bought. *What am I going to do with these?*

The kitchen, the realtor had informed me, had undergone a major renovation sometime in the early 2000s. Ivory granite countertops replaced whatever had been there before, topping refaced cabinets in a warm, dark wood. The floors were stained to match the cabinets, with the upper cabinets painted ivory to match the counters. A tuxedo-style, he'd told me. The stainless-steel fridge I'd ordered would fit perfectly.

It was rather elegant and formal, yet seemed to align with the house's demeanor.

Demeanor? Did houses have demeanors? This one certainly seemed to. My imagination is already running away with me, I thought. I'm already thinking of the house as having its own personality. The Belle Bride. *Belle.*

I began rummaging through the cabinets, hoping someone had left something behind—an old glass jar or bottle I could water these pathetic flowers in. Under the sink, I found a collection of six, Ball mason jars beside a small box of lids and rings. Apparently, there'd been a canning aficionado sometime in Belle's past. As I arranged the flowers in their humble vase, I couldn't help but wonder where the garden had been. In my earlier visit, I hadn't thought to look.

Of course I hadn't. I was a city girl. Along with never owning a horse or a dog, I'd also never had a garden. My garden consisted of three pots of herbs I kept lined up on my condo's kitchen windowsill. Basil, parsley, and rosemary. For cooking.

A stab of pain seared my heart when the memory of planning a gourmet meal for my late husband rose like smoke in my mind. It was always just the two of us—neither had ever considered kids—and I ran my web design business from home. Every night was a date night for us. Flowers, wine, a fine meal, candles . . .

Candles. I should have thought to bring a few of those. With so few light fixtures remaining in the house, would my new friend and I be eating our chicken dinner in the dark? Or in the glow of the flashlight from the glovebox of my truck?

That's right, Liv. Keep your mind on the present, the issues at hand. No need for any jaunts down memory lane. Nothing could bring Josh back.

This is why you're here. A new life. Completely different. Starting over.

It was different, all right. My ears were ringing with the incredible quiet. No matter what floor your condo is on, no matter how thick the draperies you hang, a city refuses to remain silent outside of them. I reached over the sink to raise the window sash. It had gotten quite breezy, a good thing since the temperature continued to rise with the afternoon sun. Yet all I could hear was the soft whooshing of tree branches as they brushed against one another. An occasional scuttle of dead leaves lying thick in a long-neglected backyard. And a high-pitched whine.

A whine? What the hell was that?

At first I thought it was the wind, but it was intermittent, and didn't match the wind's rhythm. I crept to the back door and peered through the glass panes toward the barn. To where I'd seen the dog. Nothing.

My heart seized when the whine sounded again, right outside the door. I looked down, and there he was, sitting on his haunches, on the top step. A white, bone-thin hound with long, tan ears connected by a round patch of color on the top of his head. He was staring up at me with soulful, caramel eyes.

So, I hadn't imagined him. It still didn't solve my dilemma as to how to deal with him. My experience with dogs was limited to passing them on the sidewalk back in the city. And then, they were always tethered to someone else. Somebody else's responsibility.

The dog whined again, his whip-like tail thumping weakly on the steps. He shifted from one paw to the other, and I noticed they were rimmed with something dark. Mud, probably. Yet his coat was such a bright white it nearly hurt my eyes.

I unlocked and opened the door, knowing the screen door would still protect me, at least buy me time if he decided to attack. He certainly didn't look aggressive. He looked hungry. Probably thirsty too, on a hot day like today.

"I don't have anything to offer you, boy," I said. "You need to go on home to wherever you live." I made a shooing motion with my hand. "Go on. Shoo. Go home."

He stood then, his tail wagging wildly, and he yipped. I heard him scratch on the aluminum base of the door, just once. The whining continued.

The mangy creature acted like he lived here. I knew it was impossible. The house had been empty for at least five years, Edwards told me. Even if the last occupants had abandoned him, he wouldn't still be here after that long.

Water. I could at least offer him water. Then I'd call the realtor, see if he had any idea who owned him. Or the number for animal control.

As I rinsed a second Ball jar from the tap and filled it, I wondered if I might end up with fang marks in my arm for my good deed. But I was being ridiculous. A complete ninny. He was only a half-starved hound dog, one with soulful eyes and a wagging tail. I would simply open the screen door a crack and slip the jar of water onto the top step. He would drink, and then he would go away.

By the time I'd filled the jar, the whining had ceased. There. He knew I was getting him water, and he was being a good, patient dog.

When I returned to the back door, though, as before, the dog was gone. A flush, then a chill washed over me. I lifted the cool jar to my cheek and closed my eyes.

Maybe my therapist had been right, after all. She'd said I needed a change—a new place, new people. When I'd told her where I was going, however, her eyes had widened. Too desolate, she'd said. Too extreme a change. She warned me. Time alone, *this* alone, might cause my mind to start playing tricks on me.

So now I was imagining vagabond dogs. What would be next? Ghosts in the attic?

Heath

It was a little past six when he pulled onto the gravel path posing as a driveway, the one leading up to the Belle Bride house. The day had turned out to be a hot one for early spring. He'd run home for a quick shower, and switched his dust-covered and sweaty work clothes for clean jeans and a crisp, cotton shirt. Still wanted to look business-like. After all, this was, technically, a potential sales call.

Although he had to keep reminding himself of the fact every time anticipation shot another stream of bubbles inside his chest. Damn it, he was attracted to her, even though she was a city girl. She probably wouldn't last three months here in rural Alabama. He never did care for city girl attitude. The independent, confident air they all exuded. Even the few girls he'd dated from Birmingham seem to hover on a higher plane —and not just from their spikey platform heels.

Not a date, Heath. Just a client consultation. He glanced over on the seat beside him to be sure he'd remembered the books: tattered copies of Southern Living and Architectural Digest focusing on plantation style decorating, a few of his period reproduction furniture catalogs, and one from a vintage lighting fixture company. The delectable aroma of the fried chicken in the back seat sent his stomach to rumbling.

Eat first, tour later, he'd decided. One thing he disliked more than cold coffee was cold chicken. And Nan's biscuits, although nuggets of pure heaven right out of the oven, turned into hockey pucks within a few hours.

He didn't spot her right away, which is why he lurched a bit and nearly dropped the bag of biscuits when a voice called, "I can smell that chicken from here, Mr. Barrow."

Scanning the porch, he found it empty. The front door was closed. It was when his gaze wandered up that he spied her through the upper gallery railing. All he could see from this angle were slender legs, bare, crossed, one foot bobbing. He took a step back.

She was sitting on ... something. A box or crate of some kind, leaning against the side of the house with her laptop balanced on her thighs.

"Good evening," he called. "I hope you're hungry. Nan's chicken was still sizzling when she handed me the box. I thought my stomach was going to stage a mutiny before I got here."

Liv clicked the laptop shut and rose, smiling down at him. "Well come on in and let's eat, then."

Heath had never been inside the Belle Bride house. Oh, he'd been in a bunch of antebellum homes in the area, and most of them followed a similar rubric: the classic floorplan popular in the day. He was surprised when he met her in the foyer to find the curved staircase rising off to his left. This upscale feature was a staple in the bigger plantation homes, but not in the smaller ones, like the Belle.

"Wow," he murmured. "Like a mini-Tara."

Liv reached to take the box of chicken from him. "I think it's why I fell in love with the place the first time I saw it."

He followed her back to the kitchen, where she'd set out plastic forks on the granite countertop. "Wow again. Did you do this?" He motioned to the counters and new cabinets.

"No. Edwards told me this renovation was done almost fifteen years ago. It sure doesn't look like anything here has ever been used, though."

"She's been empty a long time," Heath mused, studying the room. Their voices echoed in the space, he noticed. She'd be needing plenty of area rugs and soft accessories to make this place sound like a home instead of a museum.

He glanced out the windows. "A barn, too, huh? Are you a horse person?"

"I might be," she said absently as she tore the plastic wrap from around a stack of paper plates. "I hate to tell you, but unless we haul in a few more plastic crates from the back of my truck, we'll have to eat standing up. I wasn't kidding when I said I have nothing. Nada. Not a chair in the place."

"No problem. I have a couple of camping chairs in the bed of my truck," he offered.

"Oh, good," she said with a smile. "We can eat on the porch. Use one of my crates for a table."

Heath cocked his head, flashing her a lopsided grin. "They're actually referred to as galleries in these parts. At least, on an antebellum style home."

Rolling her eyes, Liv grabbed the roll of paper towels and led the way.

"To the gallery, then," she quipped.

The air cooled pleasantly as the sun dropped lower behind the house, and cricket song filled the air. Heath always thought food tasted better when eaten outdoors. What was it the city folk called it? He tried the term out.

"Chicken . . . alfredo. Right?" he said, smiling at her.

She stopped chewing and stared at him a moment, then burst into laughter. "Do you mean al fresco? Alfredo is something entirely different."

Heath could feel the tops of his ears burning hot. "Uh, yeah. That's what I meant." There he went, making a complete fool of himself right off the bat. Better stick to subjects he actually knew something about. "So, did you have a particular style you'd like to go with for decorating this place? I mean, there's always traditional plantation, and there have been lots of variations on the theme over the years. Some people even go art deco. For the contrast, you know."

She was licking bits of greasy chicken crust off her

fingers, studying him with a humorous twinkle in her eyes. Oh my, he didn't realize eating fried chicken could be so . . . erotic. He shifted in his seat and reached for his bottle of beer.

"To be honest, I don't know. I've looked at a couple of pages on Pinterest. I think I like the traditional style, but I don't want it to be too formal. This house is going to be lived in, not on display." She took a long pull from her own beer, then leveled her gaze on him. "Just by me, of course. But it will be lived in. And worked in. I'll be spending a lot of time inside these walls."

"Your work from home, then?"

She bobbed her head. "I'm a web designer. I also do some side work for a few publishers, creating book trailers and covers. I'm the queen of Serif. The princess of Gimp," she, poking her nose up in the air.

"That sounds pretty exotic," he said, not having a clue as to what she was talking about.

She pulled a paper towel off the roll she'd brought out and wiped her fingers. "They're software programs, like Photoshop. They're the platforms I learned on. These biscuits are amazing, by the way."

Carefully, she peeled back the corner of a packet of honey and drizzled its contents on the fluffy white insides of her split biscuit. The tip of her tongue peeked out from the corner of her mouth as she concentrated on the task.

Sweet Jesus. She even made biscuits and honey look sexy. He cleared his throat.

"How's your internet service, anyway?" Heath finished off the last of his biscuit and dusted flour off his hands. "It's almost non-existent in some places out here."

"Crappy," she said, scowling. "I went in for satellite internet first thing. My livelihood depends on it."

"I should probably have you take a look at my website. A guy out of Birmingham maintains mine, but he doesn't update it as quickly as I need him to when I get new stock in. I'd like to have a bit more control of the process. Unfortunately, a computer guru, I am not."

She dropped the empty honey packet in the paper bag and took a bite. Eyelids fluttering closed, she made a dreamy moaning sound. Okay, she was baiting him here. Nobody makes this much of a fuss over—

"Heath, I can't remember the last time I had a meal like this," she mumbled around a mouthful. "If ever. I've been pretty much subsisting on takeout from the pizza joint and the Thai place on my street in SoHo. And eating alone," she added.

"If you don't mind my asking . . . why alone?" he asked.

Her shrug seemed casual, but it was almost as though he'd seen a switch flipped. A door closed. She dropped what was left of her biscuit on her plate and snatched up the paper towel. "It's going to get dark here soon, and I can't give you a tour once it gets dark. Unless it's by flashlight." She hopped to her feet and grabbed her bottle of beer. "Ready?"

The house was in amazing shape for its age, and for being empty for such long chunks of time. The only room in need of more extensive repair was one bedroom at the front of the house, where she'd told him a window had been broken and only halfway boarded up with plywood.

"I guess the pigeons took up residence in here, and their poop does some nasty things to the hardwood. The cleaning crew did a really amazing job. I don't think I'll have to replace it."

Heath nodded, turning in a circle to study the elaborate crown molding edging the twelve-foot ceiling. "What plans do you have for this room?" he asked.

"My office. I'd like to put a desk right there, in front of

the windows. Morning light. The house faces east. I do my best work in the morning."

Heath combed his memory for what he had in his shop, or in his warehouse in the way of office furniture. Most of his stock wouldn't be practical for a modern computer workstation. Roll top desks and the like.

"I'm going to leave you a few catalogs to go through. You can let me know what kind of desk you're thinking of. If I don't have what you want, I can order it for you."

A long, narrow bathroom separated the two front rooms. Liv reached up and flicked a wall switch. Only one of two, tulip shaped lights flared beside a mirror over the sink.

"At least there's a little light in here," she said. "Until the other bulb gives out."

The bathroom had been modernized, but tastefully, Heath noted. A claw foot tub was fitted with rubbed brass fixtures, and a glass-enclosed shower took up the corner next to the narrow window. Subway tile in creamy vanilla covered the floors and the lower half of the walls. Nice, he thought. Classy.

As they rounded the corner into the adjacent front room, Liv reached up and pulled the band out of her hair. A blanket of honey-gold cascaded down over her shoulders, catching the last rays of evening light as she shook her head. Again, Heath caught a whiff of her scent. There it was —something fresh and earthy. Clean. Whatever it was, the aroma wrapped itself around his insides and gave them a little squeeze.

"And here," she said, pausing in the doorway and making a sweeping motion with one hand, "is the master bedroom." Then she giggled. "I really am thinking about one of those Rice Beds you showed me today."

A Rice Bed would certainly fit nicely in this space, he

thought. What he saw hovering in a corner of the room now, like a rubber island, was an inflatable mattress. It was a good one, probably queen size. The kind that came with its own internal electric pump to inflate it. He'd slept on one a time or two on camping trips. He definitely wouldn't want to make it a habit.

"I think we'd better get on ordering the bedroom furniture first thing," he said, quirking an eyebrow.

"Yeah," she chuckled. "Not sure how much sleep I'm going to get transitioning from my king memory foam to this."

She'd wandered to the front windows, which were both open a few inches. She pushed the sashes down and latched them. "Getting dark fast," she said. "And I need to grab my flashlight out of my truck." She barked out a nervous laugh and shrugged. "No light fixtures in here."

Heath looked up and saw the wires dangling like spider's legs out of the hole in the center of the ceiling. "Wow, they ripped out everything, didn't they?" Then he remembered. He held up one finger. "Which is why you're going to love what I brought as a housewarming gift."

While she retrieved her flashlight from the truck, he lifted the blanket-wrapped bundle from out of his pickup and met her at the base of the porch steps.

"Come on. Might as well take it right on upstairs to your bedroom. It's where you'll be needing it most. For a little while, anyway."

She sat on the edge of her mattress as he crouched before her, carefully laying the bundle at her feet. When he unwrapped it, she breathed out on a sigh.

"Ooh . . . the lamp I was admiring in your shop this morning." Her eyes glinted in the fading light as they met his. "There's no need for you to give this to me, Mr. Barrow. I'll buy it."

"Cut the Mr. Barrow stuff, alright? You said I could call you Liv? So, Liv, I'm Heath. And this is my housewarming gift to you. For the Belle Bride."

He crawled the few feet to the outlet on the nearest wall. Another modern upgrade, he noted. At least most of the major conveniences had already been installed.

Warm light flooded the room when he plugged it in, and the glass pendants tinkled against each other as he set it down next to her mattress. She was staring at the lamp like a drowning person sights a lifeline. Both hands covered her mouth. He wasn't sure if it was just reflection from the lamp, or if those were really tears glazing her pretty pale eyes.

"This was very, very thoughtful of you, Heath. I have to admit, I rushed into this move without much thought. No planning. If I hadn't remembered to pick up this bedding in Birmingham, I'd probably have been sleeping in my truck tonight." Her voice was dreamlike, almost a whisper.

He pondered her reaction. So extreme for such a small gesture. She seemed like a lost soul . . . and pain radiated off her like steam from hot pavement after a summer storm. What storm has she been through, he wondered? She obviously wasn't ready to talk it about it just yet.

And why, oh why, should he care so damned much anyway?

"Listen," he said, pulling his cellphone out of his back pocket. "Give me your number and I'll ring you. Then you'll have mine, and you can call me if you need anything during the night. It can get pretty spooky out here after dark."

She nodded and recited her number. Seconds later they heard the melodious notes of some classical piece Heath couldn't name echoing from somewhere on the first floor. He ended the call and reached for her hand.

"Come on. I'll help you carry in whatever else you need

out of your truck for tonight, and then you can lock up behind me."

As he backed out of the driveway, he saw the bathroom light flash on upstairs, then her shadow moving against the wall. No window treatments either, he thought. For a savvy city woman, she hadn't made very smart choices. What had she been thinking? Obviously, she hadn't been. The pain—whatever its cause—had sent her running blindly out into the wilderness, like a panicked animal. Either that or she was just plain stupid.

No, he thought. As Heath drove the five miles back toward his own place on the other side of town, he knew stupidity wasn't the cause. He just wondered how long it would be before he found out her story. If ever.

He placed his cellphone on his nightstand, double-checking to be sure the ringer was turned up all the way. Even after he turned out the light, he lay staring into the darkness, thinking about her. Worrying about her.

It had been a long time—a *very* long time—since Heath Barrow had worried about a woman. He wasn't sure if he liked the sensation, or if it scared him to death.

Chapter Three

Liv

My first evening in Camellia began as a most pleasant surprise. The man who owns the furniture store, Heath, came by and toured my house. I expected a sales pitch. To my surprise, he was anything but pushy.

In fact, I had the feeling it was really more of a social call than anything else. We ate scrumptious fried chicken and biscuits on the front porch—excuse me, *gallery*—may my cholesterol level forgive me one transgression. The beer was cold and helped smooth my nerves, settle my awkward tongue. I hadn't had dinner alone with a man since . . . before. And try as I did, I couldn't deny the attraction I felt for Heath Barrow.

He's a tall man with broad shoulders, only not in a football hero sort of way. The outdoorsy type, from what he told me. Likes to hike and camp. A trout fisherman. Not surprising in this part of the country. A loner. In some ways, he sounds a little like me. At least, the me I've become over the past year.

His Southern drawl was hard to ignore, and painted him adorable. Add that to a cap of soft-looking curls the color of milk chocolate, and eyes to match, and I could see how if I wasn't careful, I could develop quite a crush on this man. A complete stranger. Yet someone who, even though he didn't know me at all, had spent the time and effort to bring me dinner and help me embark on this monstrous project I'd set for myself.

Granted, I needed a house full of furniture. I realized I

could represent nothing more than a big-ticket sale to him. I wasn't born yesterday.

This move was going to cost a pretty penny. Completely renovate and decorate an antebellum home? Where on earth had that wild hare come from? Must have been a notion planted in my head as I thumbed through a Southern Living magazine, sitting in the doctor's office one day. I'd never even bought a copy of the magazine. Or maybe I really was experiencing a psychotic break.

It was what Carla, my therapist, had warned me about. It was why she'd prescribed the anti-depressants. Where was that bottle of pills, anyway? I hadn't taken one since I'd left New York.

I felt certain, in my heart, I wouldn't need them anymore. The excitement of adventure fizzed in my chest. I'll admit, when the realtor peeled out of my yard just hours ago, I'd been apprehensive. The seclusion—isolation, even—was completely alien to me. Alien, and more than a little intimidating.

At least now I had a friend. And a plan. This project promised to be engrossing, and fun.

Heath had agreed with me—a Rice Bed would look wonderful in the master bedroom. He was going to check his inventory to see if he had one. The dark, carved wood, paired with an armoire and chest of drawers to match would suit the massive dimensions of the room. Maybe an antique chest for the foot of the bed, he'd suggested. I loved his ideas.

The reality of a sumptuous new bed, however, seemed far off by two a.m. the next morning. My mind wouldn't settle, and I knew I was overtired. Plus, sleeping on an air mattress, no matter how thick and high-tech, threatened no competition with a pillow-top at a Marriott.

The absolute quiet was deafening. I was used to city

sounds, reflections from street lamps eking their way through the blinds, a distant horn or siren punctuating the nighttime hours. Here, there was nothing. With all the windows shut and locked, it was even difficult to hear the wind in the oaks around the house.

The errant cricket who'd apparently taken up residence somewhere on the ground floor was the only company I had. Its repetitive rant echoed all through the empty house. I concentrated on the sound, like a mantra, until I finally dozed off.

My heart exploded in my chest when the pounding on the door commenced. I sat bolt upright, clutching the blanket to my chin, eyes wide and blind in the pitch-blackness. Frantically, I reached to switch on the Astral lamp, then froze. Would I want whomever was outside my door to know I was here? I was alone, my only means of protection the pepper spray I always carried in my purse.

The next moments slowed to a molasses sludge as I laid there, my heart hammering wildly. The silence settled around me like a smothering fog. Even the errant cricket had gone to sleep.

A bad dream, I thought, trying to swallow and slow my breathing. Just a bad dream.

Until it started again. Someone was banging—loud and hard—on the heavy oak front door. Rapid, frantic knocks. Bang-bang-bang-bang-bang. The old door rattled in its frame, so violently I feared the glass of the adjacent windows would shatter. The sound echoed through the empty house like an earthquake in a cavern.

Blood racing so fast I could barely hear over the whine in my ears, I rolled off my mattress and crawled the few feet to the windows, staying low to the floor. The gallery would block my view of the entryway below, but I could at least see if there was a vehicle parked outside.

A police car, maybe. I hoped. Perhaps the local authorities didn't realize the house had been sold, and—

Bang-bang-bang-bang-bang!

No car. A half-moon winked at me from between the oak branches as they swayed. It had gotten quite windy, as if a storm was blowing in. Clouds raced across the face of the moon, chopping what little light it provided into intermittent bursts. I could see no one in the yard.

Of course, I couldn't. Whoever it was stood right outside my front door, on the porch and blocked from view by the second-floor gallery. The thought sent my heart galloping even faster. My skin slicked with a sheen of sweat as I huddled against the wall, panting.

The pepper spray . . . where was my purse?

Maybe if I stayed quiet long enough, whomever it was would just go away.

Bang-bang-bang-bang-bang!

I could hear the windows shuddering in their frames, vibrating the walls and amplified as the sound bounced off bare hardwood and up the stairwell. The next thing I feared was the sound of one of them shattering, then a hand fumbling with the lock from the inside. I slithered along the floor as quietly as I could, back to where I'd left my phone next to the mattress.

I had Heath's number. He'd said to call him. I would.

To my horror, when I picked it up and hit the button, the screen remained black. Dead. I mashed the button again and again, frantic now. Little whimpers of panic squeaked out of my throat. This had to be a nightmare. This couldn't really be happening.

My phone, which I had assured was fully charged before I'd unplugged it just hours earlier, was stone dead.

I sat frozen, unsure what to do next. I had no weapon, save for the beautiful lamp Heath had brought with its sturdy brass base. I suppose it would have to do. If I crouched inside the bedroom doorway, wielding the heavy brass shaft in both hands, I could swing it and do at least enough damage to whoever this intruder was to disable them. To get out. To my truck.

Where were my keys?

With dread, I closed my eyes and visualized them, sitting on the countertop in the kitchen. Next to my purse, holding the pepper spray. Next to the Mason jar filled with droopy flowers. Stupid, stupid, stupid.

I was going to die here. Tonight, on this first night of my new life in a strange land. It wasn't so much the dying part that scared me. It was the fear of what I might have to experience before I took my last breath.

As my rumination ebbed, I realized it had been several minutes since the pounding had sounded. I crawled back toward the windows. Lying on my belly on the cold hardwood, I rose up just high enough to see over the edge of the balcony.

That's when I saw him. A man, wearing what looked like some sort of military uniform, was striding away from the house. It looked grey. But in the dim half-moonlight, everything looked grey, even the man, from head to toe. He wore a billed, flattened cap and strode with determined purpose. My blood chilled to ice when I saw he was carrying a rifle.

He was heading straight toward the road across my front lawn. I squinted but could see no car parked there. Must have left it somewhere down the road, so I couldn't identify his vehicle. What did he want? There was nothing in this house to even steal. And what kind of thief knocks on the front door anyway?

The wind sent a furious gust to scatter old leaves and twigs tumbling across the yard. The clouds were growing thicker now, too. A giant patch drifted in front of the moon, plunging the lawn into complete darkness for a brief few seconds. When it finally slid away and I could again see the dim scene below me, the man was gone.

Huddled on my mattress, I wrapped myself in the cheap, course quilt and covered my head. I'd plugged in my phone, but saw no point in calling Heath now, or even the local police. I'd wait until morning to file a report. And get someone from the hardware store out to put a new lockset and deadbolt on the front door—and the back—first thing in the morning. Time hovered, seeming to hold its breath, as I watched the time on my phone click onward, minute by minute. How long until dawn, I wondered?

My resident cricket resumed his chirping symphony. Exhaustion eventually lulled me into a drowsy state of half-consciousness until again, my body lurched as if from an electric shock.

Whining, from the direction of behind the house. It echoed through the empty rooms downstairs and up the stairwell. The dog was back. He was more insistent now. I checked the time: five forty-five.

The dog's high-pitched pleas grew louder, resonating through the empty house. At times, it seemed as though he was crouched right there outside my bedroom door. I shuddered and slid lower beneath my blanket.

Just as the first ray of sunlight reflected off the column on the balcony, the whining ceased. A few seconds of silence, followed by a long, hair-raising howl. Then, nothing.

Good morning, Camellia, Alabama.

I must have dozed again once morning light negated the specters of the night. The next time I opened my eyes, I heard someone at my door again. Not pounding this time. A soft knock. There was no doorbell.

I slithered again to the windows. A battered Ford pickup truck sat in the driveway behind my Tacoma. A tall man—very tall, older, white-grey hair cropped short—leaned against the front fender with his arms crossed.

As I reached the foot of the stairs, I spied a woman on the other side of the window. She was as short as the man was tall. A tiny, sprite of a woman, her hair just as white-grey, styled in a severe bob that cut a sharp frame around her weathered face. In her arms was a basket wrapped in clear cellophane.

I pulled my tee shirt down over yoga pants and made my way barefoot to the door. Surely, these folks didn't mean me any harm. When she saw me approach, the woman beamed a wide, a little-too-perfect white smile.

"Good morning," she said as I opened the door. "Mr. Edwards told us we had new neighbors. I'm on the Meet 'n' Greet committee here in Camellia, and I've come by to bring you a welcome basket."

The woman couldn't have been more than four foot ten inches tall, and wore denim overalls that all but swallowed her tiny frame. Worn, leather work boots peeked out from under hems hanging a bit too long. Yet the blouse she wore underneath was fine cotton and lacey, white with tiny lavender flowers all over. She was patient, standing there with her beaming smile and waiting for some sort of reaction from me.

I swiped my hand down over my face. "I'm sorry. I didn't sleep very well, and I'm still a bit out of sorts. Last night was my first night here."

She held up one gnarled hand. "No problem. No problem at all. We don't want to intrude. Just wanted to come by, introduce ourselves, Robert and me." She nodded back over her shoulder toward the man, who was still leaning against the truck. "Our property backs up to yours. There, you see?" She pointed to the post-and-rail fence a dozen yards or so behind the barn. "That's our pasture there." Then she stuck out her hand. "I'm Betty Warren, and that there is my husband Robert. Most folks around here just call me Bitsy."

How fitting, I thought, especially when she's standing next to Robert, who went six-five if he was an inch. I shook her hand and said, "Well, I'm not exactly dressed for company, but won't you both come in? I can offer you a cup of coffee, at least."

The one thing I hadn't left the city without was my travel-size Keurig. I'd unpacked it and set it up on my bare countertop last night after Heath helped me carry in the last of the few boxes I had stuffed in my truck. Robert and Bitsy followed me back to the kitchen. She laid the gift basket on the countertop with pride.

"There's just a few things in here we figure folks might make use of when they're settling in. There's a map of the area, with a list of the historic landmarks, along with flyers from the two main places we have in Camellia for eatin' out. We have two churches, Southern Baptist in town and the Methodist out on the county road. Their latest bulletins are in here. Oh, and some local honey." She paused to beam up at her husband. "Real local. Robert here has a row of hives he keeps back at the other end of our property. Goes real good with hot biscuits."

Until now, Robert hadn't spoken a single word. A tall, imposing man, he wore denim overalls matching his wife's, only five times bigger, with a red plaid flannel shirt. After a grumble and tip of his baseball cap when he first came in the door—one blazoned with a rebel flag—he hadn't said a word as he followed Bitsy and I through the house. By the way they were both ogling the place, I assumed they'd never been inside the Belle before.

"I sure do appreciate the gift basket. And the chance to

meet my new neighbors," I said, feeling a little awkward. "As you can see, I don't have much furniture yet . . . *any* furniture." I shrugged and grinned. "I'm planning to redecorate the whole place. I stopped by Heath's Heirlooms yesterday to get some ideas."

Bitsy had made her way to the back door and was peering out toward the barn, her arms crossed. "That young fella and his family were gonna keep horses in that barn. Never did find out why they changed their minds about the place."

Robert slipped off his cap and stuck it in his back pocket. "They were city folk. From Atlanta, I think. I'd bet they figured our little town wasn't exciting enough for 'em." He turned toward me and watched me pop a pod into the Keurig. "Fancy coffee machine. Like the one they got at the new place out there by the highway, ain't it?"

"No, I'm sure they have much more complicated brewers than this one. This makes one cup at a time. Makes the most sense for just me."

"So, you come out here all alone?" Bitsy asked. "No family?"

I shook my head. "No. Just me," I repeated.

Her eyes narrowed slightly, though she tried to cover her reaction with an embarrassed chuckle. "Where y'all from, anyway?"

Judging by the rebel flag on Robert's cap, my next words wouldn't make me their most popular new neighbor.

"New York. Originally from Boston, but I've lived in New York most of my life."

They both nodded sagely, as though I'd shared with them the fact that I was also a leper.

As the first cup spurted and squealed its way into one of the foam cups I'd brought along, Bitsy waved her hand toward the coffee. "Don't bother with any coffee for us. We both had ours hours ago. We'd best be gettin' along anyway." She slid a glance up toward her husband. "Just wanted to stop by. Drop off the basket. Let you know we live right around the corner, if you need anything."

As I followed them to the door, the steaming cup in my hand, I asked, "Bitsy, do you own a dog? There's been a dog hanging around the barn and at my back door since I got here yesterday."

They both stopped and looked at me as though I'd asked them if they'd had sex this morning. "A dog? What kind of a dog?" Bitsy asked, one straggly eyebrow disappearing beneath her sharply cut bangs.

"A hound of some kind. White, with tan on its head and ears. Looks half-starved, poor thing. I'm not a dog person, myself, so I wasn't really sure if I should be afraid of getting bitten or not—"

Bitsy turned away and picked up her step as they approached the front door. "We're not dog people either. Got a couple of barn cats. No dogs, though."

"And a horse," Robert added.

"We do." Bitsy paused at the door and hit me again with her too-perfect smile. "You outta come over sometime and meet Julia. She likes people. She's been kinda lonely since her momma died last fall." She paused, casting a glance down the hall toward the back of the house. "You plannin' on having any horses here?"

I shrugged. "Don't know. I might, at some point. I used to want one when I was a kid. It's been years."

Then Bitsy surprised me by reaching out to squeeze my arm. I guess she'd decided my Yankee leprosy wasn't as contagious as most. "Why don't you come by and visit sometime? Our house isn't old and fancy like yours, but Robert built me a real nice place when he retired from the granary. We could visit over some sweet tea."

Then, as quickly as they'd appeared, the old couple was back in their truck and backing out onto the road. Robert raised a hand out the driver's window as they pulled away.

Strange people, I thought. Yet it was nice to know there was another house not too far around the bend. I was beginning to feel like I'd bought an island in the middle of the Pacific. Yet I'd been in Camellia less than twenty-four hours and I'd already met three people—not counting the realtor. The Southern culture had a reputation for friendly. So far, I had nothing to dispute the claim.

It wasn't until I was sitting on my crate on the upstairs balcony, sipping my second cup of coffee, that I remembered my mysterious night visitor. A chill washed over me, and I picked up my phone. Should I call the police? Or Heath?

Chapter Four

Liv

After the Warrens left, I showered and got dressed, making notes on my phone every time I thought of something else I needed to pick up in town—or somewhere—to get through the next few days. The appliance store in Birmingham had given me a three-hour window for my delivery, between three and six o'clock. So I knew I had most of the day to start collecting essentials.

My first stop, I decided, would be Heath's store. I needed to order the Rice Bed, along with the rest of the bedroom furniture. I wanted to do some painting in there, but that could wait until I had a decent place to lay my head at night. I wouldn't be getting much work done, either on the house or for my business, if I wasn't sleeping well.

The higher the sun rose in the sky, the more the memory of my mysterious nighttime visitor faded. By the time I climbed into my truck and headed for town, I was convinced I'd dreamed up the entire incident. Still, I was going to find out if there was a hardware store in town. I needed to arrange for new locksets and deadbolts for my entry doors. Sleepy little Southern town or not, I wasn't comfortable staying out there alone without a secure barrier between me and whatever went bump in the night.

It was a little past ten when I pulled up to Heath's Heirlooms and parked near the curb. The door was open, a "welcome" flag fluttering in the morning breeze. Immediately, I relaxed. It was nice to know I had at least one person here I could come to for help.

I found Heath at the rear of the store wielding a box cutter on several large cardboard crates stacked near the back door. He was clad in khakis that hugged him in all the right places, and the sight of him caused my breath to catch in my throat. There was simply no denying it. Heath Barrow was one damn, sexy-looking man.

He looked up and grinned when I came in.

"Good morning. How'd your first night in Camellia go?" His crisply pressed, white shirt was open at the throat. The tuft of chest hair peeking out from the open placket caught my eye for only a second.

I wondered if it was as soft as it looked. Silky, chocolate curls that matched the cap covering his head. I cleared my throat and leaned one hip against the counter.

"Gotta do something about a real bed, Heath. I'll be useless if I have to spend many more nights on a damned air mattress."

He straightened and laid the box cutter down on his computer desk. "You're in luck. I have a Rice Bed, like the one I showed you yesterday, in my warehouse. It's a repro, but a good one. There's a bureau and armoire to match. If you'd like, I can arrange to have a truck bring them both out to your place and set them up this afternoon."

I closed my eyes and breathed a sigh of relief. "Fantastic. You carry bedding too?"

"I do. Pillow top? Memory foam? What firmness? Or would you rather take a drive into Birmingham to test them out?"

Now that sounded tempting. I wondered if he'd be willing to come along—

"I've got a crew who runs the warehouse. I can call and

let them know you're coming."

My heart sank just a little. Of course, he couldn't leave his shop unattended for just one lowly customer. I shook my head.

"No. If you've got one of those new, cool memory foam jobs I'll take one. King size. This bed . . . it is a King size, I hope?"

I knew authentic reproductions might not be. I didn't think the King-sized bed was available in Victorian times.

He nodded. "You're in luck. That's the advantage of a repro over the genuine article. Come on and we'll work up a price for the package."

I spent the next half-hour sitting next to Heath at his desk while he typed in the order and negotiated price before I handed over my credit card. Concentrating on the business at hand, though, became increasingly difficult.

"These pieces, separately, usually top out over five grand. For you? As a package, this is what I can do." He pointed to a figure on the screen.

As I leaned closer, the scent of his cologne, mingled with the tang of starch in his shirt, made me a little dizzy. His hands didn't look like a man who hefted furniture every day. Broad, strong hands with long, tapered fingers. Neat, clean nails. The way the cuff of his white shirt laid across his knuckles was incredibly sexy. And cuff links. He was even wearing cuff links

—

"Liv? You with me?"

I bolted back in my chair and readjusted my ponytail. "Yeah, sorry. Look's great. You're giving me a heck of a deal. Why are you so dressed up today?"

Where the hell had that come from?

He grinned, which caused a rapid melting of everything south of my ribcage.

"Another auction. This one's in Decatur. Starts at six so I'll have to close up shop here a little early to get there in time to check out what's what. I won't have time to run home and change first." He studied me, one side of his mouth quirked. "Wanna go? I can have them deliver your furniture tomorrow instead."

Tempting. I hadn't been to an antique auction since . . . well, ever. Flea markets, at time or two. Never an actual auction.

"I can't," I sighed. "My fridge is coming this afternoon. Washer and dryer, too. Besides, I need to run back to Birmingham and pick up some other essentials. Unless there's somewhere closer where I can get basics. You know, some dishes, silverware, towels."

"There's a Walmart in Haleyville. It's only about twenty minutes up Route 13." He cocked his head, one cynical eyebrow lifting. "Unless Wally World isn't fancy enough for a city girl's tastes."

I snorted. "Not a city girl anymore, remember? I left that life behind when I bought me an old house in the middle of nowhere." Standing, I hefted my purse over my shoulder. "Up Route 13, you said? I'd better get going. What time will my bed get here?"

Heath glanced up at the grandfather clock in the corner. "I'll call the boys now. They'll get it loaded and be at your place by, say, four? Will that work?"

He stood too, wafting his delicious scent all around me. Our chairs had been pushed close together so we could both see his computer screen, and now I found myself wedged between them—and him. Close. Just a little closer than two almost-strangers should be standing. His tuft of chocolate chest hair hovered just about eye level, only a few inches from my face. I dropped my head back to meet his eyes.

"Hey, thanks for the break on the furniture," I said, my voice sounding a little breathier than I'd intended. He held my gaze, the corners of his eyes crinkling.

"No problem. I'm hoping you'll be a repeat customer," he rumbled. "Maybe I'll drag you to an auction to pick out some of your other things."

"I'd like that."

"Mornin' Mr. Barrow!"

A screechy, elderly woman's voice sliced the moment in two and we both jumped. I turned to see a stout woman clad in a bright pink dress waddling down the center aisle of the shop.

"You get my brass candlesticks in yet? Ya said they'd be here Tuesday. Today's Tuesday."

Heath smirked and pushed back his chair, retrieving his box cutter. "I was just unpacking them a few minutes ago, Dora. Give me a minute to finish up with Ms. Larson here."

As I turned to go, I remembered the one, important thing I'd meant to ask Heath. "Hey, is there a locksmith in town?"

He turned from his task and blinked. "Yeah. Billy Connelly, up near Nan's diner. Why?"

I rubbed the back of my neck, which was already starting to itch with sweat. "I'd like to have some modern locksets installed. I'll go down and see when he can come out."

Hesitating only a moment, Heath shrugged and went back to his work. "Billy's your man. Tell him I sent you down."

It was going to turn into a busy afternoon. The locksmith planned on being there between four and five. Between the appliance men, the furniture delivery, and the locksmith, my house would be full of men this afternoon. The thought was oddly comforting.

And at the same time, disappointing. The only man I really wished was going to be there would be at some auction in Decatur. I wondered absently if I was fantasizing this whole attraction thing between us. Hell, I didn't know anything about Heath Barrow. Although I *had* noticed this morning—there was no wedding band on his sexy left hand.

By six o'clock, I was again alone in my house. And now I had stuff—a washer and dryer in the utility room, a shiny new refrigerator in the kitchen, and sturdy new locksets on both my doors. I must have climbed the stairs a half dozen times to go up and just stare at my new bedroom furniture. Heath had been right. The classic lines suited the room perfectly.

And oh, was it comfortable. The stress and exhaustion of the past few days caught up with me. Even if someone had come pounding on my door during the night, I doubt I would have heard them.

I awoke the next morning refreshed and recharged. I had so much to do, and I'd only allotted myself two weeks completely off from work to get started on the renovation process. The stack of decorating magazines on my nightstand had stuffed my head with all sorts of possibilities the night before. But where to begin?

After my second cup of coffee, I was just starting to pour myself a bowl of cereal when I heard the toot of a horn. There in my driveway sat my neighbor's battered pickup truck. Robert was alone, and didn't even bother getting out. He waved at me through the open window.

"Mornin'. Bitsy sent me around to tell you she's baked her special cinnamon coffee cake. Wanted me to ask you to come by and visit a spell."

I smiled. Nice people, I thought. Friendly.

"I'd like that, Robert. I'll be by in just a few minutes.

You're right around the corner, you said?"

"Three-quarters of a mile. First driveway on your left."

Twenty minutes later, I pulled my truck onto the paved lane winding through a grove of beautiful old oak trees weaving a canopy over the driveway. At the end, I found a house much smaller than mine, a quaint white cottage with a copper roof and a wraparound porch. Bitsy stood outside her front door, waving and grinning ear to ear.

"So glad you could come. Come on in," she called.

The welcoming scents of cinnamon and coffee hit me as I mounted the steps. The relatively modern, cottage-style exterior, though, could never have prepared me for what I found inside. I stepped into a virtual museum.

A high sideboard flanked the entry hall on one side, covered with frames holding black and white photographs. Above it hung a rectangular, oak-framed mirror with a decorative top, notched and carved. It reminded me of the headboard of my new Rice Bed. On both sides, oval, convex glass frames flanked it. The large, sepia portraits featured a woman in a dark, high-collared Victorian dress, and a man with a long, grey beard.

A long, oak cabinet with a dozen or more glass-fronted drawers anchored the right side of the hall. It was massive, easily stretching ten or twelve feet long down the hall. I'd never seen a piece of furniture quite this large, and wondered what on earth its function had been. Covering its highly polished oak surface were more framed pictures. None in color, some sepia.

For a moment, I froze on the spot, trying hard to acclimate myself to the abrupt change of atmosphere. It was as though, in stepping over the threshold, I'd stepped back a hundred years or more in time.

Bitsy stood before me, still grinning, wiping her hands

on an old-fashioned apron. She waited a beat as I perused her collection before chuckling nervously.

"Bitsy, what is this piece of furniture called? And who are all these people?" I asked.

"That come from an old general store. Used to hold seeds and beans and such. And this here's my family. My ancestors. There's a few of Robert's scattered in here and there, but most of 'em are Jinkins. This here," she pointed to the oval portrait of the Victorian-clad woman, "this was Mitsi Wilbur. She married my great-great-great-grandfather, Willard Jinkins, back in 1861. Right at the start of the Civil War."

I was struck speechless. How was it even possible to trace your family history back that far? I mean, I'd heard about people going crazy on ancestry sites and sending in DNA samples. Getting a printout telling them what percentage of their ancestry came from what part of the world. As a matter of fact, it's exactly what my friend back in New York, Delphine, did for a living. She worked in a DNA lab specializing in genealogy.

These were *photographs*. Actual portraits of people who lived almost two-hundred years ago.

Finally, realizing I was gawking, I sputtered, "Wow. I mean, really wow. I've never known anybody who could trace their family history back quite this far. With pictures."

Bitsy smiled proudly. "Grandpa Willard fought in the War, and came back alive to father seven children. Grandma wasn't much one for writin' things down, but she sure did like to go have the family's photographs taken."

The concept boggled my mind. I, on the other end of the spectrum, couldn't even tell you who my mother was. Let alone my father.

Foster parents, yes. Yet they were both gone now too. As far as lineage, I ranked right up there with a mongrel dog from the pound.

"Come on back," Bitsy urged. "The spice cake is an old family recipe, and it's really best when it's still warm. Coffee's done brewin' too."

I followed the tiny woman through the house, which wasn't large but tastefully decorated—with antiques, of course. Every piece looked like it belonged more in Heath's shop than in a home.

A few moments later, I found myself seated on their lovely back porch, a mug of steaming coffee in one hand and a plate of aromatic cinnamon cake on my lap. Robert sat in a rocker, a newspaper spread open before him. The chair made the tiniest creaking sound as he gently rocked while Bitsy bustled around the small table, fixing his coffee.

"We spend mornings out here because it stays shady until dinnertime. The house is set like yours—faces east. In high summer, by suppertime, you could fry an egg right here." She pointed to the glass top of the wicker-framed patio table. "That's when the front porch comes in handy."

Bitsy's coffee was thick and black, and contrasted wonderfully with the fluffy sweetness of the cake. "Mmm. This is fantastic, Bitsy. Are there ... apples in here?"

"Applesauce. Cinnamon applesauce cake. Like I said, old family recipe." She beamed as she settled in her own chair next to Robert.

Old family. I'd been hearing more of that term since I arrived here than I'd heard in my entire life. And I had to admit, it left me feeling more than a little lacking.

A stark reminder: I had no family. My life up until a year ago had been defined by my online persona as a web designer, and as the "Mrs." half of the Larson couple. Josh's wife. His parents' daughter-in-law.

When Josh died, so suddenly, so tragically, I'd been

stripped of more than a husband. I'd been stripped of my identity.

"I'm guessing you noticed Bitsy's museum up front," Robert said dryly, studying me over the tops of his readers. "She's got more of them old pictures in boxes in about every closet of the house. Just not enough wall space to display 'em all."

"Momma never did give anything away. Or her momma before her. So, all this stuff got passed down. I mean, what was I supposed to do with it? Hold a yard sale?" She slid Robert a narrow-eyed glare. She took a forkful of her cake, then shrugged as she chewed. "Not quite sure what's gonna happen to it once we're gone, though. Robert and me, well, we never had any children. Of our own," she added quickly.

Robert's gaze lifted toward the kitchen door as the clatter of silverware rang from inside. His shoulders lifted and dropped on a sigh. "We got Benjamin," he said. "But he ain't interested in any of that stuff. He'll probably hold a big old estate sale once he puts us in the ground."

I turned and caught a glimpse through the window of a man—a large, lumbering man with shaggy dark hair moving about in the kitchen. A sharp bang followed the metallic ring of silverware, then another bang as a cabinet door slammed shut, making Bitsy wince. Seconds later he appeared in the doorway, his massive form filling the frame.

"Momma, you got any more of that apple cake?"

"Right here, Ben. Come on out and meet our new neighbor."

Benjamin looked to be in his mid-forties, though it was hard to tell. Easily as tall as his father yet grossly overweight, the pudginess of his face disguised any wrinkles hiding beneath. His hair was shoulder-length, wavy, and nearly black —or appeared to be. It was either wet or really greasy.

His stained, white tee shirt hung crookedly on his hunched shoulders under baggy denim overalls. Barefoot, he shuffled out the door on Sasquatch feet, with a plate in one hand, fork in the other. He kept his eyes riveted on the square cake pan on the table.

"Manners, Ben," Robert grumbled when he made a beeline for the cake, his plate clicking against the glass tabletop. The man paused and swung his gaze toward me, sweeping me up and down with a dull, undecipherable expression.

"Sorry," Ben mumbled, wiping one hand on his denim overalls before extending it in my direction. It was as huge as a bear's paw. "I'm Ben Warren. Pleased to meet ya."

His handshake was cool and limp, sending a little shiver down my spine. His pale, grey eyes continued to rake over me, the expression transforming from dull to appraising. The sweet cake turned suddenly sour in my mouth.

Benjamin didn't resemble either Bitsy or Robert, yet shared their last name. And I thought Bitsy said they had no children—

"You buy the old Belle place?" he asked, his heavy hand still draped around mine. I deftly slid it free and resisted the urge to wipe it clean on my napkin. I nodded jerkily.

"I did. I've still got a lot of work ahead of me. Never took on quite as big a project as this one," I said. Keeping my attention on my cake plate, I tried to ignore the icky, tingling sensation, feeling his stare as he towered over me. Apparently, I was even more appealing than the cake pan on the table. At least for the moment.

Bitsy's cup clinked on the glass table before she proceeded to cut a hefty slice of the cake. "Ben's not too good with a paintbrush or a hammer, but if you need anything heavy hauled up them stairs, give a holler. I'm sure he'd like to help you out. Wouldn't you, Ben?"

"Yes, ma'am." His response was frighteningly enthusiastic.

On a cold day in hell, I thought.

Bitsy laid a huge square of cake on his plate and held it out to him. After a beat, she shoved the plate toward him and barked, "Ben. Here's your cake. You go on back in the house now and let us visit with Ms. Larson."

I looked up and saw he'd been staring at me, his initial fervor for the cake forgotten. The sensation of a thousand skittering ants scurried along my arms and back. And this man lives less than a mile up the road from my house. I reached for my coffee and struggled to wash my bite of cake past throat muscles suddenly clamped tight.

Blinking, he took the plate from Bitsy and refocused on the cake. His fork forgotten, he scooped the cake up with two fingers and took a huge bite. "Thanks, Momma," he sputtered as he turned and lumbered back into the kitchen.

Bitsy watched him go, waiting until the sound of his heavy footfalls faded away into the house. Then she turned and leaned toward me.

"Benjamin was my late cousin's child. Minnie— Wilhelmina was her proper name—well, she died of the cancer when Benjamin was just a boy. Her no-good husband wanted to have nothing to do with the child. Ran off with another woman while Ben was spending the weekend with us." She pressed her lips together and shook her head. "We had no choice. I was lucky dear Robert here said we could keep him. Raise him. Or he woulda ended up in the county home." She smiled over at her husband, who nodded while keeping his eyes fixed on his newspaper, his face expressionless.

Bitsy shifted forward until she was on the very edge of her seat and lowered her voice to almost a whisper. "Benjamin is a little, well . . . special. If you know what I mean. Still, he earns his keep 'round here. Yard work and the like. Helps take care of Julia."

I tipped my head, forgetting who Julia was. Bitsy nodded toward the fenced pasture beside the house. "We used to keep a few horses, Robert and me. We both fancied trail riding. When we was younger. Julia was the last foal born on the place. She gets along real well with Benjamin."

I turned to peer in the direction Bitsy indicated, and spotted the distant silhouette of a horse, head down to grass, tail swishing. From this distance, it was hard to tell what color she was. In the morning sunlight, she appeared almost golden.

"I'd like to meet her sometime. I haven't been around horses since I was just a kid. "

"Maybe you could come by and Benjamin will introduce you." She beamed as though the horse was as much a part of the family as her stepson. It was touching, in a way. Though the thought of spending one-on-one time with the likes of Benjamin made my stomach twist. I shook my head.

"It's been years since I've been around horses," I repeated.

I leaned forward and set my empty plate and mug on the table. "Well, thanks so much for inviting me over for the scrumptious treat, Bitsy. It was really thoughtful of you. You too, Robert." I nodded in his direction and he, his eyes still trained on his paper, simply nodded.

"Oh, you can't go so soon," Bitsy said, hopping to her feet. "You have to let me give you the tour first."

The tour? Of the house, did she mean? I guess maybe this was a Southern custom. I slid a glance toward Robert as he looked up over his readers and rolled his eyes.

"I hope you ain't in any particular kind of hurry this morning," he remarked dryly.

Heath

He buttoned up his shirt as she watched him, careful not to catch any of his curly, dark chest hairs in the process.

"Looking good, my man. I'm so glad you found the time to stop by and see me today. Anything new in your life? You're exuding a bit more sparkle than the last time we met."

He suppressed a grin and looked away. "Let's just say life in sleepy Camellia has gotten a little more interesting lately. Potentially, anyway." He rose and tucked his shirt back into the waistband of his khakis. Then he pushed up his cuff and checked his watch. "I've got to hurry now if I'm gonna make it to Decatur."

She crossed her arms and studied him. "Well I hope life in Camellia doesn't get so interesting you won't find time to come up this way every now and again."

Fastening his cuff link, he grinned at her and shook his head.

"Never happen, Sandra. You know you've got more power over me than that. Hell, you've changed my life."

Nodding, she turned toward the door.

"And thanks—"

"No problem. Call me anytime," she said, as the door

clicked shut behind her.

Chapter Five

Liv

It was nearly two o'clock by the time I drove out of the Warren's driveway. "The tour," as Robert facetiously dubbed it, ended up taking over an hour. At least I hadn't caught sight of the intimidating Benjamin while it lasted.

Yet I hadn't been bored by Bitsy's soliloquy of family history. Moving from one faded image to the next, she'd carefully outlined her family tree, which I could hardly believe she traced back almost two hundred years in photographs. As fascinating as it had been, it left me with an empty hole aching in my gut.

I didn't have anything even remotely similar to this. It made me feel incomplete. Missing something. Something, as I grew older, that seemed crucially important in my life.

What must it be like, I wondered, to know that much about where you came from? About the people whose genetic memories resided inside you? It must be grounding.

I'll never have that. My birth mother was barely more than a kid herself and, from what my foster parents told me, never even held me after the umbilical cord was cut. They picked me up from the hospital when I was only three days old. By then, "Mom" was long gone.

My foster parents gave me everything parents could possibly give to a child in the way of love, support, and encouragement. Believing in honesty to a fault, they never held back any of the details of how I'd come to be theirs. I knew, from my very first memories, they weren't my blood relatives.

Although they explained to me my birth mother had done what was best, I still found myself waiting for her. Wondering when she'd come back for me. Certain she someday would.

I tried to imagine what she looked like, whether her hair was pale blonde and straight like mine. Or if I'd taken more after Dad. Who was he, anyway? Another kid who made an irresponsible mistake? Did he even know I existed?

My birth certificate was a lie. An ABC, they called it: Altered Birth Certificate. It reflected the names of my foster parents, with my last name matching theirs. The original was, I'd been told, sealed. In addition, my birth mother had traveled from a distant city to give birth in a place far from her hometown. She obviously hadn't wanted anyone to connect me with her.

I knew there were probably ways for me to retrieve the information, but was it worth it? If my mother hadn't even wanted to hold me after I took my first breath, then how would she react if I tracked her down and confronted her? It was a certain recipe for rejection.

I wondered about my father. Was his name on the original document? Did she even know who he was?

Now, that knowledge seemed critical to me figuring out who *I* was. It hadn't seemed to bother me when I was younger, when I still had my foster parents to ground me. And then, Josh. Now, they were all gone, and I was alone. It's why I had to get out of the city. Start a new life.

Over the last two years, without anyone or anything anchoring me within my own head, I seemed to have forgotten how to be me.

My therapist back in New York called it a mid-life crisis. Perhaps. I was at the right age—about to turn 38, my fortieth birthday looming ominously just over the horizon. I thought of it more like an identity crisis. I grew up Olivia Hawthorne, and then I became Mrs. Josh Larson. Now, I was Liv. Just plain Liv.

As I pulled up in front of the Belle Bride house, these achingly lonely thoughts spinning around in my head, a warmth spread in my chest. I couldn't explain why. What had drawn me here? Why did this particular house, in the middle of somewhere I'd never been, never even knew existed, call to me the way it did? This puzzled me.

Maybe because *this place* had a history.

Yes, the house has a history, I thought. One I can explore, unlike my own. I pulled out my phone and quickly Googled two local Camellia addresses: the library, and the museum. Yes, even a town as tiny as this one, in the middle of navigable nowhere, had one of each. Apparently, people in these parts, much like Bitsy, treasured their heritage.

If I couldn't research my own ancestry, I would start on Belle's. Besides, I rationalized, researching the home's history would help me restore her to a more authentic version of herself. After a sprint inside to grab a bottle of water and my laptop, I headed into town.

I decided to hit the museum first. After all, if I didn't know what to look up in the library, I wouldn't get very far. Camellia's museum was a faded, red brick building. Several multi-paned windows lined the front, two on either side of a covered porch. I could see lacy curtains edging the windows on the inside. Two flags flew on either side of the porch railing: the American flag, and another I assumed was a Confederate flag. It was a solid, red X on a white background. The door was propped open with an old milk can.

Once I stepped over the threshold, the musty, mildewed smell of *old* engulfed my senses. The scarred floorboards creaked beneath my feet, and it took a moment for my eyes to adjust to the dimmer light inside. Dust motes hung on the slightly cooler air.

"Afternoon."

I jumped at the raspy voice of the old woman whom I hadn't seen sitting behind a glass display counter on my left. Her wiry, white hair frizzed out about her head, defying her efforts to contain it in some sort of bun. She amply filled an antique rocking chair. Intense, bright blue eyes studied me. She didn't smile.

"Hi. I'm new in town, and thought I'd come down and learn a little bit about my new home," I said. I felt so awkward, so out of place. A nervous chuckle escaped as I continued, "I guess this would be the best place to start, right?"

The woman had been working on some sort of needlepoint project arranged in her lap. She set it on the glass countertop as she rose. The dust motes stirred and drifted into a band of sunlight streaming through the window, draping her in an ethereal mantle.

Yikes. Did I slip into a time warp here?

"Yes, it's definitely the right place." Finally, a smile transformed her face into a pattern of wizened lines. "New here, as in, resident? Not a tourist?"

I shook my head. "I bought the old Belle Bride house. I'm interested in finding out more about the place so I can do it justice when I decorate it."

The subtle lifting of one eyebrow did not escape me. She took her time, studying me, before finally crossing her arms to lean on the counter. Gradually, a smile rose to crease the corners of her eyes. "Your accent tells me you're not a Southerner. Where're you from?"

"New York." The words came out sounding like an apology.

Now both straggly brows lifted, and another long moment ticked by before she extended her hand. "I'm Nora Bentley. I was born here in Camellia. Live in the cottage right next door to this here museum."

"Liv Larson." We shook and I asked, "How much is admission?"

She tipped her head toward a battered, Eight O'Clock coffee can on the end of the counter. "Donations is all. This place is more of a hobby for me than anything else. My momma and daddy opened it back in the 50s. Just keeping a family tradition alive." She settled back into her rocker, dragging her needlepoint along with her. "Take your time. Look around. If you have any questions, don't be afraid to ask."

I stuffed a ten-dollar bill into the can and began to make my way through the museum's meager collection. It reminded me a lot of Bitsy's front hall, I mused. I wondered how many of the faded, sepia photographs hanging on these walls were kin to the lady behind the counter—Nora, did she say?

Glass display cases lined the perimeter of the room, with some scattered pieces of antique furniture in the center. Many of the items, I noticed, were military—Civil War era. Everything from muskets to tin cups to canteens.

Several relic cases rested atop the cabinets, wooden boxes padded with cotton batting and sealed beneath glass lids. Each one contained bits and pieces of God-knew-what. The yellowed index cards beside them described the items found on soldier campsites. A jumble of odd pieces, they ranged from rusted buckles to bullets to pieces of identifiable, twisted metal. A tarnished, brass bugle with a curlicue end hung from a wooden tree, along with numerous, dusty caps and hats.

In the far rear corner, two mannequins loomed ominously in a staged display. I was almost afraid to explore closer. Both wore uniforms: one blue, and one grey. They stared out at me from eyes of chipped paint above straggly beards draped with cobwebs. A shiver skittered down my spine. The Union soldier leaned on a musket with bayonet. The

Confederate held a wooden rod featuring a tattered flag.

This one was different from the flag out front. This must be the Rebel flag. No doubt the message here, I thought.

I turned toward Nora, still seated behind the front desk. "The flag out front—"

"It's Alabama's state flag. Still raises some controversy. But it's our flag, and we are duly proud of it." Only a bit of arrogance laced her words, which I chose to ignore. After all, I was a brand-new Alabamian, right? Might as well get in the mindset . . .

I turned back toward the display in the corner.

It wasn't until I'd gotten close enough to see clear down to the straw beneath the soldiers' battered boots that I spotted the dog. I froze, blinking, wondering for a moment if it was alive. Or was I was imagining the animal? Then I realized . . . the dog, although real, had left the world of the living long ago.

Someone had stuffed it. The creature lay in a natural-looking pose near the weather- and age-worn boots of the Confederate soldier. With disbelief, I crouched closer, feeling the animal's cloudy brown, glass eyes stare back at me eerily. All white except for caramel-brown ears and a matching patch across the top of its head, it was a doppelganger for the one I'd seen behind my house.

Even though the air was warm and muggy, a sudden chill washed over me. Standing slowly, I leaned to steady myself on the nearby display case. Blood whirred in my ears and I feared my heart would batter itself to pieces on my breastbone.

"That there was my great-grandfather's walker hound."

I shrieked and spun around to find the old woman standing only a few feet behind me. How had I not heard her coming? How had she moved so fast?

"Oh, I'm sorry, Miss. I didn't mean to scare you. Lots of folks are spooked by this display. My family's had it set up here for as long as I can remember. I just can't bear to tear the thing down."

Pressing my hand to my throat to keep my heart from cutting off my air supply, I closed my eyes and struggled for a deep breath.

"It's okay. I'm just a little freaked out because I could have sworn I saw this dog . . . a dog exactly like this one . . . near the barn at the Belle Bride." Embarrassed, I pinched the bridge of my nose and chuckled. "The one I saw wasn't nearly as healthy looking as this one. And this one is . . . dead."

The woman maintained an even eye contact with me, with no visible reaction. She went on as though we were friends having a civil discussion about dog breeds.

"Walker hounds are real popular in these parts. They make great hunting dogs, and are good with children, too. Very loyal. That one there—her name was Sandy—she was a breeding bitch. Raised a half-dozen or more litters of pups for my great-grandparents. When she died, Gramps just couldn't bear to put her in the ground."

She stared at me while I tried to compose myself. I must look like a complete idiot, I thought. City girl spooked by a taxidermist's handiwork and a couple of sad-looking mannequins. I rubbed my arms to try to chase the chill away.

She tipped her head. "You move down here all by yourself? Any family in the area?" she asked gently.

"No. Just me. Starting over." I stood taller and squared my shoulders. "I'm kind of a loner anyway. Since I work from home, I didn't get out much, even when I lived in the city."

She crossed her arms and leaned an ample hip against the counter, causing the old frame to creak. "You might think about getting you one of these hound dogs for a companion, then. My cousin on my dad's side still raises a litter every now and then."

"I'll keep that in mind," I said absently. Then, a thought occurred to me. "Where does your cousin live? Maybe it was one of his hounds I saw at my house—"

She was shaking her head. "No way. Ashley lives in Tuscaloosa. And he's not one to let his dogs roam about." Her eyes narrowed as she scrutinized me. "We have a dog catcher here in town. Maybe you could give him a call. Not good for animals to be runnin' loose."

If it was even real, I thought.

"I will. If I see him again."

Focus, Liv. Remember the reason why you're in here today.

"So, the Belle Bride. What can you tell me about the house?" I asked.

She turned and waddled her way back toward the front of the room. "It's been empty most of the time it's stood there, from what I know. Rumors say it was some wealthy plantation owner's wedding gift to his daughter. I know it was built in 1861. The same year as the war started."

"Hmm. The realtor told me."

It made me uncomfortable the way she avoided my eyes as she spoke, busying herself with some books and stacks of papers on the front counter. I waited, but when she didn't say anything more, I asked, "Are there any records on the house? I mean, photographs or copies of deed registries? Anything at all?"

She'd started shaking her head before I'd even finished the question. "Nothin' like that here. Library might have something." She scooted her generous form around the counter and reclaimed her position in her rocker, which groaned in protest. Picking up her needlework, she resumed her stitching.

Apparently, our conversation about the Belle Bride was over.

Heath

The auction in Decatur was a bust. Heath berated himself all the way back to Camellia for wasting his time, again. That particular auction house had changed hands about a year ago, and the quality of the merchandise had steadily declined since then. He wouldn't be making this trip again anytime soon.

At least, not for the auction.

He hadn't hung around long once he realized there wasn't a single item he was interested in buying. Checking the time on his dashboard as he revved the Ram's engine, he figured he should be back in Camellia by around nine o'clock.

Too late, he wondered, to stop by and see how Liv liked the new bedroom furniture she had delivered? He could take the back road into town . . . drive by the house. If there were lights on, well . . .

A light on, he thought, smiling. It's pretty much all she had. Unless she'd gone shopping today, or had an electrician install a bunch of new fixtures. All she had was the one bathroom vanity bulb, and the new lamp he'd bought her. The thought caused a warm spot in the middle of his chest. One that unsettled him. It shouldn't be there.

He'd already lost one love to a more exciting life than he could offer any woman here in this tiny town. A life that suited him fine. He knew, though, not everyone loved the laid-back, close-knit kind of community he lived in. Had grown up in.

Yeah, Liv had fled the city and come out here because of some heartbreak. On a whim. Fell in love with a gorgeous old antebellum home. With the *idea* of owning an old antebellum home. Obviously had plenty of money to do whatever she wanted, go wherever she wanted to go. His guess was, Liv Larson wouldn't last long in the middle of Nowheresville, Alabama.

Even if she lasted long enough to refurbish the place, get it up to a decent resale condition, there's no way she'd be staying here. The city lights would call her back. Just like they'd done with Katherine.

He couldn't risk his heart. Not again. Just the thought of what he'd gone through when Katherine had left made the twitch start at the corner of his eye. His stomach, which he knew was empty because he hadn't eaten since the sandwich he grabbed earlier this afternoon, felt bloated and uncomfortably full. He lifted his fingers jerkily to his mouth. He began rubbing his lips, over and over.

No. Getting emotionally involved with Liv Larson was definitely not a good idea. He stayed on the highway until he got to the exit leading him straight to his house on the west side of town.

Hours later, Heath was sound asleep when his cellphone ring split the night. Disoriented, he grabbed it off his nightstand, but did not recognize the number. It wasn't a local exchange. And it was two-thirty a.m. . . . telemarketers at this hour of the night? It had to be a wrong number.

Just as he reached to silence the ringer, it came back to him. The night he'd exchanged numbers with Liv.

She was hysterical. He couldn't make out her garbled, panicked words punctuating the sobs. Ten minutes later, he was in his car and headed for the Belle Bride.

Chapter Six

Liv

Once I was fully awake and knew Heath was on his way, I felt like a complete idiot. I must have dreamed this. Aftermath of my strange day at the museum, and my brush with Civil War history.

Instead of calling him back and telling him "never mind," in which case he would really think I was a nut case, I made a cup of coffee. When Heath's headlights sliced across my front windows, I was sitting on the bottom step of my beautiful curving staircase. I'd carried my lamp—his gift to me—downstairs and plugged it in the foyer.

He was wild-eyed and wild-haired when I let him in. Well, what did I expect? I'd awoken him from a dead sleep with a hysterical phone call. Now I was having difficulty remembering exactly what happened.

"What the hell, Liv? You scared me half to death. I thought somebody had broken in and was raping you."

He raked his fingers through his curls, which only made them stand up in a more disheveled mess. His denim shirt was unbuttoned, leaving his chest bare over red plaid pajama pants. I had literally ripped him out of bed. As upset as I'd been just minutes earlier, I was surprised to realize the reaction my body had to him in his state of relative undress.

He looked pretty damned sexy.

But he also looked pissed off. I couldn't blame him. All I could think to do to defuse his anger was to cover my face with my hands and lean into him. He smelled like soap.

"It was probably a dream," I said quietly. "But it's twice this has happened now, Heath, and it's really starting to freak me out."

"When *what* happened, Liv? You're not making any sense." His voice was softer now, and his hands came up to rub my back. "You had the new locks installed, right?"

I nodded, my forehead still against his chest. Warm, bare skin fuzzed with chocolate brown curls. His heart thudded beneath taught muscle.

I hardly knew this man, yet here I was skin to skin with him in the dark, in the middle of the night. Why didn't it seem weird? It should have. It didn't.

He gripped my shoulders with both hands and drew me away to look into my eyes. "You need to tell me everything. But not standing here in the foyer. Have you got any more of that coffee I smell?" He paused. "*Hot* coffee?"

I grinned and nodded as he followed me into the kitchen.

Our seating choices were limited, of course, because of the lighting situation. And with no furniture other than in my bedroom, it was a much more practical choice than the upstairs bath. I sat cross-legged at the head of the bed, while he perched discreetly near the footboard.

I took a sip of my coffee and a shaky breath. "I know this is going to sound crazy. I keep getting this night visitor. He showed up the first night I was here, and then again tonight."

He waved one hand in the air. "And? What does he want?" Irritation clearly tainted the words.

"I don't know. He pounds on my door. Like, really bangs on the wood. So hard I'm afraid the windows will shatter."

Heath shook his head and spoke as though to a small

child. "Liv, why don't you call the police? This guy is evidently a psycho—"

"Heath? He's a soldier. A Civil War soldier. In uniform."

He froze then, his coffee cup halfway to his lips. One eyebrow lifted slowly, then his eyes narrowed. "Is this some kind of joke? Some bizarre new way of getting my attention? A damsel-in-distress thing?"

His cynicism stung at first, then made me angry. "Look, I should never have called you tonight, alright? You gave me your number, and you said to call if I needed anything. I got scared. I needed somebody . . . somebody *here*." I hated how helpless and pathetic I sounded. And ridiculous.

Still, it was worth his wrath to have him sitting there, with me in this big, old empty house. Even if for only a little while. The damn banging on my door had commenced, again, at two a.m. It hadn't lasted as long. From my gallery window, I'd seen, again, the strangely uniformed soldier stomping off into the night.

He reminded me too much of the mannequin I'd seen at the museum today. Eerily similar.

Heath set his cup down on the floor beside the bed and rubbed his face with both hands. "Look," he said, "I had a crappy day, made a useless trip to Decatur, and came home empty-handed. The last thing I needed was to be woken in the middle of the night. So, pardon me if I'm a little irritable." He leaned back on his hands and looked around the room, illuminated only by the Astral lamp, which cast the four posts on the Rice bed into tall shadows on the walls. "But you've really got to get some light in this place. I mean, no wonder you're creeped out at night. These old houses can be spooky even in broad daylight."

I turned and slid a sheet of paper out from beneath the laptop on my nightstand. "Funny you should mention it. I was coming into town tomorrow morning to drop this off to you. I've picked out some table and floor lamps from the lighting catalog you left me. And some ceiling fixtures too. You said you could order them for me?"

Heath took the paper and scanned it. "Sure. I can even get somebody to install the fixtures. A buddy of mine is an electrician." He folded the list and stood, attempting to slip the paper into his back pocket. Pajama pants don't have back pockets. He closed his eyes and shook his head. "I can't believe I'm standing in the bedroom of a complete stranger in the middle of the night in my pajamas."

I couldn't help but think how right he looked standing there.

"Come on," I said. "I'll walk you out. Lock up behind you."

Wielding my handy-dandy flashlight, I led him down the stairs into the foyer. Just as I went to throw back the deadbolt, I heard a noise coming from the back of the house. I froze and turned, nearly colliding with Heath, who was right on my heels.

"Did you hear that?" I asked. Before he could answer, it sounded again. A scratching noise. At my back door.

Heath took the flashlight from my hand and said, "I hope you had this place gone over by an exterminator before you moved in. We get rats down here the size of—"

A dog's bark, then whine, interrupted him.

He looked at me. "Do you have a dog?"

I shook my head. "No, but there's one been hanging around the barn since I moved in. He's scratched at my back door before. Poor thing looks half-starved. I'm not used to dogs. When I went to get some water for him the other day, he disappeared before I got it out the door."

We stood side-by-side at the back door, peering down

through the glass panes. Heath reached up and flicked the wall switch. I was startled when yellowish light flooded the doorstep.

"Well, now I've got three working lights," I said.

Heath unlocked the door and pulled it open. There was no animal on the steps. He swept the area beyond with the flashlight. Nothing.

After he'd closed and latched the door, he said, "Leave this outside light on. Maybe it will keep whatever is trying to get in, out."

When he turned, I was right behind him, and suddenly, there we were again. Face to face. Our bodies so close I could feel his warm breath on my cheek. Musky skin, mixed with the faint scent of fabric softener from his shirt. His warm breath, smelling of toothpaste, minty and clean.

I should have stepped back, given him his space. But something inside me begged for human contact. A man's touch. I ached to be held. It was true I hardly knew this man. At that moment, it didn't matter. I stood dumbly, my hands at my sides, and waited.

The touch of his smooth fingers on my cheek drew out an unintended sigh from me. I leaned into his touch. He'd lowered the flashlight beam to the floor. His face remained a dark silhouette, backlit by the outdoor light.

Would he kiss me? Was he even looking into my eyes as I was now searching in the dark for his? The moment froze, and I closed my eyes. His fingers moved to lift my chin.

"Liv . . . I . . . I can't do this," he murmured. "God knows I want to. I've . . . I've got a lot of baggage. It wouldn't be fair to you. To either of us."

I laid my hands on his warm, furry chest, reveling in the sensation. "I'm willing to bet my ton of baggage would make yours look like a backpack. Maybe we could compare what we've got packed away sometime."

He slid a finger up to tuck my hair behind my ear, then rested his hand on my shoulder. "Maybe. But I can't be coming to your house half-dressed in the middle of the night anymore. You're too much of a temptation. I am a man, you know. We don't handle temptation well."

"I'm not asking for any commitments, Heath. In fact, it's the last thing in the world I'm ready for. We're both adults. We could handle . . ."

As I spoke, his hand began to tremble against my shoulder. Suddenly, almost violently. Was he nervous? Or cold? It was a warm, muggy night. Certainly, not cold.

Abruptly, he took a step away from me and blurted, "I've really got to go now."

After I'd locked the door behind him, I stood at the front windows and watched his headlights sweep my front lawn, then fade away down the lane toward town. Although I couldn't put my finger on the sensation, an odd sense of foreboding gathered in my chest.

Only this time, it didn't have anything to do with elusive dogs or strangely costumed visitors in the night.

Heath

The next morning, Heath opened the shop late again, in the pouring rain. Tourist traffic this early in the spring was light anyway, especially on rainy days. He hadn't slept well after his nighttime jaunt to Liv's place.

Already, this new city girl was causing upheaval in his life.

His first phone call, though, was to Dr. Donohue.

Finally, the receptionist clicked the call through. "The new drug, Sandra. It just isn't working as well. I had a couple of minor episodes yesterday, and one again last night. I think I need to go back on the old stuff," he said.

He heard her sigh. "I told you there'd be a transition period, Heath. All the journals are saying this new drug is the best thing for your condition. I think we should give it some time. Another month or so, anyway."

Heath bristled. "Easy for you to say. I have a business to run, Sandra. And I live alone. I also do quite a bit of traveling— alone. I can't afford to be out somewhere on the highway when —"

"Another month, Heath. I'm telling you, it will be worth the wait. Just plan your schedule accordingly. This formulation is documented to eliminate all of the side effects you had with the other drug."

Well, if it were true, it certainly would improve his quality of life, Heath thought. But in the meantime . . .

"Just don't take any long trips alone for the next few days. Take a friend if you need to go. Let them drive."

Heath snorted. "Yeah, and explain to them all about my *episodes*, just in case I happen to weird out on them on the way. I'm not about to do that, Sandra. I like to keep this as quiet as possible."

"Another month, Heath," she repeated. "For me. I'm telling you, you'll thank me in the long run."

Heath crashed the phone back onto its cradle and leaned his head on his hand. Side effects. Sure. It's easy to refer to them so flippantly when they aren't messing with your life, he thought. Those side effects were another one of the reasons Katherine had decided to move on.

He sighed. It hadn't been the only reason, he knew. She'd missed the life she got a taste of when she went off to Atlanta to college. The same way Liv would, he was certain. Sooner or later.

Thinking of Liv, he pulled the list she'd given him out of his shirt pocket and called in her lighting order. Then he called Ralph Potter, his electrician friend, and told him to be expecting a call from a Liv Larson.

"The old Bride place, huh? How long do you think this one will last?" Ralph barked into his ear.

Heath shook his head. "Not long, my guess. She's from up north. New York. She's already getting skittish."

Ralph made a growling sound, then chuckled. "A Yankee too, no less. Hope those fixtures come in soon or she'll be gone before I get the chance to wire 'em in."

When Heath hung up the phone, he stared at it for a moment, pondering what Ralph had said. It did seem odd about the Belle Bride. He'd lived in Camellia his whole life and couldn't remember the big old house being anything but vacant. He really thought the last family that bought it a few years ago were coming to stay.

They refurbished the barn, replaced a few floor boards on the front gallery, and then never moved in. Odd. But maybe Ralph was right. As he remembered hearing from Tom, the realtor, they were from Atlanta.

There were rumors. There always had been. Heath didn't

believe in all that bad Karma hogwash. The old timers in town had too much time on their hands, time to spin all sorts of imaginative tales. Probably most of the reason the place had been bank-owned for as long as Heath could remember. He supposed it was a blessing the money men hadn't decided to just bulldoze the place.

It was the one thing about the people in this town. They valued their history. And the Belle Bride held a precious piece of that. One folks weren't about to let go of.

Chapter Seven

Liv

Three days later I was wandering through the house holding a fan of paint chips in my hand when I heard the crunch of tires on my driveway. I watched Heath climb out of his gigantic Dodge Ram headed for my front door, hands jammed into the front pockets of his jeans.

My heart did a little flip in my chest. I hadn't seen him or spoken to him since the night I woke him in the wee hours. Since the night he almost kissed me. Maybe I hadn't screwed this thing up after all.

"Can I help you, Sir? Are you lost?" I said with a grin as I opened the door. His quirky, one-sided smile hit me straight in the swoon zone. Damn, but wouldn't I like to comb my fingers through those chocolate curls.

He glanced down at the paint fan I was holding. "Picking out colors, huh? I guess you must have made some decisions on how you're decorating the place already."

"I have. Got some great ideas from some of those Southern Living magazines you left me. Come on in. I think I've got two cold beers left in the fridge."

As I handed him the icy bottle, his eyes wandered to the new drop fixture over the sink. "I see Ralph was here. Now at least you don't have to huddle in your bedroom after dark."

A warm knot formed in my belly remembering that night. "Isn't such a bad place to hang out, though, is it?" I teased.

"It is at three a.m. when you're talking like a crazy person," he said. "Has your soldier friend been around since then? No, wait . . . I'm sure if he had, I'd have been the first to know." He winked, and again, my belly tightened.

Damn, this guy was sexy.

Still, I tried to hold it together. I scowled at him. "No, no more night visitors. And the dog hasn't been around either."

Heath tipped back his head and studied me. "Do you have any plans for tomorrow? I stopped by to ask if you'd like to go with me to my warehouse in Birmingham. You've got light fixtures, but doesn't look like you've bought anything much more in the way of furniture. Still echoes like a tomb in here."

A shiver ran across my shoulder blades. It did echo, and I figured it probably always would, seeing as the ceilings were twelve feet high. Certainly, furnishings would help. "I am getting kind of tired of eating my dinner sitting on a plastic storage crate. Really, the first thing I need to invest in is office furniture."

Heath slid his eyes away from me. "Tomorrow's good . . . I usually close the shop on Tuesdays anyway. And I was planning on dropping my car off at the shop for an oil change. Any chance you could drive?"

"Sure thing. I'll pick you up at . . . what, say, ten?"

Heath pulled out his phone, his fingers flying across the screen. A few seconds later, my phone dinged from inside my purse on the counter.

"Uh, you don't have to text me when I'm standing in the same room with you. Are you that shy?" I said, grinning.

"Address of Wilbur's garage, out toward the highway."

At ten the next morning, I pulled up to the small, ancient looking brick building with a sign over two open bays announcing *Wilbur's Automotive Repairs.* Heath stood talking to a short, balding man whose clothes were so covered with grease, their color was indecipherable. Classic, I thought. This is the kind of place you read about, typical in small towns. But you don't really believe they still exist until you see them with your own eyes.

I guess Jiffy Lube hasn't invaded this area of the country. At least, not quite yet.

"Good morning," Heath smiled as he climbed into the passenger side of my Tacoma. "Ready for an adventure? No, wait." He hesitated, rolling his eyes up toward the ceiling and touching a finger to his chin. "Adventure . . . that's guy talk. Are you ready for a shopping trip?"

God, this man was getting to me, no matter how hard I tried to resist. He was lucky I didn't pull off into the woods on the side of the road and rip his clothes off. But I was a good girl. I resisted instinct.

On the hour-long drive to Birmingham, I finally got a chance to ask the questions burning in my mind about the handsome antique store owner. I mean, I was beginning to have high hopes for some kind of relationship with him, even if it meant nothing more than a weekend in the sack. It had been a long time for me, and the chemistry sure did exist between us.

For all I knew this guy could be married with three kids.

"So, tell me about your house. You said you lived on the other side of town. Is it an old house like mine?" I asked.

"No. That's way too much space for me to handle. I just own a small cottage on a few acres. The less I have to take care of, the better." He hesitated, flashing a glance my way, and added, "What with the two businesses to run, and all."

"Two businesses. I thought the place in Birmingham was just a warehouse."

"It is. But there's also a storefront. It's right downtown, in the area they've refurbished a few years back. Gets pretty good traffic."

I raised an eyebrow. "I didn't get that from scanning your website."

"You see? I really do need your services. I'm pretty good at handling online orders, and even auctioning pieces off on eBay, but website design? I just don't have time for it." I felt his gaze warm on my cheek as he studied me, and my heartrate immediately kicked up a notch. "We'll have to set aside some time to talk about that." His voice dropped to a sultry growl as he ran the back of his hand down my bare arm.

Okay, okay, I really had to just come out and ask.

"So, are you . . . married? Involved in a relationship? I mean, I'm no prude, but I'm also not into getting tangled up with anybody else's man."

He pulled away, ever so slightly, and leaned an elbow on the door as he looked out the side window. "Not married. Used to be. Not anymore."

Should I probe further? Or was this his way of telling me the subject was off limits? Time to go back to a safer subject.

"Who runs the shop in Birmingham, then? I met your delivery crew. Hell of a nice bunch of young guys."

He turned toward me slowly with a broad grin. "You're about to meet her."

The storefront sat smack dab in the middle of a long block of two and three-story older block buildings just off 2nd Ave. Heath's store, though, was the jewel of the street. Red brick with white-trimmed, arched windows on the upper floors, it definitely made a statement. Here, instead of a decorative, hand-lettered sign labeled "Heath's Heirlooms," a long, vertical rectangle of neon featured two bright red, nested letters: *HH.*

Apparently, in Birmingham, Heath's business needed no more than that simple logo. I was immediately impressed, not to mention increasingly curious. This man was evidently not the sexy, country bumpkin I'd been assuming he was.

We parked behind the building in a tiny lot that served mostly as a loading area. This was obviously not a public parking lot. Heath directed me to snug my Tacoma up next to a shiny, vanilla Cadillac SRS tucked down one end of the raised loading platform.

"I should bring you in the front door, to get the full effect," he said as he climbed out. "But then we'd have had to meter park and walk God-knows how far. So, you're getting the back-door tour." He shrugged, then flashed me his brilliant smile again. White-hot shards of attraction shot through me like a lightning bolt. He waited for me at the foot of the steps leading up to the loading dock, and I was pleasantly surprised when he reached out and took my hand.

"Now, the back room is pretty stacked. Hard to navigate. Just stay right behind me and I'll get you through to the showroom safely."

Oh. Okay. The hand-holding was a defensive anti-slip-and-fall measure. Not a token of affection.

Drat.

We slipped inside the side door flanking two, huge bays which were, at the moment, shuttered with heavy steel, overhead doors. Again, the unmistakable scent of *old* hit me. Dust, a little mildew, and something pungent, like the mixed aromas of pine and other wood sap filled my senses.

I was surprised to realize what had appeared to be three stories from the front of the building was actually one, monstrously huge space with twenty-foot ceilings on the inside. Catwalks lined the sides, with smaller pieces of furniture suspended from ropes or chains from their steel railings. The floor level was literally mounded with antiques ranging from small bureaus to a gigantic, freestanding oak bar.

"Oh, my," I remarked as we passed the beautiful old piece. "Where on earth did you find this?"

"Came from an old saloon in Texas, actually. I've got a client getting ready to open up a pub right here in town who's seriously considering making that the centerpiece of his lounge area."

Still clutching my hand, he gently dragged me on toward the front of the building. We passed through double, swinging doors, stepping from old concrete onto plush, burgundy carpeting. I stopped and blinked in the sudden brightness.

The entire front of the store was glass, and the late morning sunlight streamed in. It bathed the warm, dark woods of the artfully arranged pieces of furniture in the modest space, and glinted off crystal pieces set on top. At least a dozen ornate chandeliers hung from the patterned tin ceiling. Here, unlike in the warehouse, it was a cozy, normal height.

"Come on. I think Cynthia is in the office sorting a new shipment of jewelry."

He headed off toward the left where a long display case flanked the wall, calling the woman's name. I leaned on the counter and waited while Heath disappeared through an open doorway.

He had dropped my hand the minute we'd entered the showroom. Apparently, no fear of a trip and fall in here.

My heart, though, did just that when Cynthia slipped through the doorway. A striking redhead with exotic green eyes, Cynthia was nearly the same height as Heath. With her spiked boots on, anyway. His arm was draped around her tiny waist as he introduced us, beaming.

Perhaps not *married*. It seemed, thought, she was definitely somebody important in his life. There was no way I planned on competing with this.

Cynthia took my hand delicately. Her fingers were encrusted with an array of ornate gemstones, most of them nestled in antique settings. She met my gaze levelly, her full, pouty lips drawing up into a sexy bow.

"Heath's told me about you. You bought the old Belle Bride mansion. Is that right?" she asked in a deeper, throatier voice than I'd expected.

Damn, she even sounded sexy.

I nodded, dumbstruck for the moment. I retrieved my hand and started messing with my hair, twisting it into a loose knot at the base of my neck. I was suddenly very self-conscious, feeling like Cinderella—*before* the fairy godmother made her appearance.

"I did, though I'd hardly call it a mansion. Especially in the condition it's in right now. Aside from bedroom furniture, I have next to nothing. Heath offered me a tour of the warehouse to see if anything caught my eye."

There. I'd established my position here. Customer. Nothing more.

"Are you planning on furnishing the place in period pieces? Or going for a more contemporary look?" Cynthia asked, clicking into full business mode as she turned to her computer monitor.

"I don't know if I can afford all genuine period, though I'd like to stay as authentic as I can. The bedroom set Heath sold me is a repro, and I wouldn't mind some more things like it," I said. "I'll need to furnish the office next. It's where I make my living."

One of Cynthia's arched, red eyebrows rose. "Oh, that's right. Heath told me you do websites. Ours could sure use a makeover. Have you looked at it?"

"I have. Tried to comb through your stock to pick out a few things, but . . . " I shrugged and winced. "It's pretty hard to navigate. One of the reasons I wanted to come here. Take a look at some pieces in person."

Heath stepped up beside me. "The warehouse itself, as you can guess, can be a bit dangerous to go exploring in. Why don't I have one of the guys help me pull out a few of the pieces I think you might like first?" he said, his eyes sliding from Cynthia's to mine and back. "You can browse in here while we do that." He turned to Cynthia. "Can you pull up the images of the plantation parlor ensemble I picked up in Decatur last fall?" He patted my arm as he headed back toward the warehouse. "It's not a true antique, but a beautiful reproduction. I think you might like it."

Once he'd disappeared behind the swinging doors, Cynthia turned to me and smiled. "It'll take me a minute to locate those images myself," she said, chuckling and shaking her head. "Our website really does need a makeover. Why don't you just browse in here while I work on that?"

So, I did. The showroom wasn't large, but was filled with lots of stuff—breakable stuff. Glass pieces and ornate lamps crowded the tops of the display cases and a few, smaller bureaus and shelving units. I clasped my hands behind me and made my way carefully down the first row.

"You've got lots of vintage jewelry, I see. Heath never mentioned he sold jewelry too," I said. The case I was peering into was filled with everything from odd-shaped hair combs to belt buckles to cameo necklaces.

"This part of the business is my pet project. I love Victorian jewelry, and it's what women were wearing in 19th

Century America. Queen Victoria kept the royal jewelers quite busy, and her beloved Prince Albert was constantly showering her with gifts from all over the world. He even designed some of the jewelry himself," she said.

I crouched to study the pieces on the lower shelf more closely. "Wow, some of these are really elaborate. And they look like they weigh a ton," I added. The multi-layered necklaces displayed on felt stands featured dozens of large gemstones with elaborate chain work weaving them together. "Does anybody actually wear this stuff anymore?"

Cynthia had come out from behind the counter to join me. "I think most of these pieces go to collectors, who display them, like we do. If you want to see some really interesting work, come look over here," she said, leading me to a counter down the other end of the showroom. The shelves in this case, instead of being lined with black velvet like the others, were draped in layers of white. Probably because most of the jewelry inside was black.

"Have you ever heard of mourning jewelry?" she asked.

I shook my head. "I haven't. Morning, like, to wear to breakfast?"

She laughed, a deep, throaty sound. "No, no. Mourning, like mourning the dead. In 1861, the Queen lost both her mother, and then her husband. She went into mourning for virtually the rest of her life. Her jewelers designed a whole new category of pieces to commemorate the dead."

I blinked. "How morbid," I said, studying the array of earrings, necklaces, and brooches that were anything but sparkly.

"How about these?" Cynthia went around behind the case and retrieved a pair of earrings, teardrop-shaped discs of dark stone with swirls of gold behind glass centers. "You know what's in there?" She pointed to the swirls. "It's hair. Blonde hair from someone who passed."

Chapter Eight

Liv

I had reached forward to touch the earrings, then quickly jerked my hand back. A shiver ran through me. "Hair? They made jewelry from dead people's hair?"

Cynthia nodded with a knowing smile. "These are a quite simple design, actually. Some of the pieces contain elaborate weavings. You know how some ladies wear birthstone jewelry? With different colored stones representing each child's birth month? Well back then, a lady might take locks of hair from her deceased parents, husband, or other family member and have them woven into a remembrance piece."

I had never heard of such a thing, and wasn't sure if I was totally creeped out by the idea, or intrigued. "Kind of . . . weird. Morbid. Don't you think?" I wrinkled my nose.

"I suppose. A lot of people were touched by the sentiment of the notion, though, and the trend traveled from England to America." She was repositioning the earrings on the white satin lining the case's shelf.

Then she reached for another, larger oval piece. This one was also black stone edged in gold with a domed, glass front. It reminded me of a tiny replica of the antique picture frames in Bitsy's front hallway. But instead of a photograph behind the glass, there were elaborate swirls of what I know knew to be . . . *hair*.

"This is one of my favorites. You see how there are two different shades intertwined? They obviously came from two different people. Parents, maybe? Children? Nobody really knows."

Surprising even myself, I opened my hand and beckoned her to let me hold the piece. It was a brooch, or a pendant, and was heavy for its size. When it touched my skin, I had the strangest sensation of warmth spread through my palm.

"What's it made of?" I asked.

"The stone is onyx, and although the frame is gold, it's a pretty low carat weight. It's why it's priced so reasonably. What's really neat, though, is there's a date on the back."

She flipped the pendant over in my hand. There, on the pitted gold surface, the date 1869 was etched into the metal. Before and after the numbers were squiggly lines I couldn't quite make out.

Pointing to them, she continued, "We're assuming these are initials, or maybe names, but even my master jeweler can't make out the letters. This piece must have been worn often, or carried around with the owner constantly to wear away 12 carat gold like that."

I was mesmerized by this piece of jewelry that should have done nothing but creep me out. Yet the warmth in my palm continued to grow, and I found myself brushing my thumbs lovingly across the surface of the rounded glass.

What was the story behind this odd tribute to two people's lives? What secrets did it hold? No one would ever know. As I studied the strands of intertwined hair, blonde and golden brown, a thought occurred to me.

"Cynthia, couldn't they use one of each of these hairs to extract DNA? Wouldn't it be a way to identify whose hair it was?" I asked.

She crossed her arms and leaned on the glass case, her ample bosom straining at the laces on the front of her fitted, velvet dress. Sighing, she shrugged. "I suppose. My jeweler does think it might have been locally crafted. But it was auctioned off at an estate sale of someone who obviously had no one to pass it down to. Besides, who would want to dismantle a piece like this unless they had some reason to believe it came from somebody in their own family?"

When she went to lift the pendant from my palm, I shrank away. For some reason, I didn't want to let it go.

"You said this one was reasonably priced. How much is it?"

I left Birmingham that day the proud owner of a lovely period reproduction office suite in mahogany. Heath told me it was from a collection called the "Leesburg," and represented a modern take on antebellum furniture. He recommended I order a chair and accent pieces in antique white to contrast with the desk and credenza I'd purchased.

I never even made it to the library, though, because I got so sidetracked by my other, unusual purchase.

Tucked inside my purse, swathed in a velvet, drawstring bag, was the piece of mourning jewelry I'd been so captivated with. I had no idea why I bought it, or what on earth I was going to do with it. Regardless, like a secret treasure a child discovers and covets, I knew I simply had to own the brooch.

Heath

Heath had his warehouse crew dig out a lovely Hooker Leesburg desk and matching chest he'd picked up from a dealer at the last big auction in Montgomery. It was a repro in gorgeous condition. Liv fell in love with it the minute she saw it.

"A leather covered top, huh? Wow, this is awesome, Heath," she said, running her fingers along the slightly dusty surface.

"Both pieces are pretty large. I think the room you're going to use for an office, though, can easily handle it. And you don't really want one with an attached hutch," Heath said, motioning to where one would have fitted to the desk's back edge. "You said you wanted morning light, right? A hutch would block that."

"I'll miss the storage . . ." She turned to the chest. Opening the piece's two upper doors, she said, "but there is plenty of storage in this thing." Her eyes met his and a beautiful smile lit up her brilliant blue eyes. "These are perfect, Heath. And within my budget, too."

Then, she shocked him. Taking a step closer, she hit him with such a typical, Southern-lady gesture, he was blown away. Lifting up on her toes, she laid both hands on his shoulders and placed a soft kiss on his cheek.

"Thank you," she murmured with a shy smile.

Demure. Ladylike. Nothing sensual about it at all. Yet still the electricity that shot from his face straight south to his loins rocked him. Her scent, warm and sweet like vanilla, made his head spin. Arousal surged strong and fast.

Fortunately, she stepped back quickly and dipped into her purse. "Let's settle up then, shall we?"

Heath had no idea she'd purchased the hair work piece until Cynthia began ringing up the sale. Now that, he thought, was something else he never would have expected her to do. Buy a piece of mourning jewelry? Most people thought they were freakish.

Even though he knew she'd come straight from the big Apple, Heath couldn't help but see small hints of Southern personality in Liv Larson.

It's time, he thought as they climbed into her truck for the ride home, for me to find out a little bit more about this supposed city girl from Yankee country.

"You told me you lived in the city. Is that where you were born?" he asked as they turned onto the highway.

The long pause made him think he'd again stepped into forbidden territory, like the night they first shared fried chicken on her gallery. She took one hand off the steering wheel and rubbed her arm as if she was cold. Then she sighed, staring straight ahead.

"I don't really know where I was born," she said. "I mean, my birth certificate says Boston . . . UMass Hospital. And I know it's where my parents picked me up. Not my real parents." She paused and slid a glance his way, almost apologetically. "I was adopted."

Heath blinked, uncertain for a moment how to react.

"Your foster parents . . . they were good to you, right? They sure raised you with class and manners," he fumbled.

She tucked her hair behind one ear and nodded. "They were very good parents, and did everything they could to raise me right. But they were older when they adopted me. My dad was in his fifties. Mom was forty-eight. They'd been trying to have a baby of their own for years. They both had health issues. It's probably a good thing they never did conceive a child."

Heath swallowed and rubbed his jaw with one hand. "They're both gone?"

"Yup. Have been for almost ten years. So, I really am on my own. No family. That I know of, anyway," she added with a wry chuckle.

"Did you ever try to find your birth mother?" he asked, and immediately saw her stiffen. She didn't say a word, just shook her head.

"No significant other?" Heath asked. "I can't believe a girl as pretty as you would have lasted long single."

He knew he was testing her. Pushing her boundaries. But damn it, he had to know. Heath was really starting to take an interest in this pretty city girl. And that both excited him, and terrified him.

Again, a long silence fell between them.

"I'm sorry," Heath said. "I don't mean to pry. It's just—"

"Well I could ask you the same question, Mr. Barrow. You're a good-looking man in a small town. Surely some pretty Southern belles have noticed you by now. You're . . . how old?" She'd folded her hands atop the steering wheel and flashed sharp glances his way as she drove.

He couldn't help but smile. "I'm thirty-five. And no, I'm not married. I was once, a long time ago."

Liv narrowed her eyes, staring straight ahead at the road. "Then who is Miss Cynthia to you? I mean, besides your shop keeper? I certainly got the impression—"

Laughter burst from him so suddenly, Liv jumped. "I'm sorry." He reached over and laid a hand on her arm. "Miss Cynthia is special to me. As special as any older sister could be to her baby brother."

They stopped at the auto repair shop for Heath to pick up his car. Liv pulled up to the office and put the truck in park, then turned to look at him. "Thanks for the warehouse tour, Heath. And thanks for helping me find the perfect office furniture. You said they'd deliver it . . . when?"

She made no move to get out, and had left the engine running. Obviously, she intended now to be the end of their day together. Heath decided he wasn't quite ready to let her go.

"Well?" she prodded.

Oops. Slipped out of the conversation there for a minute.

"Delivery? Oh, yeah. They'll bring it by day after tomorrow. I have a truck coming to pick up a few more things I've got stored in my garage."

When Heath made no move to get out, Liv's gaze strayed to the dash clock. "Your vehicle should be done, right? Do you want me to wait while you check?"

"No," he said quickly. "I'm sure it's done. But it's still early, and I've got the rest of the day off. Why don't you come by *my* house for a change? I've seen where you live." He grinned. "Turnabout's fair play, right?"

She glanced at the time again, hesitating only a moment. "Okay," she said softly. "Yeah. I would like that."

Chapter Nine

Liv

It had truly been a strange day. I'd enjoyed our trip into Birmingham more than I'd anticipated. And it wasn't just that I missed the bustle of urban atmosphere. I was developing a deep fondness for this seemingly perfect man.

Yikes. There was a big, red warning flag. There is no such thing as a perfect man. Man *or* woman. Heath, though, he seemed to be just the right combination of laid-back country and savvy businessman to appeal to me in all the right ways. Intellectually. He was warm and friendly and easy to talk to.

Then there was the physical component.

I have to admit, I breathed a huge sigh of relief when I realized the buxom, beautiful Cynthia also held the title of Heath's big sister. He'd gone on to tell me he had two other siblings. His older brother lived in Atlanta with his wife and two kids, and his younger sister, still single at twenty-nine, made her home in Dallas. His parents, he said, had retired to northern Florida, and enjoyed a lovely condo in Fort Walton Beach.

Even though they all lived in distant cities, I got the distinct impression Heath's family remained close. In today's world of cyber-communication, I suppose it's easier than ever to keep in contact with family.

I wouldn't know.

I found myself feeling, just for a moment, a wee bit jealous. And wishing, more than ever, I knew more about my own family roots.

As I followed Heath's car to his house on the other side of town, I pondered my odd reaction to the brooch I'd bought at his shop. At first, yes, I was grossed out. I mean, making jewelry out of dead people's hair? Eww.

In the end, my curiosity and interest in history overrode my initial disdain. And then, when I touched the pendant . . . I can't explain it. Somehow, the piece spoke to me. Almost seemed familiar. I wondered what its story was.

Cynthia had gone on to explain that *hair work jewelry*, as they called it, wasn't always made from the locks of a deceased person. Sometimes they were designed as sentimental pieces, with intertwining strands from family members or spouses who were still very much alive. Back in the 1800s, anyway.

It made me wish I'd known about mourning jewelry when Josh was still alive. Maybe I could have had earrings, or a pendant, made from a lock of his hair. Maybe combining locks from both of us. It wouldn't look very different from those in the piece I bought today.

My hair was blonde, and Josh's hair had been golden-brown.

I wondered: would I ever love or be loved by anyone again who would inspire me to have such a piece created? Until I'd arrived here in Alabama, I sincerely doubted it.

Now, having met Heath, I wasn't so sure. I really liked him. Was definitely attracted to him. But like I said, he seemed so perfect. *Too* perfect. I knew he had his faults, and in time, they would reveal themselves. Would they be flaws I could accept?

And was I daydreaming this whole scenario? Did he even feel the same attraction for me as I felt for him? I decided this afternoon might be the perfect time to find out.

I followed him down a winding, tree-lined road to where

his driveway cut off to the right. His house sat not far back off the country lane. It was a cute, one-story home I guess could best be described as a farmhouse. The wraparound porch, lined with quaint, lattice railing, gave it a cozy, old-fashioned aura. Surrounded by a lush, green lawn dotted with oaks, the house was secluded. I couldn't see any other homes from his dooryard.

"Welcome to my own little piece of paradise," he said as he climbed out. "It's not nearly as big, nor as fancy, as the Belle Bride. It suits me, though."

I scanned the beautiful, lightly wooded land surrounding me. "How many acres do you have here?"

"Just under five," he said. "I like my privacy. Of course, I also have to take a few extra measures of security because of the seclusion. I store some of my inventory here." He pointed to a metal building peeking out from behind the house. "Motion sensors, and wired alarms. It's also the reason I have the warehouse in Birmingham."

I tilted my head, puzzled. "Heath, you can't possibly do that much business here in Camellia. And I know the shop in Birmingham gets more traffic, but . . ."

"Thus, the website. Which is something we have to discuss in more detail. I really do need you to redesign mine. I sell a lot of items—I mean *a lot*—from my online store. I'm FedEx's most valued customer. I'm sure I could sell even more with your expert reappraisal of my site."

I followed him up the few steps and onto the porch, where matching, white-painted rockers flanked the front door in pairs.

"Do you want the grand tour first? Or something cold to drink first?" he asked, motioning to the rockers.

I sat and rocked gently, enjoying the swish of a gentle breeze through the trees in his yard. What an idyllic spot, I thought. Perfect.

There was that word again. Yikes, for real. My heart was in definite peril here.

He returned with two tall glasses of iced tea and took a seat beside me. "I love it out here. At night, I sit with the lights off and, when the moon is bright, I get to see my share of night visitors. Raccoons, mostly. A deer now and then." He sipped his tea, then turned to study me, creases between his eyebrows. "Speaking of night visitors, any more visits from your Confederate stalker?"

I shook my head, then laughed. "To be honest, I've been sleeping so soundly since I got my new bed, I doubt even Sergeant What's-His-Name pounding on the door could wake me. I think I probably dreamed the whole thing up."

He continued to study me with pursed lips. "I don't know. I heard something the night I was there. And what about the dog? Has he been around?"

"Not that I've seen." I leaned forward and looked from side to side. "What about you? No dog to help protect your treasures in the garage?"

Heath dropped his gaze to the whitewashed floorboards. "No, not anymore. I had one. A golden retriever who was my best bud for the past twelve years. Poor old boy passed away last fall. I haven't had the heart to get another one. Not yet, anyway."

He sounded so sad, so I decided to change the subject. No need to put a damper on what had been so far, for me at least, a very upbeat day. I stood and said, "How about that tour?"

The man's home was neat, comfortably furnished, and cozy. Pristine white tile lined the floors of the entire house, with braided or oriental-style rugs padding strategic places. His kitchen was white as well, with gleaming stainless steel appliances. It was so tidy and clean it looked like it was never used.

"Not big on cooking?" I asked. "Or just an obsessive compulsive, clean freak?"

He smiled, embarrassed. "A little of both, I guess. When I do cook, and the weather's right, this is my favorite place to eat." He pointed toward a side door.

We left our tea glasses on the gleaming counter. He led me through a paned, glass door onto the most gorgeous patio I'd ever seen. An arbor shaded the brick-paved space, covered with a dense, lush thicket of green vines. Grapelike clusters of purple flowers hung down everywhere overhead. A white metal patio set held center stage. The scent was intoxicating.

"Oh, Heath," I breathed, "this is breathtaking. Are they . . . lilacs?"

I wandered out under the shaded arbor, reaching up to brush my fingertips over the fragrant blooms.

"Nope. Wisteria, my mother tells me. This was here when I bought the place. I just keep trimming back the vines so they don't overtake the house."

I wasn't startled when his arms came around my waist from behind. His body felt warm and strong against me, and his breath hot on my ear. I relaxed into him, tipping my head back against his neck.

"I'd love to cook for you sometime," he murmured into my ear. "We can eat out here. Open a bottle of wine. Light some candles. What do you think?"

Warmth quickly pooled in a tight knot low in my belly. It had been too long . . . too long. I was ripe and ready for the taking. He seemed to sense it. My blood pressure spiked so fast I felt light-headed, and a little giddy. I giggled.

"Sounds like something from a sappy romance novel," I said. "But wonderful. Candles, huh? I haven't met many guys who would think of the candles."

He snorted and buried his face in my hair. "Nothing romantic about a citronella candle," he said. "Have you seen the size of the mosquitoes we have down here?"

Strong hands gripped my shoulders and turned me toward him. He gazed down into my eyes, his filled with earnest passion. He chucked me under the chin.

"I usually don't go for city girls, you know," he murmured, one side of his mouth quirking up.

"Yeah, it's where I *used* to live. But how do you know I'm even a genuine city girl? For all either of us knows—"

The words and my breath ceased when his mouth covered mine. Gentle, tentative kisses. First, chaste and soft. Then firmer, more invasive. I answered his kiss, stroke for stroke. He tasted of sweet tea and temptation like I hadn't experienced in . . . well, in way too long.

He combed his hands into my hair, and our lips parted in laughter when his fingers tangled in a snarl and my head yanked back with a painful jerk.

"I'm sorry," he said, working his fingers free. "You're just so beautiful, so tantalizing. It's been a very long time for me." His eyes on mine were penetrating, apologetic. Pleading.

"For me too," I whispered. "So, don't stop, Heath Barrow. I'm a willing participant." I paused, tipping my chin down and winking at him. "Show me what you got, country boy."

Heath

Temptation overtook him with a blind fury he hadn't expected. It was purely lust, he was certain. Damn it, he was a man. One in his prime. One who hadn't been with a woman nearly often enough over the last few years. And Liv Larson was, plainly put, irresistible.

Seeing her standing there under the mantle of wisteria made him feel as though he'd been zipped back in time to another era. True, she didn't fit the description of a Victorian lady. Her golden hair flowing free over her shoulders. Her slim, tight bottom sharply defined through the denim of her jeans. But she sure acted the part of a Southern belle, and Heath was certain it was what broke through his defenses.

There was always a constant worry. Heath's condition hovered at the back of his mind like a silent, hulking beast. His nemesis. One that threatened to do—or undo—things to his body he had no control over.

One of the things that had driven his first love, Katherine, away.

Liv's scent, mingling with the wisteria, was a nearly overpowering aphrodisiac. She tasted like sweet sin. Something he definitely shouldn't take a chance on. He simply couldn't stop himself.

She melted into his arms, molded her lithe frame against his body with such willingness. For a few brief moments Heath thought, *yes, I can do this. The new meds are working. I'm going to be able to—*

"What's wrong, Heath? Heath?"

In the next moment, he found his body rigid against hers, but not in a good way. He had "blipped out" for a minute. Or two. How long?

Her warm hand on his cheek, her concerned gaze bulleted into his eyes. The worry, the fear in those eyes—

that's what brought him back. Shame and horror engulfed his senses.

He'd had a mini-seizure. Just when he was about to make love to a beautiful woman he wanted so badly . . .

"Heath, what's wrong?" she repeated, her tone frantic. She had stepped back now. Holding his wrists at a full arm's distance. The look on her face went beyond concern. Beyond confusion.

She looked terrified.

Heath blinked rapidly and struggled to force his limbs to move. Squeezing his eyes shut, he tried to ignore the sensation the world was spinning around and around him. With gargantuan effort, he managed to lift a hand to swipe down his face. When he opened his eyes, Liv had backed even further away. She stood frozen, in a crouched stance. One he recognized all too well.

Heath was familiar with the instinctive reactions of wild animals who felt threatened. In danger. It was called the fight or flight syndrome. Liv was obviously one to take flight.

People, even those who understood his condition, were often frightened when they witnessed a seizure. Especially the first time. Yet unlike the usual reaction—concern, over-protective attempts to assist him—Liv had reacted differently. She'd completely pulled away. Shut him out.

He'd lost her before he'd even had a chance.

Chapter Ten

Liv

It was as though time stood still, before reeling backwards at a dizzying rate. One minute, I was engaged in a sensual dance of tongues with a sexy man who I very much wanted. My libido had shot straight to a ten, and I was ready for a night of wild, uninhibited sex with Heath. A kind, compassionate, fun man I found I simply could not resist.

In the next moment, everything changed. *He* changed. His rigid limbs, his blank stare, his unresponsiveness . . . oh, God, how can this be happening to me again?

Surely, I couldn't have been cursed with *two* men afflicted with the same rare brain cancer. Not in one lifetime. What were the odds?

His symptoms, though, were identical. This is how it all began with Josh. We'd been sitting across from each other at dinner—ironically, at a romantic, candlelit dinner at our favorite patio bistro—when his first seizure hit. Right in the middle of a hushed, flirtatious conversation about what he was going to do to me when he got me alone, he froze. Staring straight ahead into nothingness, unseeing, unable to hear or react to me.

I hadn't known then how serious his condition was. I had no idea what he would go through—what I would witness, helplessly—over the next, horrible six months. How quickly he would deteriorate.

Within mere weeks, even though his body was still alive, I had already lost him. He didn't know me. My husband, my beloved Josh, my other half, had simply disappeared.

Logic should have overridden emotion that night with Heath. I know it should have. But the memories clouded my consciousness like toxic fog. All I could think was, "No, no, no. Not again. How can this be happening again? Is it me? Am I some latent carrier of this awful disease?"

I don't think Heath had even completely come out of his trance when I bolted.

I pushed him away, mumbling, "I'm sorry, Heath. I just can't do this. It was a mistake for me to come here. Forgive me."

He watched me, dazed and still not completely *there*, whisk through his kitchen and out the front door. I never even closed it behind me. With tears of freshly wrought anguish and loss streaming down my face, I drove back through town and on to my house.

I know it was wrong. Heartless. Ignorant. I mean, suppose Heath needed my help? Suppose after I left, he'd collapsed on the floor and choked on his own tongue? Obviously, I wasn't thinking clearly. Emotion overrode all else. It all came back—the horrible images of Josh melting like an ice cream cone on a hot day in the sun. Dissolving from a strong, vital, viral man into a drooling mass of half-alive flesh. It happened too fast, and I wasn't ready for it. I wasn't ready to be alone.

And I sure as hell wasn't ready to take the trip it took to get there. Not again.

I sat in my truck, parked in front of the Belle Bride, my forehead pressed against my steering wheel. Sobs wracked my body until the tears would no longer come. Was I cursed? I'd been mysteriously drawn here, to this place I had no ties to, to start a new life. To forget the past. Yet the horror seemed to have followed me. I pounded my fist on the dashboard and cursed the Universe for punishing me so cruelly. What had I done wrong to deserve this?

When I finally found the strength to drag myself into the house, it was almost dusk. Cricket song wrapped around the house like a protective force field. If nothing else, I had my house. Although I had no idea why I'd been drawn to this place, I still felt safe here. Like I belonged.

Until the darkness came.

He came again that night. The Confederate soldier, in full uniform, carrying his musket with bayonet. I knew he would come because I'd heard the dog behind the house, howling at the three-quarter moon as it rose over the barn. Unable to sleep, I dragged a comforter down the stairs and huddled at their base in the dark. I waited.

I must have dozed off, because when the pounding began I bolted upright, stumbling on the blanket around my legs. He saw me then, his clear, golden-brown gaze riveting me through the glass. I rubbed my eyes and tried to focus on him, but his image remained hazy in my vision. Instead of the terror I should have felt, a surge of anger rose up inside me.

Whoever this nut case was, I was going to find out *who* he was, and what the hell he wanted. This was my house now, and it was all I had.

I threw off the comforter and stalked to the door, the hardwood planks cold and a little gritty under my feet. As I drew closer to the door, though, the figure on the other side of the window seemed to drift farther away. As though we were somehow separated by a set distance that couldn't be shortened. By the time I had unlocked the door and threw back the deadbolt, he was down the steps and halfway out into the yard. Yet he still faced me, his eyes never leaving mine.

I yanked the door open and screamed, "Who are you? What do you want?"

Still clutching his musket to his chest, he seemed to

deflate a little. He wasn't a tall man, or very heavily built. His full, dark beard gave him a gruff appearance, as did the scowl he directed at me now. Almost immediately, though, he lowered his weapon to his side.

Emma . . . I'm home Emma. Why won't you let me in?

I heard his voice, yet I didn't. It was echoey, and sounded as though it might be coming from inside my own head. And I hadn't seen his mouth move either.

This was a dream. A nightmare. It had to be. Because only in a nightmare would I have been bold enough to be standing in my open doorway, in the middle of the night, confronting a psycho in a Civil War uniform.

"There's no Emma here. And it's not your house. Not anymore. I bought this house. It's mine. Go away and leave me alone," I screamed. Again, the sobs erupted from me, and I was near hysteria.

My therapist had warned me this could happen. "Don't go off by yourself, Liv. You need people around you to keep you grounded. If you spend too much time alone, your mind will start playing tricks on you . . ."

But this wasn't Josh I was imagining. It wasn't Heath, either. It was some strange man who got his jollies dressing up like a Confederate soldier and banging on people's doors in the middle of the night.

Heath had been right. I should have notified the police.

Please . . . Emma, I've come back to you.

His echoed plea stabbed my already bleeding heart.

I dropped to my knees, the tears and the pain overwhelming me. There was no room for fear, even though a tiny voice in the back of my brain warned there should be. I covered my face with my hands.

"I'm not Emma! There's no Emma here. Go away. Go

away and leave me alone!"

The cricket song grew suddenly louder, deafening, until it hurt my ears. I covered them with my hands and prayed for the surreal moment to pass. After a few more minutes of self-indulgent pity, I opened my eyes. The soldier was gone.

When I awoke the next morning, I was on the floor inside my front door. It was closed, locked, with the dead bolt in place, as though I'd never opened it. My comforter was wrapped around me. My bare arm, pillowing my head from the hardwood, was covered with grit.

It had been one of the most bizarre nightmares I'd ever had. So vivid, and yet not nearly as terrifying as the ones I'd had in the months after I lost Josh. Hell, those started even before he took his last breath.

At least Josh hadn't haunted this dream. Nor the doctors with their pitying faces, nor the funeral director with his stoic solemnity. No weeping, sympathetic friends.

Just me, and a nutcase in a Confederate uniform. I struggled to my feet and padded to the kitchen. While a cup of coffee brewed, I dug in my purse for my cellphone. I had to call my therapist. I was quite sure, between what had happened yesterday with Heath, and this morning, I was experiencing a nervous breakdown.

When my fingers brushed against the velvet pouch inside my purse, I froze. The pendant. A sudden calmness washed over me. Extracting it, I laid the piece in my palm and felt the same, warming familiarity as I had the day before. The metal glowed even brighter than it had in the shop, as though it had been polished and renewed somehow. The glass dome gleamed and reflected the brilliance of morning in my kitchen.

When I heard the knocking on the front door, I wondered—had the soldier returned? Perhaps he could tell me more about this piece of jewelry from an era he obviously identified with. Would he still be wearing his very convincing looking reenactment costume? Maybe it hadn't been a dream after all ...

It was Heath standing on the other side of the glass, shoulders hunched, hands stuffed in his jeans pockets. A real person, yet somehow, possibly, worse than any nighttime imagining.

Heath

After the seizure subsided and he'd come back to himself, Heath realized Liv was gone. She'd bolted, just like the terrified animal she'd reminded him of as she stood there, staring at him. The front door stood open. Dust still hung in the air from where she'd spun out of his driveway.

How bad had it been, he wondered? He couldn't be sure, not since he'd been on this new medication. With the old drug, his episodes had been gradually becoming more severe. It's why Sandra wanted him to try the new one. The muscle spasms and staring spells had begun to leave him temporarily paralyzed. And instead of lasting minutes, the last few, bad seizures had taken him out of awareness for over an hour.

Now, he felt ashamed, embarrassed, horrified. Yet a little angry too. He could understand if his episode had frightened her, but for her to just up and leave him? Her escape made her seem awfully shallow.

Just like Katherine. It was all about her. She never really worried about him hitting his head or hurting himself thrashing around on the floor. When his seizures interrupted *her* day, Katherine had simply been repulsed by him. He had become an unpredictable nuisance.

Katherine, he reminded himself, had known about Heath's epilepsy. Liv did not. He had to go see her. Tell her what was wrong with him. And let the chips fall where they may.

He drove the few short miles to the Belle Bride wondering what kind of reaction he would get. Hands trembling, though not from a seizure but from pure anxiety, he stood on her front gallery and watched as she peeked out of her kitchen. She stood there, without moving, for a very long moment. Would she even open the door for him?

His breath whooshed out in relief when he saw her padding toward him, barefoot. She was wearing, it appeared, nothing more than a long tee shirt. And oh, those long, slender legs. A knot formed in his stomach, one wrought of anxiety, and sadness, twisted taught by pure, physical need.

She opened the door and immediately swung away from him, crossing her arms over her chest. "I guess I owe you an apology," she mumbled. "I sort of freaked out on you yesterday."

"May I come in?" he asked.

Liv nodded, her back still toward him.

"We need to talk, Liv. I haven't been entirely forthcoming with you about my . . . my condition. I should have told you right away, just in case something happened while we were together. I was so hopeful, with this new medication—"

She spun toward him then, her arms pulled back, her chin raised. "Are you dying, Heath Barrow? Because if you are, I'm sorry, but I've just been through that. It's why my head's in such a mess. I can't . . . I just can't . . . Not again . . ." Covering her face with both hands, her words dissolved into sobs.

Heath took two strides and folded her against him. Oh, my God, what has this poor woman been through? He'd known there was pain, though he had no idea the cause.

Stroking his hand down her tumbled hair, he murmured against her ear. "No, no, Liv. Nothing like that. What I have is treatable. Controllable. Just a little . . . well, scary at times."

A half-hour later they sat in her bedroom, since there was still no furniture in the parlor. Her back against the headboard, and he at the foot of the bed, they both clutched mugs of coffee and avoided each other's eyes. Heath took a deep breath, and then began.

"Liv, I was diagnosed with epilepsy when I was about fifteen. At first, the symptoms were so minor, my family figured I was just another spacey teenager. They even grilled me about drug use. It wasn't until I had my first grand mal . . . then they took me for testing."

Liv lowered her cup and stared at him, wide-eyed. "Epilepsy. My God, I never thought . . . oh Heath, I'm so sorry."

Heath looked away. He couldn't bear to see the reaction he knew was coming. The one he'd seen on Katherine's face the first time he told her.

"I know it's probably very scary to watch, but I've been fairly well controlled with drugs for the past five years or so. They're developing more and more sophisticated treatments for this condition. My doctor wanted me to try this new med they just came out with. There's a transition period. I should have told you."

Then she heard her . . . giggle. Huh? He had no idea how to feel about her reaction. She thought this was funny?

In the next moment, she'd slammed her mug down on the nightstand and lunged for him. He barely kept from sloshing coffee everywhere as she landed in his lap and threw her arms around his neck. Laughter jumbled with sobs as tears streamed down her face.

This, surely, was the strangest reaction he'd ever seen. People either pitied or shunned him. As if he were a leper, or a rabid dog. It's why he stayed here in this small town. Kept to himself as much as possible.

It's why, ever since Katherine left, he'd remained alone.

She was all over him now, kissing his neck, his face. Running her fingers through his hair. He barely got the mug set down on the floor before she began unbuttoning his shirt.

"Liv . . . Liv, it can happen again. At any time. It's more likely to happen when I get . . . aroused—"

She silenced him with a wet, deep kiss that drained all the blood out of his head and straight down into his loins.

Yeah, he thought. Like that. Exactly like that.

To hell with it. It had been ages since Heath had been with a woman and in that moment, lust overrode all other thoughts and worries. Her mouth was lush and wet, and she tasted of freshly brewed coffee.

Nice, hot coffee.

Their tongues tangled in a sensuous dance as she worked the last button on his shirt free and slid the cloth off his shoulders. He combed his fingers into her tangled hair and answered her passion, stroke for stroke. Her nails raked lightly down his naked back, and it raised goosebumps along his flesh. He'd become painfully hard in his tight jeans, pressing on her bottom as she wriggled closer on his lap.

My God, he hoped he had the self-control to hold it back. Make it good for her. For at least a little while. He broke the kiss, breathless.

"Liv . . . Liv, it's been a while. Let's take it slow—"

She cupped his face in her hands, then flashed a devilish grin as she wiggled her bottom on his hardness. "I can tell. It's been a long time for me, too. I say, let's just go for it."

Before he could draw another breath, Liv reached down and grasped the hem of her long tee shirt, lifting it over her head on one smooth movement. As the cloth sailed through the air behind her, Heath found himself gazing at the most perfect female body he'd ever imagined. Completely nude.

She was slim, sinewy, yes. Yet undoubtedly female, with full, rounded breasts tipped with perfect, peach-colored nipples. Her small dimple of a navel marked the center of a perfectly flat tummy. At its edge sparkled a tiny diamond.

Ooh, mama.

He stood, lifting her with him, and laid her head down gently on the pillows. It wasn't until he got his jeans unzipped that dread clotted in his stomach. He groaned.

"I don't carry condoms around with me, Liv," he moaned.

Her expression morphed into one of tragic disappointment. "And I'm not on the pill. Not since . . . well, for years now." Her mouth twisted into a pout.

His shoulders drooped as he checked his watch. "And I'd run up to the drugstore, but I've got to open the shop in less than an hour."

Her pout grew more exaggerated. She crossed her arms over her breasts as if she were cold. "What time do you close today?" she asked.

Heath sighed in exasperation as he carefully—painfully—re-zipped his jeans. "I've got a truck coming to pick up a shipment at four. So, five maybe? Five-thirty?" He moved to sit next to her on the bed. "I'm sorry, Liv. I just never expected . . . after what happened yesterday . . ."

She reached up and cupped his face. "It's okay. I don't deserve you anyway. Not after running out on you yesterday. When you might have needed me." She sat up and reached for a nightshirt she had flung over the headboard. As she pulled it over her naked body, she asked, "What should I do if you have a seizure when we're together, Heath? I've dealt with men with other . . . conditions, but never epilepsy." Her eyes cut off to the side and she said wistfully, "If only that had been the problem with my late husband."

There it was. She was a widow. And her husband had obviously died of some disease that cut him down in a horrible way. It explained the pain he saw in those clear, blue eyes. He rubbed her arm.

"Do you want to talk about it, Liv? Maybe I should know

your demons, too," he murmured.

She slipped her arms around his neck and dropped her forehead to his shoulder.

"No. It's a time in my life I'd rather put behind me. It's why I'm here. I wanted to start over. Get as far away from my old life as I could."

He wrapped his arms around her and rocked her. "I'm so sorry, Liv. How long ago did you lose him?"

"Two years. A very long, lonely two years ago."

Smoothing his hand up and down her back, he buried his face in her hair. "I don't know what to say," he said helplessly. "I lost my wife, but she ran out on me. She didn't get sick and die."

Liv drew back and gazed into his eyes, hers brimming with tears. "Still doesn't stop the hurt. That might even be worse. The rejection part, I mean."

He pinched her chin and searched her face. "It's okay. I got over it. My condition is treatable. My doctor swears this new medication will eliminate what few episodes I've continued to have." He pressed a soft, chaste kiss on her lips, and then said, "And epilepsy won't kill me. It's not considered terminal."

Only to a marriage, he thought wryly, remembering Katherine's drawing away from him. He checked his watch again. "Listen, why don't I run by the drugstore on my way to the shop, and then we can meet somewhere for dinner. We can either come back here or go to my place afterwards." He paused, searching her face. "That is, if you're willing to try this again."

Liv's face warmed with a quirky smile. "I sure as hell am." She kissed him then, deep and wet and hot, reigniting the desire in his belly.

He broke the kiss and drew back, grinning sheepishly. "At this rate, I'll have to go home for a cold shower before I head to the shop," he said wryly. Only peripherally was he aware of the twitch the had begun in the corner of his eye.

Her eyebrows drew together and she touched a finger to the side of his face. "Is this how they usually start? This happened to you yesterday, just before . . . are you okay to drive? Should I drive you into town?" she asked.

Heath closed his eyes and sucked in a breath. Before, with his old medication, he experienced odd facial twitches often. The majority of the time, the drugs prevented the brain misfires to progress any further. With this new med, who knew?

"What should I do, Heath? When you do have one of your episodes? Is there an epi-pen or something I'm supposed to administer?"

Her concern made him smile. He shook his head. "I wish it were that simple. There's really nothing you can do, Liv. Just know—I can't hear or see you while it's happening. I have no idea what's going on when one hits." Sliding his gaze from hers, he added, "Fortunately, I haven't had a grand mal in a very long time. Hopefully, it stays that way."

Her shoulders rose and fell with a frustrated sigh. "Water. Let me get you some water, and leave you alone for just a moment. It'll probably help if I'm not staring at you like you're a bug on my ceiling." She hopped up and whisked out of the room. He heard her bare feet slapping on the wooden stair risers.

Heath twisted his head from side to side, then rubbed the back of his neck. The twitch was subsiding already. Maybe this new medication was finally kicking in.

When he heard Liv's scream echoing throughout the house, his blood ran cold.

Chapter Eleven

Liv

I turned the corner into the kitchen and came face to face with my nighttime visitor.

The soldier was here, right *here* in my kitchen. Except now, it was broad daylight, and I wasn't dreaming. This time, I knew he was real.

Or was he? When the scream erupted from my throat, he didn't react at first, just continued to stand at the counter, staring down at the items there. My purse, my truck keys, a discarded hair tie. And yet, although I could see him clearly, down to the mud caked along the soles of his boots and the gleam of the bayonet slung over his shoulder, I could see *through* him too.

The temperature reading, in neon green, on my refrigerator's digital display glowed through his form, as though the numbers were emblazoned on the soldier's wrinkled, grey jacket.

I backed away, screaming again as his face lifted toward me.

Emma. I'm home, Emma.

Just like in my dream, his words echoed more inside my head than in my ears. He was a sturdy, compactly muscled man, but not very tall. Young, and handsome, he stared at me over the grim smile splitting his dark, unkempt beard. Wisps of wavy brown hair curled up from under the edges of his soldier's Kepi cap.

Vaguely, I heard Heath's footfalls rumbling down the stairs and through the hall. Still, when I took the next step backward and slammed into him, I lurched and shrieked as I spun around.

"What? What's wrong, Liv?" Heath grabbed my shoulders, raking his eyes over me quickly before looking past me into the kitchen. "What? What frightened you?"

For a moment, with my heart pounding painfully in my throat, I couldn't speak. I fell against his chest and pointed behind me, toward the soldier.

"Liv, what is it? I don't see anything."

Sure enough, when I turned back toward the counter, the soldier was gone.

Overwhelmed, I burst into tears. "I'm losing my mind, Heath. He was there. Right there," I screeched, pointing with a shaky finger. "The whacko dressed up like a soldier. He was . . . right . . . there."

Heath quickly stepped around me and strode with long, sure steps through the kitchen, ducking to peer around the appliances and opening the tall pantry door. When he disappeared through the doorway into the parlor, I hurried after him.

The last thing I wanted to be was alone if the weirdo reappeared.

Ten minutes later, Heath had scoured the entire house, twice, with me in close pursuit. No sign of any soldier. He'd checked the deadbolts on both the front and back doors. They were secure.

When he met my gaze again, there was pity in his eyes. "You've been through a lot. Even more with this move, Liv. Everything is so different here, I'm sure, than the life you're used to. It didn't help, me wigging out on you yesterday." He took me into his arms and tucked my head under his chin.

"You need to get some rest." He kissed the top of my head as he pushed me away. "And I need to get on to open the shop."

"You think I'm crazy, don't you?" I asked, my voice trembling. I wasn't sure which emotion was stronger—the fear, the confusion, or the anger.

Then there was the worry. What if I *was* having a nervous breakdown? My therapist had warned me—

"Call me at the shop later. If you still want to get together for dinner, there's a nice little, Mom and Pop restaurant out by the highway. You can meet me in town and we'll drive out together."

I nodded dumbly and watched him unlock the door and step onto the gallery. The front yard was practically glowing with golden, morning light. Birdsong twittered from the trees. A battered pickup truck rolled slowly by, and Robert and Bitsy waved and tooted the horn before disappearing around the bend.

Life appeared maddeningly peaceful. Normal. The only speck of crazy was me.

"Your neighbors?" Heath asked as he descended the steps. "The Warrens. They've been in the shop a time or two. I didn't realize you'd met them already."

I nodded. "I think Bitsy's antique collection could put yours to shame," I added under my breath.

Heath didn't hear me. He was already climbing into his truck. "Call me," he called. The engine roared, and he was gone.

I locked the door, then turned and leaned back against it.

Face it, Liv. It's time to call the therapist.

I made my way through the house and opened the back door. The section of grass still shaded by the house's shadow twinkled with morning dew. In the distance, I caught sight of the Warren's horse, grazing peacefully.

Normal. The entire world around me was peaceful, normal. And then, there was me.

I scrolled down my contact list until I found my therapist's number, and dialed the phone.

"Good morning, Arlene. This is Liv Larson. I was wondering if Dr. Greene is in today?" My hands were shaking. The last time I'd seen Carla Greene, I honestly thought it would be the last time I'd need to speak with her.

"She is, Liv. As a matter of fact, she's just had a cancellation . . . hold on a minute . . . yes, she's in her office. Hold on and I'll ring you through." The cheerful, friendly sound of the doctor's receptionist sent a pang of homesickness through my chest. I chewed on my thumbnail and waited.

"Olivia Larson! So good to hear from you. Are you back home in Manhattan yet? I had a feeling you wouldn't last long in Rebel country." Carla's slightly snarky tone doused my homesickness instantly. I'd expected a lecture—*another* lecture. Her I-told-you-so tone caught me a bit off guard.

"Yes, I'm home. Not in Manhattan, though. I'm in my pretty antebellum house here in Camellia. Just thought I'd give you a call and touch base." There. The long pause told me she hadn't expected that either.

"Really. Are you doing okay?" The doctor seemed genuinely shocked. "How wonderful, Liv. I really do hope it works out for you down there. I'm just worried about you. Are you getting out and meeting people? It's not good for you to be alone too much."

I hesitated. Who had I met? The realtor, the neighbors, and Heath. Pretty good for being here less than a week, right?

"As a matter of fact," I said, "I am. I've already been to my neighbor's house for a visit. I've been spending quite a bit of time with the nice man who owns the antique shop, too."

"That's good, Liv. Really good. A man, huh? Already?" Carla sounded almost . . . jealous.

"Yup," I shot back proudly. "Good-looking, single, and a few years younger than me, too."

"Sex is great therapy, Liv. I've been telling you to revive your love life for two years. Who figured you'd leave a city with thousands of men to find one out in the boondocks of Alabama?"

We shared a laugh, but it died quickly, and was replaced by an awkward silence.

"Still on the anti-depressants I prescribed?" she asked.

I cleared my throat. "Actually, I'm not. I started weaning myself off of them, like you recommended, about two weeks before I left the city." It was a bold-faced lie. The last pill I took was the night before I pulled out of Manhattan, almost a week ago.

Oh, my God. I'll bet that was it. She'd warned me about the withdrawal effect. That was probably what my Confederate soldier was. A withdrawal symptom.

Suddenly I wanted this phone call to be over. It had been a mistake to even contact her. How could she possibly help me from over a thousand miles away?

As if she'd read my mind, she asked in a gentle voice, "Do you need me to call a script in to a pharmacy down there for you?"

"No, Carla, really, I'm good. But you could do that? If I needed you to?"

"One time. Since you've been on the meds for over six months. You understand, though, I can't officially consider you my patient anymore. So once is all I can do." The snark and the chill had returned to her voice. "Until, of course, you come home."

Until? Glad she had so much faith in me, I thought. How had I even chosen to keep seeing this nasty bitch?

"I *am* home, Carla. I won't be coming back north. Thanks for speaking with me today."

I ended the call and pinched the bridge of my nose between two fingers. Why hadn't I thought of the meds? And why on earth had I chosen to ignore all sensible advice and just stop taking the anti-depressants, cold turkey?

Sighing, I turned back toward the kitchen for something cool to drink and came face to face with my Confederate nightmare. Again. He was standing, as he had been before, hovering over my things on the counter.

Jerking to a halt, I sucked in a shaky breath. This was just an imagining, I told myself. Ignore him and he'll disappear.

Instead, his eyes narrowed and he gripped the butt of the musket slung across his shoulder. His next words both shocked and perplexed me.

Why would you ever consider going North, Emma? Why?

Great. Now my hallucination was not only eavesdropping on my phone conversations, now he was chiding me. I squeezed my eyes shut, hard, and opened them again. He was still there. His form had become more solid now —I could no longer see the digital readout on my refrigerator through his coat.

Okay, so he's not going to just disappear. Maybe I needed to acknowledge him. Then he will go away.

"First off, my dear hallucination, I'm not Emma. My name is Olivia. And since you are nothing more than a result of drug withdrawal, I'd really appreciate it if you'd go away." Even though I was trembling all over—probably another side effect —I folded my arms across my chest and lifted my chin.

Here I was thinking the soldier was the local nutcase who liked to play dress-up. Now I realized the only nutcase in the house was standing in her kitchen doorway—in nothing but a tee shirt. Talking to a ghost.

"If you're not Emma, then what are you doing in our house?"

Even his voice, deep and rich, had more solidity than it had before. He almost sounded . . . real.

A scowl twisted his features as he scanned me head to toe. "Who are you? And what are you doing in our house, half-naked?" He motioned toward me with a sharp movement that made me jump. "With your hair down! Shameful. Have you become some Yankee's whore in my absence?"

I stumbled back a step. This was ridiculous, and the emotions warring inside me flitted from fear to shock to anger so quickly I felt lightheaded. Probably another withdrawal symptom. What was next? Would I pass out? I squeezed my eyes shut again, raking my fingers into my hair and pulling as hard as I could.

If I just ignore this, it will pass. He'll disappear, just like he did before.

When I opened my eyes, his form was translucent again. His next words were mere echoes inside my head.

I've come home from war, Emma. I've come home to my bride. Where are you, my love?

With my next blink, he had disappeared.

I stood there for a long time, staring at the place where the soldier had been—where I'd *imagined* he'd been—waiting for my heart rate to slow from its staccato rhythm, and the whirring of blood in my ears to subside. Then I stepped into the kitchen, carefully avoiding that spot, and grabbed my purse. I dug inside until I located the bottle of anti-depressants, fumbled a pill out of the vial, and downed it with water from the tap.

Perhaps weaning myself off them gradually was a good idea after all.

Heath

Heath arrived at his shop fifteen minutes past opening time to find the Warrens, Bitsy and Robert, standing on the sidewalk waiting for him.

"Mornin', Mr. Barrow. We seen you there at the Belle Bride house, leaving. So, we figured we'd wait for you," Bitsy said brightly. The tiny woman clung to her husband's arm, grinning up at Heath from beneath her bowl-like cap of silver hair.

Heath cleared his throat. "Yeah, I've been helping Liv—Ms. Larson—pick out furniture for her house."

And seriously trying to get into her pants.

Of course, when the Warrens had driven by this morning, Liv hadn't been wearing any. Just a long tee shirt, her hair a rumpled mess. Heath felt the heat rising up his neck as he unlocked the shop door.

"So, what can I do for you folks today?" he asked as he flipped the door sign from *Closed* to *Open*.

Robert stepped into the shop ahead of his wife, his thumbs hooked in the straps of his overalls. Bitsy wandered off to examine the milk glass pitcher and bowl on the sideboard flanking the front window. When neither of them answered his question, Heath turned to find Robert staring at the floor, his booted feet planted wide.

"Something wrong?" Heath asked.

"No, no," Robert replied, shaking his head. "Just came by to ask you a question, is all." Robert lifted his gaze to Heath's, one eyebrow raised. "We were just wondering . . . do you ever need any help here in the shop? I mean, moving this heavy stuff around is more than a one-man job, I'd think."

Heath stared at him, stunned. Surely, this man, who had to be at least in his mid-seventies, wasn't asking him for a job.

"I . . . I don't understand, Mr. Warren. I mean, I do have men who work for me in my warehouse in Birmingham. If I ever need help, I wait until they're coming into Camellia with a truck . . . " Heath trailed off, thinking.

Then it hit him. Their son.

"We were just thinking, it might do our Ben good to get some part time work. To keep his mind occupied, you know," Robert mumbled.

Bitsy was suddenly right behind Robert, peering out sheepishly from around him. "He's not good with numbers, or reading, or anything like that. And he's not really good with people, but, well, lifting heavy things. He's right good at doing those things."

Most people are probably intimidated as hell by Benjamin, Heath thought. The man was as big as a grizzly bear, and his mind was a bit slow. Heath thought back to the last time he had to crate up a bureau for the FedEx truck. He'd struggled with the thing for almost two hours, and still had a sore spot between his shoulder blades.

"You know," Heath said, "I don't need anybody on a regular basis. There are occasions, though, when I could use some help. Why don't you have Ben come down and talk to me." Heath strode around the counter to his desk and checked the calendar. "I've got a truck coming in tomorrow. They'll be pieces to unload—office furniture going out to the Belle Bride, by the way—and then a few big things to load back on the truck. To go back to Birmingham. Why don't you tell him to be here, say, around three?"

Bitsy fairly vibrated off the floor with excitement. "That's real nice of you, Mr. Barrow. Real nice," she squealed, clapping her hands.

"We'll have him here, three o'clock tomorrow," Robert said, turning toward the door. He stopped short when Bitsy, who was now reattached to his arm, didn't budge.

"Just a minute, Robert. The milk glass set you got in the front window," she said to me, pointing. "What you gotta get for it?"

"Now, Bitsy, the last thing we need is more dust-gatherin' stuff—"

"It's not for me, Robert," she glared up at the tall man, and Heath could swear he saw the man shrink back. "It's a housewarming gift for Ms. Larson. That's a right nice set. I think it would look real pretty in the dining room of the Belle Bride. Don't you, Mr. Barrow?"

Chapter Twelve

Liv

I realized it was probably mostly in my head, but in just the few short hours since I'd taken the anti-depressant, I was feeling more stable and centered. I spent about an hour cruising Heath's website, trying to decide on furniture styles for the parlor and dining rooms. I was getting mighty tired of eating my meals hunched over my countertop in the kitchen, or perched on a Tupperware tub on the upstairs gallery.

And Heath was right about his website. It sucked. Half of the images didn't load, and many were distorted or blurry. Navigation was a nightmare. Finally, I gave up and Googled Victorian furniture, and bookmarked the styles that caught my eye. I'd just show Heath what I was looking for, and ask if he had anything suitable.

I wondered how so much of his business came from online orders. You'd never guess as much, judging by his site. I was looking forward to tackling the redesign, which I could probably start on next week. My office furniture was due in tomorrow.

Once I was more relaxed, I found my mind drifting back to the handsome man with the chocolate colored curls more and more throughout the day. I'd wanted him so badly this morning. Still, I wasn't taking any foolish chances with my health, or with my future. I'd decided a long time ago—children weren't in the cards for me.

How could I offer a child a decent future when I didn't know anything about my own family history? Besides, I was the offspring of a female who had given me up without ever even holding me. Something deep inside told me that didn't bode well for my own qualifications for motherhood.

I spent an extra-long time getting ready to head into town for my dinner with Heath. Instead of my customary uniform of jeans and a blouse, I flipped through the things I'd hung in my new armoire until I located the pretty, pale green sundress I'd bought last summer. Its short, flirty hem showed off my legs, especially when I paired it with strappy white sandals with heels a tad higher than I usually wore. Since the dress buttoned up the front, I could choose to leave a few undone at both the top and bottom.

Which, of course, I did.

By the time I climbed into my truck at a little past five, my entire body was humming. It wasn't dinner that had my appetite up. It was libido, pure and raw.

Sex is good therapy, Carla had said. I'd, hopefully, squelched my Confederate soldier delusions by going back on the meds. At least temporarily. Tonight, I definitely intended to indulge in some other, more pleasurable therapy as well.

We rode in Heath's giant truck down the short stretch to the main highway where I discovered *Maisie's*, the local dining hot spot. He looked delectable in a white button down shirt, starched and pressed so crisp it looked like it might be painful to move in. His jeans, I noticed when he'd climbed into his truck, were just as meticulously creased—he must have his clothes done in Birmingham.

And oh, how they fit him in all the right places. He'd left the top buttons of his shirt undone as well, revealing those super-soft looking chest curls. The minute I pulled the truck door shut behind me, his scent enveloped me, an enticing mixture of some spicy cologne and his own, musky male aroma.

"You're looking mighty fetching tonight, Ms. Larson," he said, smiling as he shifted the truck into gear and pulled out onto the road. He kept stealing glances over to skim down my body, his gaze punctuated with stops at my thighs and cleavage. I didn't have much in the latter department, but it was all mine. Thank the Lord for Victoria's Secret.

"Why thank you, Mr. Barrow. You're looking pretty dashing yourself." What was it about being in the South? Nostalgia and tradition reigned here, and infused itself into your very being through the steamy air. I felt like a proper Victorian lady, even though I was dressed . . . how did my hallucinatory soldier describe me? Oh yes. *Like some Yankee's whore.*

No, dear Rebel. Almost two hundred years have passed. We "ladies" have claimed the right to dress, or undress, in any manner we please. Sexual freedom is no longer reserved for the male of the species.

Maisie's was a pleasant surprise. The place was quaint and cozy, the tables dressed with paisley patterned tablecloths that matched the window treatments. A small vase holding a fresh daisy sat beside a lit candle in the center of each table.

It was early for dinner—at least it would have been in the city. Yet even at not quite six o'clock the place was already pretty well populated. The next nearest "nice" restaurant, Heath explained, was twenty miles farther up the road, so Maisie's did a booming business.

We didn't discuss the debacle that had been our morning, neither the squashed sexual interlude nor my ridiculous fantasy soldier encounter. I didn't mention the soldier's "return" after Heath left. I also avoided sharing with him my suspicions about my drug withdrawal symptoms.

The man had enough to worry about with his own medication issues. I did, however, ask him casually if he'd had time to stop at the pharmacy. His quick smile was his only answer, and it sparked a fire in my belly. And it had nothing to do with the spicy cocktail sauce I was dipping the shrimp appetizers in.

"I took a look at your website today," I began. "I really need to get busy picking out dining room and living room—I guess the proper term is *parlor*—furniture. You're right. The site leaves a lot to be desired."

Heath frowned. "I know. I told you, I'm a furniture guy, not a computer geek. I just haven't had to time to check out references on any of the web designers so far. You," he paused, pointing a shrimp tail at me, "I believe I can trust."

"Why is that? I mean, you hardly know me, Heath. I've bought some furniture from you, eaten fried chicken and biscuits with you, and then . . . run out on you when you had a seizure." I huffed out a breath. I was just being honest. It was flattering to consider, though, the thought . . . maybe, just maybe, he'd done some background checking on my business skills. That it wasn't just my potential buying power or my body coloring his decision.

He rolled his eyes toward the ceiling and said, "Oh, well, let's see. There are at least five top U.S. companies on your client list, for starters." He proceeded to name them, ticking each off on his fingers as he did. I flushed with pride, and a little embarrassment. "From what I could glean from the Internet," he continued, "your design company may be small, but it's also focused. As well respected as those like Grey Global and Tombras."

Now I could feel the heat rising up my neck. He was going overboard on this flattery thing. I had a successful web building business with a solid reputation. Still, I wasn't on any of the Fortune 500 payrolls.

I slid him a sly smile. "Flattery won't get you a discount on my fee," I said, "but unlike the popular saying, it may get you somewhere . . . tonight." I winked.

The spark of desire I saw in his eyes only served to fan my own flames. How had I not noticed how much of a hole the lack of sexual energy had left in my life? No wonder I'd felt like such a ghost ship these past two years.

We feasted on prime rib that was, even according to my "city girl" standards, pretty damned tasty. Unlike the fancy potatoes Chantilly or boring steamed broccoli I often ordered with the meat, this steak was served with spicy sweet potato salad (which I'd never even heard of), green bean casserole, and cornbread. It was hard not to make a pig of myself, yet I didn't want to present myself a few hours from now, naked, with a bloated belly.

"There's no way I'm going to be able to finish all this, Heath," I said, leaning across the table.

He grinned. "I have all the modern conveniences. Even a refrigerator."

"So, your place, then?" I asked, secretly relieved we wouldn't be going back to the Belle Bride. Not for this first night together. Not after my strange hallucinations over the past few days. I hadn't experienced any withdrawal symptoms anywhere else.

He nodded and I smiled.

"That would be fantastic."

An hour later, I was strolling through Heath's front door once again, holding my to-go box against my vibrating—and still reasonably flat—belly. I was so ready for this. I'd asked him twice on the way there if he was sure he'd picked up condoms at the drugstore. He assured me his protection department was well stocked.

There was no way I'd be able to stomp down the flames if he got me going like he did this morning. Not again.

I was amused to see his hands were shaking as he took the Styrofoam box from me to stash in the fridge. Then I paused. His epilepsy . . .

"You alright?" I asked, laying a hand on his arm. He closed the fridge door and turned, grabbing my gaze. After the slightest of nods, he answered by pulling me against him and ravaging my mouth with a demanding kiss. I could feel his arousal hard against my belly.

"I'd like to think I'm better than alright," he growled, moving from my mouth to run his tongue along my jawline. "Way better than alright," he said, dipping his tongue into my ear and nipping the lobe. Heat and dampness pooled between my legs. I groaned.

With gentle fingers, he lifted my hair and continued his way down my neck, bathing my skin with warm kisses and teasing strokes of his tongue. I was melting from the inside out, and my knees felt wobbly. It didn't help I was still teetering atop those a-bit-too-high heeled sandals.

He must have felt my swoon, because in the next moment he swept me off my feet and perched me—on the kitchen counter? Well, it was the closest horizontal surface available. The thought flashed through my mind: I'd never done it in the kitchen. It was a nice, clean kitchen, but still—

"Let me get you nice and relaxed before we get started," he purred into my ear. "Just lean back and try to make yourself comfortable. I mean, as comfortable as one can be when sitting on Corian."

I giggled. The cold, hard surface under my bottom was an odd contrast to the heat rapidly building in my sex. Sex on a countertop. Who knew?

Heath was not one to rush anything. He took his time, planting kisses along my collarbone toward my cleavage, then nipping lightly at the fabric before undoing a few more of the top buttons. My nipples were already straining against the lace bra I wore. They were more than ready for some long-deserved attention.

He surprised me then by skimming past my breasts and lowering to a crouch before me. Slowly, methodically, he began sensual massage, caressing my calves and ankles before slowly unfastening the buckles on my sandals. They hit the floor, one at a time. Flames erupted low in my belly. I'd heard the feet could be an erogenous zone, but this was the first time for me. The guys I'd been with were always in a hurry to get to the other, more interesting areas of my body.

I wiggled my bottom against the rapidly warming surface beneath it and moaned. My breath was coming in short, hot bursts. "Heath, you're killing me," I murmured. "And I hate to complain, but I don't have a whole lot of padding on my backside."

His low, rumbling chuckle vibrated against the thin, sensitive skin on the top of my foot. "Well, let me take care of that," he said.

Rising, he grabbed a thick, clean terry towel from the drawer beside me (Wow, impressively lush dishtowels. Unless he planned on this all along . . .) One, strong arm grasped my waist and lifted me, and my legs automatically wrapped around his waist. It was his turn to groan.

"You're testing my control, Ms. Larson," he rasped into my ear. He apparently had no intention to take this to the bedroom just yet. As I clung to him, arms wound around his neck and face buried in those soft curls, he arranged the folded towel along the counter beneath me. Gently, he set me back down, and again dove into my mouth with his hot tongue.

Desire coiled inside me, setting my body on fire as he explored my mouth with increasing urgency. I dropped my head back, breaking the kiss, gasping for air as my heart pounded frantically against my ribs. Heath took advantage of that moment to flip open the buttons on my dress, one by one, to my waist. He eased the fabric off my shoulders, revealing my bra, one made of pale, sheer lace. Groaning, Heath closed his eyes as he ran his thumbs over the stiff points showing through the lace.

I nearly came undone right then and there. My nipples had always been uber sensitive, and they had been feeling very neglected for a long time. I shuddered, my hips bucking against him of their own accord.

"I'm gonna lose it, Heath. It's been too long . . ." I choked out in a frantic whisper.

He immediately moved his hands away, trailing gentle fingers up my arms to my shoulders. "Oh no. Not yet. We need to make this last much, much longer." Slipping the bra straps down, he released my swollen breasts. A breath whooshed from him. "You are so beautiful. I want to explore you a little more first."

His eyes locked with mine, he methodically finished unbuttoning my dress and helped me slip my arms free. The cloth pooled around my hips as his gaze trailed down my belly to the lace thong panties. He sucked in a breath, taking a moment to readjust himself in his jeans.

"You need to get comfortable too, there, Tiger," I purred, anxious for a peek at what lay beneath the impressively mounded denim, straining to be free.

"Not yet."

He then lowered his mouth to my nipple, at the same time sliding his hand down between my legs. I gasped when his finger slid into my wetness. The dual onslaught of sensations took me by surprise, and shattered my control. My orgasm was immediate and mind-blowing. The waves of pleasure racked my body with shuddering intensity, again and again.

Screams echo more in a kitchen than in a bedroom was the first coherent thought rising to the surface as I came down, shuddering and burying my face into his neck.

Heath

Heath had felt decadent when he bought those oversized, overpriced new kitchen towels on a whim. He'd been browsing at some fancy bed-and-bath store at the mall in Birmingham and bought them on impulse. Now he was thinking they were a pretty smart investment. He hadn't had any idea how he'd use one for the first time.

The plain fact of the matter was . . . he couldn't wait to get her naked. After watching her lithe, sexy body ripple under clothes now for over a week, he'd gotten the full view just this morning—only to discover there wasn't a damn thing he could do about it. Not then.

He didn't want extensive foreplay or oral sex with this woman. He wanted to be inside her, part of her. Claim her as his own: body, heart, and soul.

Geez, where had that come from?

Okay, he'd admit it: he was hornier than hell and hadn't had a woman in . . . well, years. In truth, he'd also been a little hesitant about even trying to have sex with any woman after the rejection Katherine put on his head. His old meds had sometimes made him mentally cut out at the worst possible moment. Tonight, he was banking on the fact the new ones would carry him through.

And so it seemed only natural to follow his instincts when she looked up at him with those huge, blue eyes in his kitchen, trapped between him and his countertop. Her pouty mouth just begged to be kissed. The concern in her eyes—for him. Now that was something he wasn't used to, and it melted a little part of his heart. At the same time, the rest of his body peaked to full arousal in seconds. Once he tasted her, warm and pungent with the wine they'd been sharing, he wanted to get started. Right now.

Those spiky sandals had been tantalizing him all night.

They added a delicious wiggle to her hips when she walked, showcasing her long, shapely legs. She was obviously as cocked as he was, so when he ran his thumbs over those hard, pebbled nipples and she nearly came, he figured he'd better slow things down a bit. Make this last. Tease her from the ground up. Literally.

A little voice in the back of his head kept screaming, *Danger, Danger*, like a robot on some old sci-fi series. Liv Larson was just way too classy, too sexy, too city. He'd been down this road before. His body, however, responded with a simple *Fuck You*.

Or, more accurately, *fuck her*.

Heath knew taking her, the way he wanted to, deep and hard, wouldn't be nearly as comfortable for her on his kitchen counter as atop his memory foam mattress. But damn, it sure was hot thinking about the prospect. No. Not this first time, he decided. He wasn't sure how much control he could hang onto, and the last thing he wanted to do was make this an uncomfortable memory for her.

Once she came apart in his hand, her sex pulsing hot and wet around his fingers and her nipple stiffening in his mouth, he knew better. Once he got started, he couldn't promise to be gentle.

When her shudders finally subsided from the-longest-orgasm-he'd-ever-witnessed, he scooped her off the counter and headed to his bedroom. Damn, this woman was hot. His own condition was rapidly becoming painful inside of jeans that were more than a little too snug in the crotch area. He cuddled her and she curled against him, trembling still, gasping for air as she snuggled into his neck.

"You alright?" he asked.

She answered with a nod, wrapping her arms tighter around his neck. Heath couldn't help feeling as if he were dreaming all this. Liv Larson had dropped into his life out of a wet dream. He just hoped to hell he never had to wake up.

She looked like a goddess, propped on his bed against a stack of pillows, naked, her legs spread open for him. With shaking fingers, he managed to shed his shirt, and eased his jeans down over his now-painful erection. Liv stared the whole time as if she'd never seen a naked man before, blue eyes wide, biting on one thumbnail. The flash of heat and anticipation he saw in her blown pupils shot his own libido even higher.

God, he hoped he could pace himself. Hoped to hell his new meds did their job.

Then, she surprised him. As he went to swing one leg over her body and straddle her, the sizzling hot, city girl switched up the rules. In one swift movement, she rolled him onto his back, strong fingers digging into his biceps. And then she was on top. She was in control.

Heath kind of liked that.

Pressing her warm, wet center not over, but beneath the base of his throbbing erection, she began a sort of . . . petting. Smiling, she ran her fingertips lightly over his chest, his belly, and down his arms. She carefully avoided touching his stiff shaft, which was maddening. The fluttery sensation along his skin, now damp with a sheen of sweat, was exhilarating, and he found himself panting. This wasn't going to last too long— not nearly long enough—if she kept this up.

The whole time her blue eyes stayed locked on his, a mischievous hint of a smile curling her bee-stung lips.

"You doing okay?" she asked, noticing his chest rising and falling at an ever-increasing rate.

Again, her concern, and it seemed genuine, pierced his heart with bittersweet pain. Apparently, even though she hardly knew him, Liv was unafraid or unconcerned about how his condition might interrupt their joining. Heath was seeing a side of this woman he hadn't seen before: pillow-soft emotion with an iron-core of strength underneath.

He could say nothing, his mouth dry, his heartbeat deafening him. What he did know was if she kept bumping her flat, smooth belly against his arousal he was going to lose it. He reached up and grasped her arms.

"I want this to be good for you, Liv. If you keep this up it will be over before I can do that." He reached for the protection he'd left on his nightstand.

Then he switched it up on her, swiftly sweeping her onto her back and settling himself between her legs. He'd wanted to tease her more, make this last longer. But he could feel his control slipping.

When he buried himself inside her, she let out a gasp before wrapping her legs around his waist. For a long moment, he couldn't move, though it had nothing to do with his condition. This was sheer torture, wrestling his impending release into submission. Breathing slow and deep, his body relaxed over her as her fingers danced lightly across his back. It was as if she understood. As if she'd read his mind.

When he finally did begin to move inside her, propped on his arms so he could hold her gaze the entire time, Heath felt a crack form in the armor he'd so carefully fastened around his heart. This wasn't just sex. And the way she was speaking to him with her eyes, silently, passionately, he knew it wasn't just a physical act for her either.

Chapter Thirteen

Liv

I awoke in my own bed the next morning, brilliant sunshine streaming across my pale green coverlet. Stretching and yawning, I felt decadent. Completely relaxed—more so than I'd been since I'd arrived in Camellia. It's amazing what an evening of hot sex can do for your state of mind.

I'd resisted Heath's repeated requests for me to stay with him, sleep in his bed last night. Still, he had insisted on following me home. We spent another half-hour making out in the foyer, which would have led to another coupling against the wall if not for—again—the lack of protection.

"Keep them in your wallet. Your truck. Your pockets. Your shop," I growled at him, poking his chest with one finger as he backed out my front door. "I'll buy some tomorrow so I have some here. So we're always prepared."

Now, lying in my bed in the warm rays of the fully risen sun, I was glad I'd insisted on coming home. Heath was way too tempting. I wanted to keep our relationship light and physical, at least for the foreseeable future. I wasn't ready to endanger my bruised heart again. Not yet. Maybe not ever.

Time would tell.

I hadn't slept this late, or this well, in forever. Counting the days in my head, I realized my self-determined vacation would be over in just a few days. Then I would be back on schedule, working regular hours every day in my office. On my new desk. Which should be arriving—

I bolted upright to the sound of a truck pulling into my driveway. A big truck. Glancing at the clock, I realized it was 10:29 a.m.

Holy crap, I really had overslept.

I pulled an oversized tee shirt over my head as I swung out of bed, wincing a little at the soreness between my legs. Then smiling at the pain. A good pain.

"I'll be down in a minute!" I called through the cracked-open door leading to my second-floor gallery. Two burly men who I thought I remembered seeing at Heath's Birmingham warehouse were climbing out of the truck's cab.

The now empty cab. My heart sank just a little. I'd kind of hoped Heath would be on the delivery team.

I've got to stop this, I thought as I pulled on a pair of gym shorts. Sex only. None of this bleeding heart, emotional yearning.

With Heath Barrow, though, I knew it would be difficult to restrain my emotions from getting all tangled up. He was just too perfect. Too freaking perfect.

To my surprise, when I opened the front door to the delivery crew, I realized I *had* recognized at least one of the men, and not from Heath's warehouse.

"Benjamin?" I squeaked out, surprised I'd actually remembered the Warren's son's name. He looked a sight different from the first day I'd met him. For one thing, he was wearing shoes. Big shoes. I wondered absently where one would find work boots that big. His shaggy, dark hair was clean and contained in a band of some sort at his nape. His Big Foot persona had been somewhat tamed by his clean, farmer-style denim overalls.

"Howdy, Ms. Larson," he grumbled, reaching out to engulf my hand in his giant paw. He was smiling at me.

I reflexively smiled back. "I didn't realize you worked with Heath," I said.

"I do now," he answered proudly, puffing his massive chest up even more. "We done brought your office furniture. Where do you want it?"

As I followed the two men into the house carrying one section of my expansive new desk up the curved stairway, I couldn't help but notice how Ben seemed uneasy. His normally slow movements became jerky, and he kept searching the hall and stairwell as if he were looking for something.

"Haven't you ever been inside the Belle Bride before, Ben?" I asked as they slid the desk into the spot I designated in my office.

His eyes darted around the room nervously. "No, ma'am. Never been inside." He rubbed his hands on the bib of his overalls and shifted toward the door. "Come on, Syd. Let's get the other pieces in and done."

I directed the men where to place the furniture, and the pieces were perfect. I had them position the desk so there was enough room between it and the front window to pass between . . . maybe I'd put a plant stand there, and cover it with orchids. The other man helping Benjamin had puffed and struggled as they maneuvered their way up the winding staircase with the heavy wooden pieces. Benjamin looked as though he might be carrying a light bag of groceries.

The man was huge, and intimidating. The fact he was a little lacking in the brains department added to my already heightened sense of uneasiness around him. As did the fact that every time I glanced his way, I caught him staring at me with an almost hungry expression.

Yikes. And I thought my Confederate soldier was scary.

A half-hour later I stood in my office admiring my shiny, new mahogany desk, facing the east window. Heath had been right. The morning light bathed and bounced off the dark wood beautifully. I almost couldn't wait to get my computer and office tools set up.

Then I remembered: all I'd brought with me was my laptop and the wireless printer. There hadn't been enough room in my truck for the oversized monitor I needed to produce intricate graphics. Or the ergonomic keyboard. Or the blotter. Or the paper trays.

I sighed. Time to go shopping. Again.

I really was going to have to get back to work in a few days if I wanted to keep all my website clients happy. And not go broke.

A Google search on my phone told me the nearest decent-sized office supply store was in Birmingham. Guess I was heading back to the city today.

An hour later, showered and dressed, I swept my phone off the counter and dropped it into my purse. I noticed the velvet bag containing the hair work brooch was still lying on the granite surface, right where I'd left it. I fisted the bag, feeling the strange, tingling warmth the piece gave me. Maybe I'd stop by Heath's warehouse while I was in Birmingham. If Cynthia was working, maybe she could tell me a little bit more about this strange, unique kind of jewelry.

I made it my first stop, not wanting to leave the big box I knew my new desktop computer would come in sitting in the open bed of my truck. Not in the middle of a city. I'd lived in Manhattan long enough to know that wasn't a good idea.

"Well, hello there," Cynthia said as she slipped out of the back room a minute after I'd entered the shop. "Back to browse some more?"

Today she was wearing another shape-hugging dress, this one in a vivid royal blue with lace edging the low, scooped neckline. It looked vintage, like the green one she'd been wearing the other day. I wondered if she wore vintage fashions to enhance the atmosphere of the shop, or if it truly was her personal style.

I smiled as I slipped the velvet bag out of my purse. "I am. I'm also very intrigued by this piece I bought from you the other day. I wondered if you had any more information on its background."

She pursed her pouty lips, furrows creasing the pale skin between her eyebrows. "I'm not sure if I had any notes on that piece or not. I think I picked it up at an antique show in Decatur. I do keep a log book on every piece I buy, though. Let me grab it and see if I wrote anything down."

She disappeared into the back room and returned a few moments later carrying a lovely, leather-bound journal. The cover was deeply embossed with what appeared to be a Celtic knot pattern.

Even her notebooks are antiques?

"Seen Heath lately?" she asked casually as she began to flip through the pages.

Every inch of him, I thought. I could feel the heat rising up my neck to make my cheeks burn. I quickly turned to wander back along the jewelry display cases. I didn't want to lie, but ... Noncommittal, I figured, was the best path to take.

"We live in a small town. It's inevitable I'll run into him now and then." I tried to sound distracted, flippant. When I felt her eyes on me and looked up, I realized she must know her baby brother pretty well. She had one hand on her hip and one tawny eyebrow arched.

"Well I wouldn't credit the small-town atmosphere entirely. You were all Heath could talk about when I spoke to him yesterday. Seems pretty taken with you." She cocked her head as she continued to peruse the contents of her notebook. "Heath's a nice guy, Liv. But he got tangled up with a big-city gal once before. It didn't bode well for him." She shot me a pointed glare and sighed. "Of course, it's really none of my business. I'm sorry I said anything."

Hmm, I thought. Pretty protective older sister. Heath had said his family was close. In that moment, I knew I should be feeling indignant at her boldness. Instead, all I felt was . . . jealous.

What it must be like, to have family watching your back all the time. Worrying about you. Would it be comforting? Or would it make me feel smothered?

Guess I would never know.

The silence continued until Cynthia's eyebrows drew together as she ran a manicured finger down a page of notes. She began to tap the paper.

"Here. It wasn't Decatur. It was one of Empire's auctions in Athens. Last fall." She glanced up and turned the notebook in my direction, pointing. "You can read what I wrote down about the lot. There were five pieces, in all. The other four I believe I've already sold."

I returned to the counter and skimmed the page, covered with a loopy but meticulous longhand. Three sentences, none of which meant anything to me at all.

Estate lot from the Bernard family: five pieces, one hair work. Samuel Bernard: died earlier this year, no living kin. Will declares proceeds to go to the Confederate Veterans Memorial Park in Greenville, Alabama.

I read the sentences aloud, then looked up at Cynthia. Her shoulders lifted in a shrug.

"I know there was a lot of talk about the unveiling of a new monument there last fall. It came right after all the racial unrest and violence in Virginia, so some folks got their noses bent out of shape over it."

Although I wasn't completely unaware of the current news, I tried to avoid watching the repeated airings of the *bad* news. Of course, that also meant I didn't watch or read much news at all these days.

"Where is Greenville?" I asked. "I mean, is there a museum there? If this Bernard fellow willed his estate to the Memorial Park, there might be somebody he knew. Someone who could tell me more about the history of the jewelry."

Cynthia picked up her iPhone and leaned both elbows on the counter, thumbs flying across the screen. "Greenville is down south of Montgomery. It's over three hours from here," she said. "Not sure what you'll find what you're looking for there, though. I understand the property is actually privately owned."

Heath

Heath was whistling—actually *whistling*—as he unlocked the antique store's door that morning. His doctor had apparently been right. The new meds for his epilepsy were working. He'd been able to perform flawlessly last night with a brand new, super exciting sexual partner, without a single sign of a seizure in sight.

Yet as he went through the shop, turning on some of the antique lamps he always kept lit throughout the space, he couldn't ignore the niggling bolus of worry quivering deep in his chest. This time it didn't have anything to do with his health. At least, not his physical well-being.

He'd been all for fanning the flames of a fling with the pretty new girl in town. A fling. Sex with no strings. He realized after making love to Liv last night that maintaining a rein on his emotions might be more difficult than he'd anticipated.

There it was. *Making love.* In the bright light of morning, those were the words his mind spoke to describe the incredible experience of last night. Not a roll in the hay. Not a quick piece of ass. *Making love.*

And from the looks of things, Liv Larson wasn't going to be leaving Camellia anytime soon. She'd bought a house, for God's sakes. And was now in the process of furnishing the place, making it her own. Next week she would go to work—for him—redesigning his website. Insinuating herself into his carefully shielded world in a multitude of ways.

What had he been thinking?

Obviously, he hadn't. Not with his brain, anyway. He'd acted like a typical, hormone-driven, horny male.

Heath did his best to keep his mind on his inventory list for most of the day. When Ben and his other man, Syd, arrived at a little past noon to swap out the pieces he'd had brought from the warehouse, he'd just finished deciding what he would be sending back to Birmingham.

"How'd it go at the Larson place?" Heath asked as he met the two men on the street in front of the shop.

"Real good," Syd replied. "The set fits perfectly in her office."

"I had a feeling it would," Heath said, smiling. Then he turned to Ben. "How's your first day on the job going, Ben?"

Ben kept his eyes trained on his work boots, scuffing one on the concrete beneath them. "Good. Easy. This ain't so hard, Mr. Barrow."

"I'm glad, Ben. I won't need you every day . . . a few times a week, maybe. I'll call and let you know a day ahead. Will that work?" Heath asked.

Ben nodded and shrugged awkwardly.

He really has no social skills at all, Heath thought. It was smart of his parents to find a job for him. And it made Heath feel good he could help out.

Syd clapped his hands together and said, "Okay, Ben, let's get these pieces unloaded. We'll leave them here on the sidewalk, then grab what Heath wants to go back to the warehouse." He laid a hand on the big man's arm and said, "Now, there's a lot of stuff packed into Heath's shop, Ben. We have to be real careful getting things in and out."

Ben nodded and mumbled, "Yes, sir."

By the time the men had done the furniture transfer, it was well past two o'clock. The process of maneuvering pieces in and out of Heath's crowded shop got complicated. Like Jenga with bureaus and sideboards. Heath was pleasantly surprised to find that although Ben was mammoth in size and strength, he was also cautious and careful. He managed to complete the entire task without scratching a single piece, or breaking any of the more delicate items Heath had on display.

Heath was feeling pretty pleased about the new arrangement when Ben's father pulled up to the curb and tooted the horn. As he peeled off bills to hand to the big man for the day's work, Ben looked down at him wearing a silly grin.

"Thank you, Mr. Barrow. I like working for you," he said as he took the money and stuffed it in the pocket of his overalls.

"You're welcome, Ben. And you can call me Heath. I'll probably need you again in a day or two. I'll call."

As he turned toward the door, Ben paused. "We gonna have any more stuff goin' out to Miss Larson's place?" he asked. "She's nice. A real pretty lady."

Something in the tone of his voice set Heath's nerves on edge. Something about the way Ben, who usually avoided eye contact, was now holding his gaze. There was a glimmer of . . . *something* there. It made the hairs on the back of Heath's neck prickle.

"She is. A real nice lady. I'm not sure when I'll have anything else to deliver out her way."

And I don't think I'll be asking you to go on any more deliveries to Liv's house, he thought.

Heath had just plopped down into his desk chair when his phone buzzed. The caller ID said, *Cynthia.*

"Hey, bro," she said brightly. "Syd headed back this way yet? I'd like to cut out a little early this afternoon."

"He is. Should be there within the hour," Heath replied.

"How'd it go with Bigfoot?" Cynthia asked.

Heath sighed. "That's mean, Cyn. Ben's a pretty good worker. The Warrens are nice people. I'm glad I decided to give the guy a chance."

"Hmm," was her reply. "Well, I've seen him a time or two when I've been in Camellia. He creeps me out."

The long pause on the other end of the line told Heath he was about to get a big sister lecture. The business was his —she worked for *him*. Still, Cynthia didn't usually hold back anything when it came to voicing her opinions about his management moves. So, he was surprised when her tone went soft.

"How are you feeling?" she asked. "On your new medication, I mean?"

"Good, Sis, thanks. Really good." Heath winced. Had he really growled out those last two words?

He heard his sister clear her throat. "Heath, this woman."

Ah, here it comes. And he thought it would be about Ben. Heath had felt his sister watching him that day, the way he'd interacted with Liv when they came to the shop. She'd given him "the look" more than once. She knew him just too damn well.

"How much do you know about her?" she continued. "It's pretty obvious you've got the hots for her. And she's not just passing through, Heath. She's bought a home here, and—"

"Cynthia, please. I'm a big boy. I can take care of myself. I'm not about to get all gooey on another city girl. I'm smart enough to keep lightning from striking me twice. You should know that," he said, trying to keep the annoyance out of his voice.

"She was here again, you know. Today. Said she had to pick up some things for her new office. She's all agog over the hair work piece she bought. Wants to trace its history. I'll bet she's on the phone with some friend at Sotheby's back in New York right now. Figures she's latched onto a big payoff. Typical city girl." He could almost hear the scowl in her voice.

When he ended the call, Heath couldn't help thinking

how much Liv Larson *didn't* fit the mold of a typical, slick city girl. She had the New York accent, yet that didn't fit her either. She seemed too at home here, in this tiny Southern town, in her big old antebellum house.

He spent the rest of the afternoon trying hard to ignore his sister's concern. Fact of the matter was, what she'd said worried him too. Ever since he'd met the tall, lithe lady with the blue, Anime eyes. Ever since the first night on Liv's gallery, watching those eyes dance as she ate fried chicken and biscuits. And now, after he'd *had* her. After he'd crested a wave of indescribable passion, lost in her eyes . . .

Liv Larson was a conundrum. A damned sexy, irresistible conundrum. And Heath had a feeling his heart was in big, big trouble.

Chapter Fourteen

Liv

I drove back to Camellia with all the whistles and bells I needed to set up my home office: a huge iMac Pro, an ergonomic keyboard, wireless mouse, a desk blotter, paper trays, and a variety of small baskets to hold my new repertoire of pens, mechanical pencils, paper clips, highlighters, and stapler. A whole new office regime for a whole new life.

I had restrained myself from buying another piece of hair work jewelry in Heath's shop. Honestly, it wasn't much of a struggle. There just weren't any other pieces on display that spoke to me the way the one I'd bought did. I couldn't help wonder how, or why, I felt so strangely connected to this particular piece of jewelry.

It was barely two o'clock when I rolled back into town headed for the library. I'd never made it there the day I visited the museum. To be honest, I'd been too creeped out. Seeing the stuffed dog, one that looked exactly like the one I'd seen wandering around in my backyard . . .

My backyard. Yeah, I was owning the Belle Bride. Viscerally, it seemed. Now, I guessed, as long as I kept taking my anti-depressants, I wouldn't get any more visits from Confederate soldiers.

The library was open, it's red and white flag flapping boldly from its stand on the porch railing. These folks were big on flags, it seemed. I guess once yours has been trampled, burned, and desecrated in just about every way possible, one might feel that way. Alabama's state flag being so similar to the

Rebel flag was a controversial topic, to be sure. Still, the Civil War was part of our history—a big part. One in which human rights, and morals, were put to the test and fought over.

I pondered the violence over memorials in the recent news, as Cynthia had mentioned. I could understand the emotions on both sides. But history was history. It was a record, and should not be ignored, or destroyed. At least the Belle Bride had a history. It was more than I could say for myself.

After parking in the small gravel lot, I paused, casting a glance at my computer box in the back of my truck, then up at the sky. It was a cloudless, hot spring day. And I was back in Camellia now. Surely, my goods would be safe for the few minutes I'd be in the library.

I strolled up to the entrance and through the heavy, oak-framed doors with thick glass panes. I'd been a big fan of libraries ever since my first visit to the New York Public Library. Though this one was a mere pebble compared to Manhattan's gigantic planet of an athenaeum, it still held the comforting commonalities—the woody aroma of old paper, and the sodden hush of sound surrounding me like an invisible hug.

I wondered how much this library had ventured into the modern, technological age. Would there still be card catalogs? Or would all of their holdings be accessible via computer monitors?

There was a little bit of both. Beside the librarian's desk, a monstrous, semicircular oak pedestal reminiscent of an old judge's podium, were two, small modular desks sporting what looked to be relatively new computer monitors. There was, however, a bank of cabinets against the far wall holding dozens, if not hundreds, of tiny, rectangular-shaped drawer fronts. An old card catalog.

I smiled and sighed, then slipped my phone out of my

purse and pulled up my notepad. I'd recorded what few details about the history of my hair work brooch there before leaving Heath's Birmingham store.

The librarian appeared from some hidden room behind the elevated behemoth of a desk shortly after my arrival. I'd followed the instructions for accessing the online catalog of holdings from the index card taped to the desk next to the keyboard. But after performing searches for both the name "Samuel Bernard," then just "Bernard," I was coming up with no viable results. I frowned. The librarian cleared her throat.

"Is there something I can help you with, Miss?" she asked in a shaky, old-lady voice. I looked up to see her peering down at me from her elevated podium, a pair of readers dangling from a beaded chain around her neck. Her gray-streaked brown hair formed a sort of static halo around her beefy, ruddy face. I couldn't tell if she was frowning at me or if it was just her heavy jowls pulling her thin-lipped mouth down into a scowl.

"Hi there," I said, in a voice a little too loud for a library. I winced and looked around, but there didn't seem to be anyone else there I might disturb. I swallowed and continued in a hushed tone. "I'm looking for some history on a family named Bernard. Samuel Bernard."

The woman blinked and jerked back as though I'd slapped her. She slipped her readers on, then off again. I watched as she scanned the small library's space just as I had done a moment before. Then she cleared her throat and held up one finger before disappearing behind the podium.

I jumped when a small door behind the two new computer desks swung open, and the librarian emerged. She pulled the faded, pink cardigan sweater she was wearing closer around her shoulders as she approached and planted herself before me, the monitor acting as a barrier between us. Her name tag said *Florence Edington, Head Librarian*.

"What's your interest in Samuel Bernard?" she asked, planting two chubby fists on her ample hips. She said the name with a sense of familiarity, and regarded me with a suspicious glare.

I scrambled to grab my purse off the floor where I'd dropped it when I sat down at the computer, and dug inside for the velvet bag.

"I bought this in an antique shop in Birmingham," I said, holding the bag up before loosening the silken strings. The brooch, when it tumbled out into my palm, caused the same, warm tingling sensation as it had since the day I first laid eyes on it. I held it out for her to see. "The clerk in the shop where I bought it said it came from the estate sale of Samuel Bernard. I'd like to find out more about him, and his family, if I could."

Slowly, her gaze flashing from me to the brooch and back, Ms. Edington slid her readers up on her nose and leaned closer to my open palm. Her mouth rounded in a silent O, then she covered it with her hand. Her eyes riveted mine, but she said nothing.

I waited a full minute before prodding her. "Well? Do you know anything about this family?"

I was shocked to see a watery sheen fill her eyes. Silently, she nodded. Then she pointed to the brooch in my hand and, almost timidly, asked, "May I?"

My palm felt suddenly cold as she lifted the piece and cradled it with both hands, as if it were a priceless relic. Her head began to oscillate, side to side, as she turned the brooch over and caressed the almost completely faded-away engravings on the back. Finally, with a huge sigh that lifted her shoulders and dropped them in a whoosh, she grabbed my gaze and smiled.

"I haven't seen this piece in thirty years," she said, her voice thick with emotion.

Excitement had begun to bubble in my chest like seltzer. Was it possible I would find the answer to my questions in the library, but not in a book?

"So, you've seen this brooch before? Did you know Samuel Bernard? The notes from the estate auction said he had no living kin when he died," I said.

Her thin lips pressed into a line. After a long pause, she said, "He did not. I was his bookkeeper. For years and years after his dear wife passed on. I'd bring him reading material from the library. He didn't get out much after she was gone. Sadly, Samuel was forced to move into an assisted living facility in Decatur after the stroke stole his mobility. I don't drive, you see, so . . . " she paused, producing a crumpled tissue out of the pocket of her cardigan, "I never got the chance to go visit him much. When I read his obituary in the Camellia Chronicle last spring, I hadn't seen Samuel in almost twenty years."

Liv

Later that afternoon, I sat at my new desk, the brooch cradled in its velvet bag set carefully beside my laptop. I hadn't even taken the time to unload all of the new equipment I bought out of my truck. After leaving the library, I couldn't wait to get home and start researching a man named Samuel Bernard.

Why this seemed so important to me, I had no idea. Yet the hair work jewelry had touched me so, left such a mark on my emotions. For one, I'd never imagined such a thing—jewelry made out of dead people's hair? It was macabre and bizarre. Like carrying around, or wearing, tiny fragments of your deceased loved ones in miniature, glass-lidded coffins. At first, the very notion had really creeped me out.

Then I'd been struck by a sense of awe. Imagine: This brooch contained the actual remnants of not one, but two people who lived over a hundred years ago. Who was this Samuel Bernard, and why had he owned this piece? Cynthia said the proceeds from his estate sale had gone to fund a Confederate Memorial Park. Was he simply a collector of Civil War era memorabilia? Or was this a family heirloom, one he couldn't pass on to an heir because he didn't have any?

Even though I'd never met the man, never heard of him, I knew what that felt like. This man had been a kindred spirit. And since I now owned a piece of his legacy, had felt strangely compelled to buy it, I yearned to know more about him.

After bashing around on the Internet like a fly in a hot car, I'd completely lost track of the time when two things brought me out of my frenzied search, simultaneously. The sound of a truck pulling into my driveway, the door slamming shortly after. And a boom of thunder that shook my entire house, making the windows rattle.

Crap on a cracker. All of my new office equipment was still in the truck. And although the smaller items had fit inside the cab, the box containing the desktop computer was in the bed. The open, uncovered bed.

I dashed down the stairs and burst through my front door. I was more than relieved to find Heath lifting the large box off my tailgate just as fat drops of rain began pelting the cardboard. He made it up the steps and under cover just before the sky opened up.

"Guess I happened along just in time," he said, a little out of breath from his jog across the lawn carrying my new iMac Pro. The box probably wasn't heavy, but it was awkwardly large. "What the hell did you buy here?" he shouted over the increasing pounding of the rain.

"A computer with a nice, big screen so I can do justice to your website redesign," I called back.

He set the box down carefully up against my front door, away from the pelting drops bouncing off my steps and railing. But just then a gust of wind sent a veritable wall of water our way, and we both dove to our knees to shield the box. I pushed open the door and we crawled over the threshold, pushing it through to safety. I kicked the door shut behind us. We both lay sprawled on the hardwood floor, dripping and laughing and out of breath.

"My God, I'm so glad you came by. I'm sure I'd never have gotten this thing inside before it was completely ruined," I panted.

"My pleasure," he murmured.

He was beside me then, propped on an elbow and peering down into my eyes. Droplets of water slid off his chocolate curls and drizzled down his cheeks. My gaze followed them down to his mouth, to those sculptured lips I already knew could morph from gentle to demanding in a heartbeat. Warmth sparked low in my belly.

"Cynthia said you went by the warehouse again today,"

he said, one side of his mouth quirking. "She thinks you're stalking me. Should I file a restraining order?"

I chuckled. "No, silly, I knew you wouldn't be there. I wanted to find out more about the brooch I bought from her the other day."

One of his brows lifted. "And? Did you?"

"I did. And now I'm obsessed with finding out more about the man who used to own it. My obsessing almost got my new computer trashed."

He cocked his head. "Why?"

I sighed and turned my head to stare up at the ceiling. "I wish I knew. There's just something about it that's . . . haunting me."

He brushed the back of his hand along my jawline, sending a rocket of heat through me. "Well, I can understand your being spooked by it. Hair jewelry is macabre, yet Cynthia says it sells well. The unique and bizarre always sell, I guess." His fingers lifted my tangled hair and traced the edge of my ear. "Um, can we take this conversation off your foyer floor? This hardwood is . . . hard."

I laughed as he pulled me to my feet, then shrieked and fell against him when lightning flashed through my front windows. The thunder crack was almost simultaneous—it sounded as though it had struck right in my front yard. Heath held me and staggered away from the windows until his back hit the far wall.

"Wow, that was a close one," he breathed out, holding me tight against him.

We stood that way for long moment, listening to the rain pounding on the roof and pelting against the windows. I tucked my head under his chin, pressing my ear to his chest. The steady thudding of his heart was calming, reassuring.

Until suddenly, it sped up. Like, crazy fast, out of control. At the same time, his arms went rigid around me. His entire body stiffened, and he began to shake, violently. Then his knees gave way, and it took all the strength I had, hooking my arms around him and lowering him to the floor.

Oh, no.

"Heath? Heath?" I called his name over and over as he was stared straight ahead, unseeing, unresponsive. His body slumped to one side, sliding along the wall, which had saved him from collapsing hard on my unforgiving wood floor. I shimmied around to where I could guide his head onto my lap.

Horror, sheer terror clutched at my chest as memories of my late husband's similar episodes flooded back into my mind. Sobs burst from me as I rocked back and forth, knowing there was nothing I could do but wait. Wait until he came back to me from whatever place his mind went when one of these seizures racked his brain and body.

I combed my fingers through his curls, hoping to somehow untangle the web of misfiring neurons in his brain. I couldn't bear to watch his face, his eyes when they drifted back in his head. Alive, yet dead to me, to this world. Instead, I squeezed my own eyes shut and let the tears flow freely as heaving sobs shook my chest. All I could hear was the din of the rain, and the jittering of Heath's heels and elbows against the wooden floor.

I can't go through this again. The thought kept repeating itself in my mind, over and over. The logical part of my brain knew Heath's condition was not fatal. He was not dying, would not deteriorate, day by day, until he would disappear from this world entirely. Still, my body reacted with the same awful dread I'd felt as I watched my husband disintegrate before my eyes.

I can't go through this again.

The wave of nausea hit me as suddenly as the lightning struck the yard. I scrambled out from under Heath, laying down his head as gently as I could. I barely made it to the hall bathroom before retching convulsed my body until I felt as though I might turn inside out.

Heath

When Heath regained consciousness, it took him a few moments to remember where he was. When realization dawned, he was confused. Then it all came rushing back in an ominous, mysterious jumble.

He was at the Belle Bride. Liv's house. There'd been a box in the back of her truck—a big box. The sudden rain. Scrambling like children through the front door on their hands and knees. Wrapped around her, her warmth and her scent all around him. She'd been here with him, just moments ago . . .

Where the hell was she now? And why am I on the floor?

He heard her then, the awful sound of her retching in the bathroom just a few feet from where he lay. Scrambling to his feet, he realized with disgust . . . his jeans were soaked, and not from rain. He'd been lying in a puddle of his own urine. Another seizure. The worst in a very long time. So much for the new medication being his salvation.

All he'd wanted to do was to find out how Liv liked her new office furniture. Invite her to his house for a drink, maybe dinner. He didn't expect for his visit to end with his having a grand mal seizure in her foyer. And then, for him to piss himself like a toddler, all over her floor.

"Liv?" He stood outside the bathroom door, which was pushed partway closed. "Liv, are you okay?"

My God, he'd disgusted her to the point of vomiting. He couldn't blame her. In that moment, Heath was pretty disgusted with himself too.

She emerged a few minutes later, her face blotchy, her eyes swollen and red. When she reached for him, though half-heartedly, he immediately backed away.

"No. Don't. I . . . I had an accident on your floor. Liv, I'm sorry. I'm so, so sorry."

"Are you okay?" she squeaked. "I didn't know what to do. I felt so helpless."

"There's nothing you could have done, Liv. Nothing anyone could have done."

Except watch me turn into one of the Walking Dead, right there on your foyer floor.

Together, silently, they used an entire roll of paper towels to sponge clean and dry the hardwood. The rain had slowed to a feeble drizzle outside, and the silence in the house was deafening. All Heath could think was, *this is over now. I've repulsed another woman who can't tolerate a condition I can't seem to do anything about.*

He wondered what was going through her mind. No, he didn't have to wonder. He already knew.

Heath shuffled into the bathroom and removed his soaked boxers, depositing them in a Ziploc bag Liv provided. She gave him a towel to cover the seat of his truck so the wet denim wouldn't soil the seat. Few words passed between them. There was nothing he could say to make this go away.

"I'm sorry, Liv," he said again as he headed for the door. He was shocked when he felt her hand on his arm.

"Heath, no. I'm the one who should be sorry. I'd like to say I don't know why I reacted the way I did. Unfortunately, I know exactly why." She dropped her gaze to the floor. "I need to explain—"

His throat closed, thick with emotion, as he cupped her face in his hands. "No, you don't," he croaked, then turned and headed for his truck.

Chapter Fifteen

Liv

I sat on the bottom step of my curved staircase and cried for a very long time. Until my ribs ached, and my tears dried up, and my throat was sore. Until dusk dimmed the grey light outside my windows, plunging my house into murky twilight.

The problem was, I wasn't really sure who I was crying for. Was I feeling sorry for myself? My widowhood, my state of aloneness in this world? Or for my apparent bad luck in moving halfway across the country to land in a town where I'd encounter a man with a condition so reminiscent of my late husband's illness?

Was this *just* bad luck? Or was I cursed? *What lesson should I be learning here?*

Before complete darkness fell, I dragged myself into the kitchen and plucked a bottle of beer and two cheese sticks out of the fridge. I glanced at the huge box sitting inside my front door. No, I just wasn't up to struggling the new Mac upstairs tonight. I left it in the foyer and trudged up the stairs to my office. I'd work off my laptop, as I had been doing for the past few weeks.

As I rounded the upper portion of my staircase, I became aware of a pocket of cold air hanging in the upstairs hallway. *Cold* air? Doesn't heat rise? Shouldn't it be warmer up here?

As I drew closer to my office door, which stood half open, the hairs on the back of my neck prickled. Electricity seemed to spark in the air around me, making my skin pucker and tingle. Once I pushed open the door, I knew why.

My Confederate nightmare was there, in my office. His figure was translucent, as it had been before. I could see the frame of the window through the crumpled, grey jacket he wore. He was staring at my laptop, and didn't react to my presence. I froze, yet oddly, was not afraid.

This was a withdrawal symptom, I remembered soberly. In my state of post-coital euphoria this morning, I'd forgotten —again—to take my anti-depressant meds. This hallucination was nothing more than a recurring, waking nightmare.

I'd just close the door and go back downstairs, take my pill. I would eat my cheese stick dinner and drink my beer. Maybe not the beer. Not after taking anti-depressants. Hell, I might not wake up in the morning.

I sighed. I just needed to down the pill and spend the rest of the evening buttoned up in my cozy bedroom. Surely, in the bright light of morning, Soldier boy would be gone.

I never got that far. As I took a step backward, the figure wheeled on me, clutching his gun in both hands, a scary looking bayonet pointed in my direction. Almost immediately, though, his posture relaxed. He lowered his weapon, and his face softened. He smiled at me, a strange kind of recognition dawning.

Emma. I'm home, Emma.

The words echoed in my head, as they had before. It's where this whole delusion was coming from, after all. I took another step backward, and he raised both hands, his gun swinging from the sling around his shoulders.

Wait. Please. Tell me . . . who you are. You're not my Emma. You look like her, but you're not her.

I cleared my throat. Should I interact with a hallucination? What was the psychiatric world's stance on this sort of thing? I'd have to look it up . . . at a later time. When I didn't have to walk *through* an apparition to get to my laptop.

I figured, why not? What could it hurt?

"My name is not Emma. And I don't know who you are, or why my mind keeps conjuring you up. I don't even know an Emma," I said, my voice shaky. I was also feeling very, very foolish.

He pointed at me, squinting.

You must know something, woman. Or you wouldn't have this.

He moved so abruptly, I jumped. Wheeling toward the desk, he swung his arm toward the velvet bag next to my computer.

I pinched the bridge of my nose, squeezing my eyes shut. So that was it. My errant imagination was weaving an elaborate tale involving my fascination with the piece of macabre, Civil War jewelry. I really have to wean myself off these pills S-L-O-W-L-Y.

I whooshed out a breath in relief when I opened my eyes. The apparition had disappeared. Saints be praised.

Heath

His appointment with his doctor was at one p.m., and Heath closed the shop at noon and put a sign on the door saying, "Closed Early Due to Emergency." Last night's seizure had left him embarrassed, sad, and unsteady. It didn't occur to him until he went to climb into his truck that it probably wasn't a great idea to drive all the way to Decatur by himself.

What if he had another seizure at the wheel? He hadn't even felt the one coming on last night. Driving the thirty-odd miles to Decatur . . . it was a chance he really couldn't afford to take.

And he couldn't ask Liv to drive him. Not now. He wasn't sure he could even face her, the embarrassment was so raw. Who, then? He had a few friends in town, but most of them were working on a weekday. Cynthia was running the shop in Birmingham, almost an hour away.

Then it hit him. There was someone who sort of owed him a favor. Firing up his engine, he headed out toward the Warren's house. After giving their son a job, surely, Robert wouldn't mind giving him a ride to Decatur.

He tried not to look as he drove past the Belle Bride, but couldn't help notice Liv's truck in the driveway. A fresh wave of humiliation washed over him. He'd really made a spectacle of himself last night. Enough to send her into the bathroom vomiting.

Robert Warren's ancient, blue Ford was parked under the carport, and Heath breathed a sigh of relief. He didn't know the Warrens well, but well enough that he could ask them this favor. He would have to, he knew, explain to Robert what might occur on the way to Decatur. He wasn't sure if they knew about his epilepsy.

Heath had tried to keep his condition a private matter, but wondered sometimes how many in town knew anyway. It was the way people looked at him . . . treated him. Everyone was so nice. A little too nice. He had a feeling his ex-wife had made it common knowledge why she was leaving him. Her excuse, and the final blow to his character.

Bitsy answered the door on the first knock, beaming up at Heath with youthful glee. Like a tiny, old fairy, he thought wryly. He didn't think he could ever remember seeing Bitsy Warren anything but happy.

"Is Robert busy, Bitsy?" he asked as he followed her into the hallway. "I could really use some company driving up to Decatur this afternoon. It shouldn't take long . . ."

Bitsy's brows drew together as she studied his face. "Everything alright, Mr. Barrow? You're looking a little peaked today."

Heath shuffled his feet nervously and kept his eyes on his work boots. "I actually do have a doctor's appointment. She's trying me on a new medication, and after some of the side effects I've had, I'm thinking it's not such a good idea for me to make the drive alone," he mumbled.

When he looked up, Bitsy was nodding sagely. "All right. Robert's not doing anything important. He was plannin' on replacing a few boards on Julia's paddock this afternoon. That can wait, though." She reached up and patted Heath's arm. "Why don't you come in for a glass of tea while he changes out of his work clothes?"

Twenty minutes later Heath was sitting in Robert's old but functional pickup truck, heading north on Highway 278 toward Decatur.

"Not doing well with your new meds, Bitsy says," Robert said, glancing over at Heath. "This the same problem you been dealing with all your life, Heath?"

Robert Warren had an easy way of making you feel as though talking about an illness like epilepsy was no big deal.

And it wasn't, until your body grew immune to the medication keeping the seizures at bay. Like what had happened to him over the last few years—numerous times. Heath rubbed his forehead.

"I'm beginning to lose hope, Robert. Seems like nothing they've put me on keeps these damned episodes from happening, again and again. Last night, I had a bad one. Worst one I've had in years." As painful as it was to talk about it, Heath was relieved to get it out. Robert had a fatherly way about him . . .

He was shaking his head, his lips set in a grim line. "Damn shame. They can put satellites out in space but they can't come up with drugs to cure the common cold. Or control somethin' like what you got. Damn shame, it is."

Heath sighed. "My appointment shouldn't take long. I think there's a little coffee shop right around the corner from my doctor's office. I can meet you there when I'm done, if you like," he offered.

Robert nodded. "Sounds good, Heath. Hey, you tell that doctor she's got to do something for you, now. So you can get on with your life, you know?"

No shit, Heath thought. Although he had a feeling his chances with a certain new girl in town had been irreparably damaged last night.

"Your vitals are all on the mark, Heath. And your blood levels are good. Are you sure this wasn't just an isolated incident?" Sandra asked as Heath re-buttoned his shirt. "What were you doing when this happened?"

Heath closed his eyes and sighed. "Holding a very pretty woman in my arms and listening to the rain," he said sadly. "After the spectacle I made of myself, it's probably going to be the last time I get a chance to do that again. With her, anyway."

Sandra narrowed her eyes at him. "Listen. You're not a freak, Heath Barrow. And you have absolutely no reason to be embarrassed or ashamed because you were cursed with epilepsy. It's not contagious, it won't kill you, and it doesn't make you a monster."

"I know that. But not everybody feels the same way. Not everyone understands—"

The doctor crossed her arms over her chest and cocked one hip. "Listen to me. Just because one woman couldn't live with your occasional episodes, it doesn't mean every woman is going to feel that way. If somebody really cares about you, they will understand. They won't shun you for something you were born with. Something you have no control over."

Yeah, Heath thought. Right. I guess Liv Larson isn't a caring, understanding woman, then. During his first episode, she'd turned tail and run like a scared rabbit. After the second one, she'd puked her guts up.

Sandra sat down at the computer in the examining room and was typing notes onto Heath's chart. "I can increase the dosage one more time. If it doesn't keep the big seizures at bay, Heath, I don't know . . . we're running out of options here."

Heath's heart sank. I'm running out of options too, he thought. Other than the sentence of a life lived alone. Limited in his ability to go places at the wheel of his own truck.

Stopping short in her typing, Sandra suddenly swiveled in her chair to look at him. "You said it was raining when this happened. Was there lightning?"

Chapter Sixteen

Liv

The whining woke me. At first, I thought I was dreaming. I lay there, in the dark, listening to the wind rustle the branches in my front yard. Was it the wind I'd heard?

No. It commenced again, echoing through the near-empty ground floor rooms and into the stairwell. A dog. *The* dog was back. My skin pebbled with goosebumps.

Wrapping a small throw blanket around me, I swung my legs out of bed and scuttled to the stairs in my bare feet. My alarm clock read 2:03 a.m. The house was surprisingly bright, lit by what was probably a near-full moon. I cast a quick glance over my shoulder toward my office. The door remained closed, as I'd left it after my hallucination last night.

My anti-depressant pill had worked its magic rather quickly after that, relaxing me to the point where I'd felt comfortable enough to soak in a long, hot bath in the old, footed tub. I'd never even gotten to the new Southern Living magazine. I fell asleep so hard and fast, I didn't think I had dreamed at all.

Moonlight fell in long, icy bands across the hardwood in the foyer, illuminating the high-ceilinged space nearly all the way back to the kitchen. The whining—again at the back of the house—was followed by scratching on the metal frame of the screened door.

Instead of going to the door right away, I tiptoed silently through to the parlor, where I could peek out the farthest tall window. From this vantage point, I could see my back stoop.

What I saw there set my body quaking.

The dog—the same lanky hound with the tan patched head—sat on the top step, his white body glowing in the moonlight. Something about him seemed . . . odd. His unnaturally white fur pulsated, as though lit from within. And when he moved, lifting a paw to scratch at the door, his leg left a glowing trail in the darkness. Like the tail of a comet.

I rubbed my eyes, squeezed them shut, and opened them. Surely, this apparition would disappear just like the Soldier Boy. Yet the dog remained, whining pitifully and reaching his left paw up at regular intervals to scratch at my door.

Over and over and over again. In the same, perfectly timed, rhythmic pattern. It was as though I was watching a video clip running in an endless loop.

I shrieked and stumbled away from the window when another sound split the night—the whinny of a horse from mere yards away. Seconds later, the beast appeared from around the corner of my barn—glowing white, just like the dog. Its hoof beats shook the floor under my bare feet as it galloped across the short distance to curved bank of steps leading to my back door.

Was this the Warren's horse? They said she liked to challenge the fence separating our properties. Was she loose? Should I do something?

The horse skidded to a stop a few feet from the steps, causing the dog to stand and turn. His wagging tail left the same comet-like tail of light as he stretched up to touch noses with the horse, who snorted and tossed his head. A strange flash of light blinded me when their noses touched.

I realized then my view of the paddock fence was not obstructed by the horse's massive body. I could see right through it.

I stood in frozen, shocked silence as the two animals enjoyed an apparent happy reunion. The dog leapt off the steps and danced around the horse's legs as it pranced in place, curling its tail over its back and nickering softly. Then the horse turned, swinging its elegant neck in a gesture that seemed to beckon the dog to follow. The dog barked and jumped around the horse as it trotted away from the house, the pair leaving a glowing trail of light in their wake.

As they neared the barn, their images became more and more translucent until, just before they reached the paddock fence, they evaporated. I blinked and rubbed my eyes. When I opened them again, all I saw were the fence boards, softly illuminated by moonlight.

I awoke lying on my hardwood floor—again. This time it was in my empty parlor, near the far window facing the back yard. My feet were freezing, bare and sticking out from the plush throw blanket I had wrapped around me. My cheek and the upper arm pillowing it were gritty from sand on the boards.

Sitting up, I wiped the grit off my face and stared out toward the barn. Yesterday's rain had washed the world clean, it seemed, and droplets glistened on the tall reeds growing unchecked along the rail fence. In the distant field, I saw the golden horse Bitsy had called "Julia," head down to the grass, tail swishing away at the flies.

I needed to check the fence, I thought. Their horse got loose last night and had been romping around in my back yard. God knows what could have happened to her if she'd wandered out onto the road. Running upstairs, I pulled on a pair of shorts and slipped my feet into a pair of moccasins.

A close inspection of the entire length of rail fence separating the Warren's property from my own revealed no breaks, no downed rails, not even a gate that might have swung open. "Julia" watched me with mild interest for the first few moments, lifting her head but not bothering to turn her body in my direction. By the time I'd walked the fence line, up and back, three times, she'd again lowered her head to her grazing.

The late morning sun was warm and brilliant in its cloudless sky, yet fear's icy fingers still tickled my neck and shoulders. What was it I'd seen last night? And why did I have the feeling I wasn't alone out here in my own backyard? When a twig snapped in the wooded patch down the other end of the barn, my heart did a somersault as I whirled around.

Great. Now I was letting some scurrying, furry thing scare the bejesus out of me in broad daylight. This has gone far enough.

Enough with the self-doubt. Enough blaming these strange visions I'd been experiencing on my med withdrawal. To hell with all of that. I'd never been one to believe in the supernatural: ghosts, or hauntings, or poltergeists. I'd always been the logical one. The one who looked for scientific reasoning for any strange occurrence.

Now, I was done questioning my own sanity. It was time to get some real answers from some real people. By a little past noon, I was showered, dressed, and in my truck. My first stop was at the Warren's house.

Robert's old blue pickup truck wasn't in the driveway, yet Heath's gigantic black Ram was. I hesitated. Was I up to seeing him again after yesterday? I still hadn't digested all that had happened. I was still mortified by my ridiculous, over-the-top reaction to his obviously uncontrollable episode.

I was here to get some answers, I reminded myself. To hell with formalities. If Heath was here, it would be a lot easier to face him with other people around than alone anyway.

I knocked and heard the light tread of footsteps, just before the door swung open. Bitsy grinned up at me.

"How ya doing, Ms. Larson? Come to visit and sit a spell?" she asked brightly, opening the door wider.

"Actually, well, sort of, yes, Bitsy. I'm not interrupting anything, am I?" I asked.

"Nuh-uh," she answered quickly. "Nobody here but me."

I took a deep breath. "Well, I was wondering if I could ask you and Robert some things about the Belle Bride house. About its history," I said, stepping into Bitsy's literal hall of history. I motioned to the photos surrounding me. "You folks have been here in Camellia all of your lives. For generations. Maybe you can tell me a little bit about the house just up the road."

Bitsy's straggly eyebrows drew together and she rubbed her chin. "Robert ain't here," she repeated. "He's gone to Decatur today. Just left, as a matter of fact. Come on in and have a seat, though. I'd be happy to answer whatever questions about your house that I can," she said.

I followed her into her kitchen where she asked if I wanted sweet tea or something stronger. My eyebrows shot up.

"Something . . . stronger?" I asked, puzzled. It was barely past noon.

"Well," she drawled, shifting from one foot to the other and rubbing her hands together, "it's just you look a little . . . well, a little upended, is all. Like Mr. Barrow did when he got here a while ago. It's got me upset, you see. More excitement than I usually get in a day. I thought it wouldn't hurt to slow the carousel down some while we talked."

I blinked in surprise. "Mr. Barrow was here?" Then I realized, *dumb question. His truck is sitting in your front yard.*

She nodded enthusiastically as she lifted a pitcher of what looked like lemonade out of the refrigerator. "Yes 'um. He asked if Robert could drive him up to Decatur this morning."

That's all she said. Drive him to Decatur? For an auction? And why in Robert's old truck? Surely, Heath's giant pickup could hold more than the old Ford if he was hauling back any furniture.

I watched as Bitsy reached up and opened the cabinet over the range hood. Inside was a fully-stocked shelf of liquors. She moved a few bottles aside and extracted a . . . mayonnaise jar? Only it wasn't holding mayonnaise. It was filled to the brim with crystal clear liquid.

"You like lemonade, right?" she asked nervously, setting the jar down on the counter gently and unscrewing the lid. "I made some from fresh lemons just yesterday. It sure tastes a sight better with a smidge of Robert's special 'shine added in."

Shine. Moonshine? At noon on a Friday afternoon? Oh well, I'd spent the night watching ghost animals romp around in my yard. How much more bizarre could my life get?

We sat on the back porch, the same place where I'd shared Bitsy's delicious homemade applesauce cake the day I'd first come to visit. Only this time, we sat at the table, leaning toward each other, elbows tented over Mason jars filled with moonshine-tainted lemonade.

Damn, I might just be able to get used to this Southern living after all.

Bitsy took three long swallows of her drink before wiping her mouth on the napkin she'd set the jars on. Then she lowered her voice and asked, "What is it you wanna know about the Belle Bride?"

I took a deep breath and rested my forehead against my hand. "Bitsy, I'm either losing my mind, or my new house is as haunted as Stephen King's Overlook Hotel."

The reaction I'd expected was a guffaw, in which case I would have felt like a complete fool. The one who'd skittered out of the local museum with nightmares following her home. The Yankee girl spooked by her big old, antebellum house.

The reaction I got was scarier.

Bitsy took another three, long swallows of her southern cocktail—holy smokes, this tiny woman could drink—before leaning on her arms and staring into my eyes.

"I can't tell you anything about the house except what's local lore. Rumors, you Northern folk would call them. Nothin' that can be proven. All I'm telling you is . . . well, neither Robert, or me—or Ben, especially—we won't go anywhere near the place once the sun sets. No ma'am." Shaking her head vehemently, she drained her glass.

I blinked, then took a sip of the concoction she'd set before me. I'd never tasted moonshine before. My initial impression was that I was drinking a lemon martini—in bulk, over ice, and out of a Mason jar. The first sip cleared my nasal passages and burned all the way down. After the second sip, I knew I shouldn't drink much more and drive, even the short distance up the road to my own house.

"So, what's the local lore, Bitsy? Do people say it's haunted? Because I can tell you, there sure have been some strange things happening since I moved in."

Bitsy smiled sadly and nodded, closing her eyes. I wondered for a moment if she might pass out on me. This moonshine was rocket fuel. In a moment, though, she seemed to have gathered her wits about her and levelled her gaze on me.

"They've been trying to sell the place for, oh well, it's gotta be over twenty-five years now. Nobody's ever lasted long there. It's been bought and sold, bought and sold. The bank always ends up holding the paper, and the buyers always leave town without warning. Sometimes in the middle of the night." She dropped back in her chair, folding her arms across her birdlike chest. "I woulda warned you, Ms. Larson. I didn't know you. And it all happened so fast."

I waved away her apology. "This has nothing to do with you, Bitsy. It's just, well, it would have been nice if Mr. Edwards had shared a little more about the house's history with me before I committed to buying it." I hesitated, sliding my gaze past my hostess to the open field behind her house. "Fact is, it would have been a lot smarter if I had done a little more research before I bought the place," I murmured, more to myself than to her.

She leaned forward and patted my hand. "Some things, though, they're just meant to be. I had a real good feeling when I met you that day. It seemed like, well . . . like you just sorta belonged to the Belle Bride." She paused and cocked her head. "I was hopin' you wouldn't be bothered by whatever's been chasing off the previous owners of the place."

"And what has that been, Bitsy? What's been chasing people out of the Belle Bride?" I asked.

She stared at me, as if trying to analyze something she could see that wasn't visible on the outside. Then she shook her head and made a tsking noise. "Shoulda known the day you asked me about the dog. The dog, well . . . the dog is always the first one to show up."

"The first one," I repeated. "Then what?"

She raked her silver bangs off her forehead and rested it on her hand. "Oh, I'm not really sure 'bout the details, Ms. Larson. Nobody wants to talk about it, you see. A lot of it could just be legend . . . because of the house's early history."

"What early history, Bitsy? Neither the museum nor the library seem to have any records on the Belle Bride at all. At least, not that they're willing to share with me."

Irritation began its seltzer-like sizzle in my chest. I knew I'd made an impulsive, poorly planned move by leaving

Manhattan and buying a historic house in the middle of nowhere. Now, I was feeling more the fool than ever.

The older woman sighed heavily and peeked at me from between her fingers. "Not so sure about actual written records. The rumors about the place are well known around here. It's why none of the locals have ever bought the house."

"What rumors, Bitsy?" I slammed a hand down on the patio table, and Bitsy jumped. I knew I'd fairly shouted, but this was ridiculous. This was all information I should have had well before I signed the deed. *Why hadn't I done more research?*

"You okay, Momma?"

I whirled in my seat, heart racing, to see Ben's giant form standing in the doorway. *Filling* the doorway. Why hadn't I heard those heavy foot falls?

"Oh, Ben. You're back." Bitsy said, seemingly as startled as I was. "The fence line all good?"

Even more caveman-like than the day I first met him, today Ben wore only a baggy pair of denim overalls, with no shirt underneath. He was, as before, barefoot. His beefy arms and chest were sheened with sweat, small flecks of grass stuck to his pale skin here and there. My stomach did a slow turn.

He was nodding in response to Bitsy, yet he didn't take his eyes off of me as his face spread into a slow, toothy grin.

"Hey there, Miss Larson."

I swallowed and tried to ground myself by curling my fingers around the cool drink on the table. "Doing fine, Benjamin. I just stopped by to chat with Bitsy here for a few minutes."

"I know. I saw you leave."

A feeling of cold dread landed like an iceberg in my chest. "Wha-what do you mean, you saw me leave?"

Bitsy reached across the table to lay a hand on my

arm. "Ben was walking the fence line for me and Robert this morning. Checking to make sure none of them boards had come down. Wouldn't want to have Julia romping around in your backyard, now, would we?" She spoke quickly, the last words coming out around a nervous chuckle.

Were these people spying on me? Maybe the feeling of being watched I'd experienced this morning had been real. The thought was even more disturbing than phantom soldiers and dogs.

I took another sip of the nuclear-powered lemonade followed by a deep breath. Paranoia. Another withdrawal symptom . . .

"So, you were there this morning? When I was out behind my barn?" I asked Ben. My voice sounded high and squeaky, which I hated.

His grin broadened. "Uh huh. What was you lookin' for, Miss Larson?"

I cleared my throat. "Actually, the same thing you were, apparently. I saw . . . or thought I saw a horse behind my house last night. I thought maybe Julia had gotten through the fence somehow, and—"

Ben was shaking his head as he reached down to readjust himself through the crotch of his overalls. My stomach lurched again.

"No ma'am. Couldn't a been Julia. Them boards are set real firm."

His eyes drifted down to my chest, and I instinctively crossed my arms.

Bitsy suddenly clambered to her feet, then swayed a little. She snatched up her empty glass, motioning toward mine. "I'm going for a refill. Can I get you something else, Ms. Larson?"

I shook my head and started to rise. My curiosity about the history—the legend—about the Belle Bride had been quickly doused by this new seeming threat. It was time for me to leave, before Ben continued his mental undressing of me.

"I think I'll go, Bitsy. Sorry, the moonshine is a bit much for me, especially this early in the day."

Her face screwed into a little-girl pout before quickly brightening again. "It's okay." She set down her own glass and lifted mine. "Shame to waste it, though," she said, and took a long swallow.

I wanted out, now. But Ben was still blocking the doorway into the house. I glanced around and couldn't see an exterior door on the screened patio.

Odd, that. I was discovering there were quite a few odd things about my new neighbors.

I pulled my truck keys out of my pocket and jingled them, glancing between Bitsy and Ben.

"I guess I'll be going, then."

It took another ten seconds before Bitsy finally looked up and said, "Go on, Ben, and let the lady through." She scanned him up and down, as though it was the first she'd noticed his grimy condition. "Get yourself washed up, boy, if you plan on eatin' lunch at the same table with me."

Ben flinched as though she'd slapped him and stumbled back a step. "Yes, ma'am." He turned and headed back into the kitchen. Then he stopped and hit me with another grin over his shoulder. "Nice seeing you again, Miss Larson. Stop over anytime."

Heath

Heath left Sandra's office with mixed emotions, not sure whether to feel relieved, hopeful, or confused. She'd given him a prescription doubling his medication, which she said he could act on, or not, depending on how he felt. She still seemed to believe this new drug would stop his symptoms. It was just a matter of time, she explained, until his body had absorbed enough of the drug for it to work to its full effect.

It was interesting, though, she'd asked about the thunderstorm. Heath had forgotten that he seemed to be more susceptible to seizures during violent electrical storms. Mostly because he hadn't suffered a grand mal in several years—the last one he had, he remembered, had happened during such a storm. And last night, a lightning bolt had struck directly in Liv's front yard. It was entirely possible, even probable, the electricity in the air had triggered his attack.

Still, his heart was heavy with the realization that, just as Sandra had pointed out, a woman who really cared about him would be understanding, and concerned, about his condition. Especially during a seizure. There was just no excusing Liv's reactions to the two seizures she'd witnessed. She obviously wasn't a very compassionate person. She was, just like Katherine, a self-centered city girl.

It would be difficult, Heath knew, to go on with Liv living here in this small town. Wanting her as he did, yet knowing that when it came to his medical issues, he disgusted her.

Which is why his heart tumbled painfully in his chest that afternoon when he spotted Liv's truck driving by his shop. He'd gone back into town after he and Robert returned to Camellia. His men were supposed to have delivered some pieces he'd ordered to replace the ones he'd recycled into the warehouse yesterday.

He was standing on the sidewalk, unlocking his door, when he saw her rust-colored Tundra rolling down Main

Street. Pausing, he turned, his hand poised to wave. She drove right on by as if she hadn't even seen him.

Guess she's written me off. At least I didn't let my heart get in any deeper before now, or I'd think this pain in my chest was a heart attack instead of just the heartache of rejection.

Chapter Seventeen

Liv

I drove through town in a daze, anxious to get home and jump into the shower—again. My skin felt crawly when I left Bitsy's, with her giant son gawking at me from the cottage's front porch. I wondered if Benjamin was really dangerous, or just creepy.

He was a simpleton. He couldn't help that. Still, he was a full-grown man with, one would assume, the normal male urges. And it was becoming more and more obvious every time I saw him—he'd definitely noticed I was a woman.

The thought that he'd been watching me this morning made my chest clutch and my heart sputter. The snapping twig hadn't been some small, furry animal. It had been Ben. Must have been. There simply wasn't any way I would have missed him out in the open pasture, checking fence.

And watching me.

After scrubbing myself raw in the shower, I planted myself at my new desk and tried to keep my mind occupied with a little online research. I didn't like the sound of the term Bitsy had used about the Belle Bride—*legend*. A gossip-enhanced folk tale may not exist in print anywhere, but surely, there had to be some records on the history of the Belle Bride. It didn't take me long to discover, via a quick Google search, that sellers were required by law to disclose any documented "ghoulish activity."

Apparently, my realtor, Thomas Edwards, hadn't disclosed all he knew about the house he'd sold me. Neither the legend nor the neighbors. It was time I got some answers. Grabbing the thick manila envelope containing my sales contract, I drove into town, praying Mr. Edwards was in the office.

I parked my truck in front of the Thornfield Real Estate Agency, and was relieved to see the "Open" sign hanging crookedly in the window. Now I just had to hope my agent, the caricature car-salesman-turned-realtor, Thomas Edwards, was in.

The woman staffing the tiny reception area said he was, in fact, in his office. Moments later, Mr. Edwards came around the corner. His sparse hair was combed in stringy strands over his scalp, and he was dressed more casually than he'd been the day of the closing. In fact, he looked downright rumpled, like he might have slept in his dress pants and plaid shirt. His expression, though, once he caught sight of me toting the packet of papers he'd handed me that day, transformed quickly from relaxed to guarded.

"Ms. Larson. How nice to see you. How you getting along out there at the Belle Bride?" he asked. His tone was tight, clipped, belying the smile he'd pasted on his face.

I held up my packet of paperwork. "It's exactly what I need to talk to you about today, Mr. Edwards. I need you to help me find, somewhere in this contract, the disclosure stating my house is haunted."

Edwards' smile evaporated as he cleared his throat and slid a glance toward his receptionist, who kept her eyes fixed on her computer monitor.

"Why don't you just come on back to my office, and you can tell me what this is all about."

The office, as Edwards had called it, was little more than a closet with a compact desk and two chairs, one on either side. After quietly closing the door off the hallway, he motioned for me to take a seat, then wedged his way to the chair behind his desk.

"There, now. Are you having problems at your new house? I believe the home inspectors cleared it of all the usual issues—plumbing, fire hazards, termites—"

"Mr. Edwards, let's cut through the bull crap here. What I want to know is the history of the house. And not the romantic, fantasy story of newlyweds and rich plantation parents you gave me when you sold it to me. I want to know about more recent history. How long since the Belle Bride has actually housed a family?"

I tried to keep my tone as even and crisp as possible. Still, I couldn't help feel somewhat foolish. I mean, I was here to ask if anyone had ever reported seeing ghosts on the property.

If there was a documented haunting, I was entitled to back out of my contract. Or at least file for damages. I'd learned that from my brief scouring of the Internet on a search for "Ghoul Disclosure."

If there was no evidence of strange happenings before me, then I was just another kooky Yankee trying to stir up trouble for the small town of Camellia.

Edwards avoided eye contact as he turned to his computer screen, ignoring the contract I'd plunked on the desk between us. "Well, let me see what I can pull up here. If you go to the County Records System, there's a list of all the property transfers for any address in Camellia going back, oh, say, the last fifty years or so."

Irritation spiked in my chest. "And you know damn well that unless you're a realtor, or have been a voting citizen in this county since at least the last election, gaining access to the county site is about as easy as sifting sugar of your syrupy sweet tea," I huffed. "I already tried the County records system."

Edwards' gaze flashed between me and his screen with increased rapidity. "Is that a fact," he stated quietly. It was not a question.

"The fact of the matter is, Mr. Edwards, I've encountered some strange visitors out at the Belle Bride. Someone pounding on my door in the middle of the night. Odd-looking animals romping around in my backyard. A weirdo who likes to play Civil War dress-up who apparently has a key to my house, and shows up at odd hours."

Crap. I hadn't meant to include that part. I was pretty sure my Confederate Soldier was the fabrication of my mind sans sufficient levels of fluvoxamine. But was I?

At this last point, Edwards swiveled away from his keyboard to face me, concern knitting his brow. "You've had intruders? Inside your house? Have you reported this to the local authorities, Ms. Larson? Has anything gone missing?"

I closed my eyes and huffed out a breath. *Nothing, except perhaps my sanity* was the thought flashing through my mind. I shook my head.

"No, nothing's been stolen, and to be honest, the soldier thing may have just been a nightmare. It's a different experience for me, living in a big house all by myself. In the middle of nowhere. I'm used to city noise—"

"You know," Edwards interrupted, "I asked you when you bought this place what a city girl like you was going to do in a big old plantation home, all by yourself." He sat up straighter in his chair and quirked an eyebrow. "Now, just because you're finding out that small town living isn't for you doesn't mean there's grounds for you to be backing out of your sales contract," he said. With a little more snip in his voice than I found acceptable.

He jumped back when I slammed my fist down on the pile of papers between us. "You're dodging my question here,

Mr. Edwards. What I want you to tell me is whether or not anyone of the previous, apparently short-term owners of the Belle Bride have reported anything falling under the category of *ghoulish activity*."

At the mention of the phrase, Edwards flinched. He was apparently as aware, as I now was, that sellers had to disclose all possible flaws about a house— structural or otherwise. In 1991, a New York judge granted a buyer the right to back out of a sale because the seller did not disclose the house's history of paranormal activity. Since then, bizarre as it may seem, realtors have been advised to include this kind of disclosure to prospective buyers.

Nobody had said anything about ghosts, or ghouls, or hauntings in connection with the Belle Bride when I'd toured the home, nor when I'd signed the sales contract.

Edwards slid his gaze back to his computer, and then his expression brightened. "Here are the sales records the county has on file, Ms. Larson." He turned the monitor so I could see the screen. The list was a long one.

"Can I get a printout of that?" I asked, uncomfortable about scanning the tiny print with Edwards staring at me the whole time. "And while it's printing, what can you tell me about my neighbors? The Warrens?"

Several beats of silence ensued, punctuated only by the clicks of Edward's mouse. He cleared his throat, then swiveled to face me.

"I've known Bitsy and Robert Warren ever since I was a kid, Ms. Larson. They are exactly what they appear to be: cordial, simple Southern folk. They'd do anything they could to help you out, make you feel welcome—"

"I'm talking about their son, or stepson, or whatever he is, Mr. Edwards. I'm referring to Benjamin. Has he ever been in any trouble?"

To my relief, Edwards' expression showed purely innocent shock, then confusion. He held my gaze steadily. "Benjamin?" He shook his head, a flash of sadness crossing his features. "Ben is a simpleton, Ms. Larson. Granted, he's very . . . imposing. Intimidating, even. But I can assure you, Ben Warren wouldn't harm a bee if it stung him."

Okay, so add paranoia to the list of withdrawal symptoms from anti-depressant drugs. The list itself, it occurred to me, was becoming depressing in its own right.

Twenty minutes later Edwards walked me to the door, seemingly anxious to get me on the other side of it. I had the six-page printout of the sales record of the Belle Bride tucked into a manila folder balanced on top of my sales contract.

"Ms. Larson, there is nothing in your contract stating any history of hauntings or anything of that sort associated with the Belle Bride. Because there's nothing on record. It's been bank-owned for, well, at least the last ten years or so. And I'm fairly certain a bank wouldn't have encouraged the spreading of any ridiculous rumors about a property they were holding the paper on. It just wouldn't be smart business."

I spent the rest of the afternoon studying the deed records on the Belle Bride. The facts I discovered were sobering. It seemed that since 1980—almost thirty-eight years ago—the house had been largely standing empty. The property had changed hands fifteen times, with no owner claiming the address as their primary one for a period of more than two years. The last family before me, I remembered Edwards telling me on closing day, hadn't even moved in. They had made improvements to the barn to house their daughter's horse, then changed their minds and put the house on the market before ever moving in.

I wondered if the dog, or the horse, or both, had scared them away from the barn. The soldier, perhaps? I itched to contact them and ask them why they'd left. Yet although the family's name was listed, there was no other information as to where they'd gone after leaving Camellia. Initiating a search for them could send me down another dead-ended rabbit hole.

As I sat hunched over my new desk, scanning the records from the most recent ones down, I also noticed that even though the property had sold to fifteen different buyers in those thirty-eight years, there were huge gaps in ownership. Sometimes five years or more went by before a new deed owner went on record. In between, usually after the house had been on the market for over a year, the deed showed as being the property of the First National Bank of Birmingham.

The purchasers had obviously quit paying the mortgage, and the Belle Bride had gone into foreclosure. Exactly ten times.

It wasn't until I got to the last page that my heart shot up into my throat, and a sheen of cool sweat slicked my skin. This was, simply, too much of a coincidence to fathom. I really thought I was imagining the information on the page before me. I rubbed my eyes and took a few swallows from the bottle of water before leaning closer to examine the last entry on the list.

Recorded Date	Type/Desc.	Doc #	Seller
Deeded to:			
09/29/1980	Warrantee Deed	1952068	Samuel Bernard
1st Natl Bank of Birmingham			

I slumped back in my chair, a wave of dizziness washing over me. I knew coincidences occurred, all the time. Most often, I believed, coincidences were meaningless, vague connections created in people's minds. This one, however, sent chills skittering up my spine, and set my heart to thumping frantically against my ribs.

Samuel Bernard, the man whose hair work brooch lay wrapped in its velvet bag on the desk beside me, had owned my house. I didn't know for how long, because the record before me ended there. Older records, I supposed, I could uncover with additional research. Perhaps the librarian could help me with that. Tell me how long Bernard had owned the Belle Bride. Tell me who he'd acquired it from.

The chilling fact remained, right there before me. Bernard had sold the Belle Bride in the fall of 1980—to the bank. It hadn't been a foreclosure, but a legal transfer of warrantee deed.

It appeared, from the copy of the officially stamped document in my trembling hands, that Samuel Bernard had given up ownership of the Belle Bride the same year—on the same date—as I was born.

Heath

That evening, Heath found doubling up on his meds just made him sleepy as hell. He sat on his back patio, chin resting on his hand. As he stared out over his pretty backyard, he found himself counting the minutes until he could climb into his bed and pass out.

It was barely seven o'clock, and still light outside. He couldn't go to sleep now or he'd be up at two in the morning, wide awake. Talk about feeling like an old man in a young man's body ...

It was depression dragging him down, he knew. Even though Sandra had spent a good, long time trying to reassure him the new drug would be his salvation from this damned, insidious disease, he was still uncertain. She'd also inadvertently lectured him against Liv, though she hadn't known who "the pretty woman" was.

He jolted awake when his cellphone began buzzing on the table next to him. Damn it, he'd dozed off anyway. Snatching it up, he didn't recognize the number on the screen. Probably just another blasted telemarketer, he thought, and ended the call.

Secretly, his heart squeezed. He'd hoped to see Liv's number on the screen.

If somebody really cares about you, they will understand. They won't shun you for something you were born with. Something you have no control over.

Well, Katherine had. And now he was pretty sure Liv was doing the same thing. In fact, Liv's reaction had been even more hurtful than Katherine's. At least his ex-wife had levelled with him, told him she just couldn't live with the uncertainty his condition left hanging over their lives.

What about a family, Heath?

Katherine's words echoed in Heath's memory.

What happens when you're caring for our children and I'm not around? A seizure would most certainly terrify a small child, but it could be a death sentence for an infant or toddler.

Well, Liv wasn't going to give him a family either, from the way she'd talked. She had no interest in becoming a mother. She'd said so the first day they'd almost made love.

He had to quit thinking about the sexual romp they'd had as *making love*. It was sex, that was all. Pure, raw lust, nothing more.

It was something, he knew, he needed more of. He was, after all, a healthy, otherwise normal thirty-five-year-old male. He had needs. Not that prospects in this small town were plentiful. Everybody knew everybody else, it seemed. Camellia wasn't the place to hang out at the local bar to simply "hook up" with a girl for the night. Hell, the nearest bar wasn't even in town, but eight miles up the road in Quincy.

Cynthia had suggested online dating services. At first, Heath had scoffed at this idea. Still, maybe his sister had a point. He could disclose his condition, right up front. Surely, there were other women in the world—those working in the medical profession, maybe, who wouldn't run like scared rabbits when a seizure hit.

Rising heavily from his patio seat, Heath yawned and stretched. Maybe he would go in and fire up his computer right now. Might as well get started on this new venture right away.

Chapter Eighteen

Liv

The next morning, I took the deed list Edwards had given me, my hair work brooch, and a notebook to the library. The librarian had told me she'd known Samuel Bernard—quite well, in fact. Surely, she would be able to shed some light on his ownership of the Belle Bride.

"Well, good morning, Ms. Larson. Nice to see you again," Florence said, her eyes bright over her readers. She was up on her desk-podium thing, studying some colorful catalog spread out before her.

I smiled back. "Ms. Edington, I discovered just yesterday what seems like an awful coincidence. Not awful, really, just awfully strange," I began, sliding out the list of deed records. "It seems I bought the Belle Bride, then came into ownership of a piece of mourning jewelry owned by Samuel Bernard, who actually owned the place at one time. In 1980." I handed her the last page of the list, where I'd highlighted the earliest recorded owner in bright yellow. "Did you know Mr. Bernard when he lived at the Belle Bride?"

The librarian's white eyebrows drew together as she took the paper from me, shaking her head. "No, I didn't. Didn't know he ever owned it. I didn't start working for Mr. Bernard until the late 1980s." She handed the paper back to me. "Why? Is it important?"

My shoulders sagged. "Not really. I just thought it was odd, is all." I drew a breath and looked around the old library, which was, as before, empty of patrons except for me. "A coincidence, I guess."

I was startled when I heard rustling from the room behind the podium, and saw Ms. Edington turn around. "Come on out here, Ruthie, and meet one of our newest residents."

Skirting the edge of the counter came a young woman who appeared to be in her late twenties. She brought to mind Vivian Leigh from Gone with the Wind, with masses of waving, raven hair and large, dark eyes set in a perfectly heart-shaped face. The only thing that destroyed the Scarlett O'Hara image was the shapeless, faded grey librarian's smock.

Her full lips curved up in a smile as she offered her hand. "How do, ma'am. I'm Ruth Edington." Her voice was soft and lilting. "I'm Ms. Edington's granddaughter."

"So nice to meet you, Ruth. I'm Liv Larson," I said. I hadn't seen this gorgeous young woman around town before. "Are you here visiting your grandmother?"

She shook her head. "No, ma'am. I've come home from college. I just graduated from the University of Alabama."

Ms. Edington straightened her shoulders and puffed up like a proud hen. "Ruthie here just earned her Master's in Library Science. She's going to be taking over here at the library when I retire at the first of the year."

Oh, I thought, this is good. She is about ten years younger than I am, but she's been living in a big city. Maybe we'd have some interests in common. Maybe we could become friends...

"That's exciting, Ruth. So, you'll be staying here in town. I'd love for you to come out to see my house. Of course, once I get it furnished," I stumbled, laughing. "I just moved in a few weeks ago, and it's not quite company-worthy yet."

"Ms. Larson here bought the old Belle Bride place, Ruth," Florence said.

The girl's dark eyebrows lifted. "Oh. Wow. I've always wanted to get a peek inside that place," she said. She slid a sidelong glance toward her grandmother before adding, "I mean, more than just peeking in the windows like we used to do when we were kids."

I left the library on a lighter step, and with a purpose. I really did need to finish furnishing my house. Dining room furniture, sofas and chairs for the parlor, occasional pieces for the foyer. Some nice artwork for the walls. The only way I could start making a life for myself in this new town was if I started making friends—other than the one man who made my brain go to mush every time I was around him.

Our last evening together had ended in disaster. I shouldn't have reacted the way I did, and it was time I got over those flashbacks to those last months with Josh. Heath was not Josh, and he didn't have a brain tumor. Remembering how Heath had slunk out of my house that night in shame, I felt terrible. How heartless of me. I needed to explain. I needed to let Heath know his seizures freaking me out had nothing to do with him, or his condition.

It was time for me to spill my own demons. Maybe if I did that—let another person see those scars on my heart—the healing could begin. Right now seemed like a good time to start.

Heath was unpacking some glassware from a huge box filled with Styrofoam balls when I burst through the front door of the shop. He looked up, his automatic smile fading quickly when he saw me. My heart clenched.

What a cold, heartless bitch he must think I am. And who could blame him?

"Hey," I said, glancing around the shop to be sure we were alone.

"Hey," he replied, then went back to whisking the bits

of foam packing off an ornately painted vase. "Help you with something?"

God, how it killed me to hear the ice in his tone. This man had been inside me, making love to me, less than a week ago. Now he acted as though he didn't even know me.

"Yes, Heath, you can. I have some explaining to do. About . . . the other night. I reacted rather badly—"

"There's no need to apologize, Liv. I understand. My condition can be . . . off-putting," he said, avoiding eye contact. "It's okay. I understand. But we do live in the same small town, and I do still want you to revamp my website. So, I'm hoping we can maintain some sort of civil relationship."

Civil relationship?

He straightened and turned toward me, extending his hand. *A handshake?* He wanted to reduce our foundling relationship to a handshake?

I blinked rapidly, my brain scrambling for the words. "No, Heath, you don't understand. There's a reason why I reacted the way I did." I glanced at the grandfather clock behind his desk. "It's almost lunch time. Why don't we go down to Nan's and grab some lunch? Then I can explain—"

My words were cut short by the sound of the door opening behind me. Heath's gaze wandered over my shoulder, and a huge smile lit up his face.

"Hey there. You're a few minutes early. I'll be ready in just a minute or two."

I turned to see the young woman I'd just met at the library. She was sauntering down the shop's center aisle toward us wearing a flirtatious smile. Ruth Edington's librarian's smock was gone, revealing a pastel, floral-print sundress in some sort of silky, flowy fabric. Its cap sleeves fluttered over sculpted, tanned biceps, and its hem did the same, revealing slender, shapely legs.

Crap on a cracker. He's moved on already?

"Liv, this is Ruth Edington. She's Florence's granddaughter—"

"I know. We've met. Like, fifteen minutes ago," I said weakly.

Scarlett—I would always think of her by that name, not Ruth—beamed brightly at me as she moved closer to Heath, hooking herself to his upper arm. Her gaze wandered appreciatively over his face.

"Liv tells me she's in the process of furnishing her new home. Guess you're helping her with that, huh?" she said, never taking her eyes off his.

"I am," Heath said, then glanced at me and cleared his throat. "And right now, I'm closing up for an hour to take Ruth here to lunch. To celebrate her homecoming to Camellia."

I drove home feeling more miserable than I had in months. An idiot, is what I was. Why couldn't I just have come out and shared the gory details of my husband's illness with Heath that first day I told him I was a widow? If I had, then maybe he would have understood my freaking out at his seizures.

It still wouldn't excuse my reactions. But at least he wouldn't have blamed them on himself.

Now, with pretty, young Ruth Edington back in town, it was obvious Heath's interests had wandered elsewhere. If she grew up here, she probably knew about his epilepsy. More than likely, she would have the capability—and the willingness—to be supportive, and understanding.

In Heath's opinion, unlike me.

I was going on the assumption, of course, that the glittery ring on Ruthie's left hand was merely a family heirloom . . .

Heath

"Really great to see you, Ruthie," Heath said as they slid into a corner booth at the diner. "It seems as though you've been gone forever."

He watched appreciatively as Ruth leaned towards him, crossing her arms on the table. The flowered sundress had a lacy neckline maintaining all aspects of prudency until she tipped forward, gifting him with a view of pale, soft-looking mounds.

"It's good to be back," she said, one side of her pouty lips quirking up. "I wasn't crazy about life in Tuscaloosa. I've never been one for the city life, you know."

"I'm not surprised," Heath replied, "but it was a smart move to get the best education. I'm sure your folks are very proud of you."

Heath couldn't believe the girl he'd known in pigtails had blossomed into such an attractive woman. He racked his brain for how many years she'd been behind him in school . . . or had she even started high school when he'd graduated? How many years *were* there between them?

He cleared his throat. "What are your plans now you've got your sheepskin?" he asked.

"I'm going to live with my grammy until I can find a place of my own. She's retiring soon, and guess what? You're looking at Camellia's new head librarian." A smile lit up her entire face, and he noticed the tiny gap between her two front teeth he'd always thought made her look so endearing.

One thing was for sure. The adorable little girl he knew as Ruthie Edington sure had grown up. And all of his male sensors were reminding him of just how nicely.

Chapter Nineteen

Liv

I knew as I climbed into my truck it was time I spilled some of this on a sympathetic ear. The alone time since I'd left New York—three weeks now—had been enough. Not enough to convince me I'd made a mistake, yet enough to make me question my resolve to start over, leaving every aspect of my old life behind. Including my friends.

Delphine picked up her office phone on the second ring, just as I was pulling into my driveway. She worked for a DNA testing lab in Manhattan. I had no qualms about calling her in the middle of a workday: Delphine Paulson didn't just work for the lab. She ran it.

"Del?" Her name came as a squeak as I threw the truck into park and killed the engine. For the next few seconds, I couldn't speak as I desperately struggled to hold back the sobs rumbling deep in my chest. Leaning my forehead on the steering wheel, I concentrated on sucking deep, slow breaths as I listened to my friend's frantic questions rattling into my ear.

"Liv? Olivia? What's happened? Oh my God, are you okay?"

I swallowed the huge ball of pain in my throat and managed five garbled words.

"I'm sorry, Del. You busy?"

Of all the friends Josh and I had hung out with over the past five years, Del and her husband Bill had become the closest. And they'd stayed close, even when things got ugly. They'd been there, waiting with me in the Emergency Room the night they ran the first battery of scans and tests, after Josh's first bad seizure. Del held me as I cried, cried *with* me, when the reality of Josh's diagnosis hit home. They'd stood by me, one on each side, literally holding me up, beside my husband's casket.

I had expected Delphine, of all the people I told about my move, to be the most supportive. She was, after all, from the South. Born and raised Delphine LeBlanc in New Orleans, Del moved to New York to attend Sarah Lawrence College for her Masters degree in Human Genetics. Not long after graduation, she met her soulmate and future husband, William—Bill—Paulson. He was the corporate attorney handling the legal affairs of Del's new employer, Manhattan DNA Diagnostics.

Bill was also my husband, Josh's, partner and best friend.

"Liv, honey, where are you?" The soft, familiar lilt of Del's accent made my throat close down to a pinpoint. I was barely able to get out the next, single word.

"Home."

"Oh, thank God. Home, as in, here in New York?"

I hauled myself out of the truck with the phone against my ear. The midday sun had turned my Tacoma into a truck-shaped, high-temp oven within just a few short minutes. The last thing I needed to add to my pathetic state was heat stroke.

She must have heard the bang of the door slamming shut, and then the quiet. The quiet that was definitely not on a busy Manhattan street.

"Oh. You're still in Alabama."

A half-hour later, I sat cross-legged on my second-story gallery with an almost empty beer bottle in one hand and the phone still pressed to my ear.

"Okay, so tell me this again. You're experiencing some really weird withdrawal effects from your anti-depressants, and you're super depressed about it. You have one weirdo in Civil War drag stalking you by night, and a Bigfoot clone stalking you by day. And you're wondering why the hell I'm so worried about you?" Del's New Orleans accent always kicked up a notch when she was upset. I doubt I'd ever heard it get *this* bad.

Add to that the absurdity of the tale I'd shared with her, and the fragile emotional state I was in. I guess neither of us should have been surprised when I burst into a fit of hysterical giggles.

"I'm a mess, huh?" I sputtered.

Del wasn't laughing. "I'm getting on a plane, and I'm coming down there, Liv. I'm flying down there. We're going to pack up your stuff in your truck, and I'm driving you home. Where's the nearest major airport?"

I could hear the click of her computer keys. Del wasn't kidding. She was deadly serious, and I knew if I didn't do some fast talking, she'd be texting me from the airport in Birmingham to come pick her up.

"No, Del, I'm not coming back. I belong here. Don't ask me why I believe that. I just do. Okay, my move has been a little dramatic, but my entire life has defined that word for the past few years. I'm probably over-reacting. I just needed to talk to you."

The clicking of the keys ceased. "Liv, I'm really worried about you. I mean, you live in a part of the world where people go missing and nobody ever finds out what happened to them." She snorted. "Believe me, I know. I'm from New Orleans. At least you aren't surrounded by a bayou."

I sighed. She was right, of course. Other than Heath

and the Warrens, with their behemoth of a son, I didn't know anybody here. Oh, and then there was the realtor, Edwards, who I knew I couldn't trust if my life depended on it.

I hoped it didn't.

"You're welcome to come down . . . visit. See my house. But I'm not coming back to New York, Del. I don't belong there. Not anymore."

The words had come out of my mouth with such conviction they surprised even me. How could I be so sure of this? How? Why? *Why?*

"Why, Liv?" Del parroted my thoughts back to me. "I don't know whatever made you pick Alabama in the first place. What makes you think you belong in a place you've never been before?" She paused for a long, silent beat. "But . . . we don't really know that, do we? For sure?"

It was true. I did not know where I'd been born. I knew where my parents had taken possession of me, at three days old. Where my birth parents had been from, where they'd been born and raised, I had no idea. I knew my mother was an unwed teen. It's all I knew. She could have been from Maine or from California. It was anyone's guess.

"Even if I'd been born here, Del, how would I remember that?" I said weakly, toying with the loose edge of the label on the beer bottle. "Though I have to tell you, it's almost like I'm following some kind of . . . instinct. I know, I know, I chose Camellia because it's where the dart landed on the map. I could have gone anywhere I wanted. It's just, when I got here, something . . . *clicked.*"

I could hear the tapping of Delphine's fingernails drumming on her desk—one of her many idiosyncrasies I'd come to know about her over the years. Del was a believer in synchronicities, which was kind of odd, seeing as she worked in the field of science. You would think logic would rule her life. Instead, she was a big believer in following gut instincts.

Genetics don't lie, she'd always told me. What that had to do with hunches and intuition, I had no idea.

"Isn't it time you let me run some tests on you, Liv? I mean, I know you have no interest in finding—or contacting—your birth mother. Still, if you knew where she was from—"

I barked out a wry laugh. "No, Del. Not going there. We've already been through this. I need to keep my sights set on the life ahead of me, not what's in my past."

Even as I said the words, the image of Bitsy's front hall—her own private, family museum—flashed into my mind. She had no children of her own. All she had was her past, and it was very important to her. It kept her grounded, it seemed.

Other than the days when she dragged down the moonshine jar.

Del had continued her rant, which again mirrored the thoughts floating through my brain. "It helps to know where you came from, Liv. I know it seems like clinging to an irrelevant past. Honestly, it means more than that. Just look at how many people are obsessed these days with determining their heritage. Knowing one's cultural identity is so, *so* important for a person's mental health. Hell, it keeps my lab in business."

I dragged in a deep breath and raked my fingers through my hair. Maybe Del was right. It really did bother me, not knowing who I was. Where I was from.

What had she called it? My *cultural identity*?

It was a fact: My mental stability had been somewhat tenuous over the past few years. How could it not have been, considering what happened to my husband? Perhaps this was a problem I'd been dealing with, without fully realizing it, all of my life.

I sighed, then conceded. "What would you need from me?" I asked.

Heath

Heath's lunch with Ruthie Edington had been stimulating, interesting, and ultimately—disappointing. They were about halfway through their club sandwiches when Heath noticed the sparks of light flashing off the young woman's left hand.

Shit, why hadn't I noticed that sooner?

"Pretty ring," he said, tipping his chin toward her hand. "Is it a family heirloom?"

Being an antiques guy, Heath immediately recognized the floral-shaped, milgrain setting as vintage. Or a damn nice replica. Once he actually *saw* it. The rock nestled in its center had to be better than a carat of blue-white brilliance.

How the holy hell had he missed that?

"No, actually it's not," Ruthie replied, patting her mouth with her napkin before daintily proffering her hand. "But we did have it fashioned after one that used to belong to my grandmother. It's my mom's now, and she offered the setting for us to use. The stone Keith picked out, though, was way too big for Mom's ring."

The toast on Heath's sandwich seemed suddenly too dry and scratchy in his mouth.

She's too young for you anyway, you idiot.

Eight years' age difference wasn't huge, but Ruthie was a very *young* twenty-seven. She came from one of the wealthiest families in Walker county. And with her looks and brains, she probably had an entourage of young men begging for her hand. What had he been thinking?

"Congratulations," he managed after forcing the dry bread down his throat. He lifted his tea glass and drank deeply. "Who's the lucky guy?"

After he'd escorted Ruth back to the library, kissed her

cheek chastely, and told her to be sure she kept in touch, Heath dragged himself back to his shop. He really was an idiot. Asking that young girl to lunch, he admitted, was a knee-jerk reaction. The truth of the matter was he was heartbroken over the disastrous ending of his fledgling relationship with Liv.

What must she think of him now, he wondered? Barely days out of the sack with her, Liv had come into his shop and he'd flaunted a pretty young, new toy in her face. At least, that must be how it seemed to her. Now she probably thought he was not only epileptic, but heartless. Shallow. Flippant.

She'd come into the shop to tell him something, he remembered. Something important—at least it had seemed important to her. Should he call her? Text her?

Grow a set, Barrow, he told himself. When you close up shop this afternoon, take your sorry ass over to the Belle Bride. Ask the woman in person what it is she has on her mind.

Tamping down the butterflies churning around in his stomach, Heath closed his shop promptly at five and set out toward the Belle Bride. He found Liv in her usual spot, perched on her upper gallery, portable computer in her lap.

She has office furniture now, he thought. Maybe she didn't care for it after all.

Liv looked up when he pulled into the driveway behind her Tacoma, and he hesitated. Would she ignore him? Tell him to go away?

He was pleasantly surprised when she closed the laptop and scrambled to her feet. By the time he'd stepped out of his vehicle, she was leaning on the railing, smiling down at him.

"Well, good afternoon," she said, her voice a little quivery. "Or evening, I should say. Is it after five already?" She glanced at her watch.

Heath whooshed out a breath and returned her smile. "I'm sorry I blew you off at lunchtime, Liv. Ruthie . . . her family and mine are old friends." He hesitated, adding, "I should have asked you to join us." He cringed inwardly, hoping she wouldn't call him out on his little white lie.

Liv's eyes narrowed. "Don't give me that, Barrow. Your chest was more puffed up than a peacock's. Guess you didn't notice the engagement ring until later, huh?"

Damn these perceptive—and eagle-eyed—women.

His shoulders slumped. "Okay, busted. Still, I'm still here to apologize for blowing you off. And to find out why you came to see me."

One side of her mouth quirked up and she tipped her head toward the door. "Come on in. I think I've got a couple cold beers left in the fridge."

Chapter Twenty

Liv

I have to admit, I was relieved—elated, actually—when Heath showed up in my dooryard. My reaction to his episodes really had been inexcusable, but maybe now I was beginning to understand why my head was so messed up. And ready to face it, head on.

Losing Josh was certainly a huge factor. As for the weird imaginings, the anti-depressant drugs probably had something to do with those too. What Delphine had explained to me, for the umpteenth time, over the phone this afternoon finally broke through.

"Before you can love anybody else, you have to love yourself, Liv," she'd said. "I know you and Josh hit it off, and what you had was great. Yet you were really nothing more than an extension of *him*. Mrs. Josh Larson, not Liv Larson, in her own right. In order for you to go on with your life, you have to learn more about who you really are. You need to understand your cultural identity."

I felt like now—finally—I understood that, accepted the fact. And I was taking steps to remedy the situation. A giant step.

It took me hitting rock bottom, again, thinking I might have lost my chance with Heath to push me into the decision. Before we'd hung up, Del promised my genetic testing kit, complete with all three types of DNA tests, would be arriving in the mail via FedEx the following day.

Heath stood on my doorstep wearing a sheepish, I've-been-a-bad-boy look on his face, hands stuffed in the front pockets of his jeans. God, he looked good. Crisply pressed button-down shirt, long sleeves turned up to his elbows, in a pale shade of sky blue. His jeans, though dusty and smudged with what was probably furniture polish across one thigh, fit him snugly in all the right places. When his eyes met mine, the sincerity I saw there melted a little edge of my heart.

"Can I come in?" he asked, knocking me out of my hormonally-charged trance.

Cripes. I've been standing here admiring him like he was an ice cream cone on this hot Alabama afternoon.

"Of course, silly. I'm sorry. I've been doing some online shopping and my brain's still got that monitor buzz thing going on." I stepped back and we walked together toward the back of the house. Yup, furniture polish. And mixed with the musky scent of his sweat, it was incredibly enticing.

"Shopping for what, exactly? More furniture?" He glanced into my empty parlor while I twisted the caps off two beers. "Still really echoes in here."

I handed him one bottle and took a long pull off my own. "Yes, it does. I need a sofa. Or maybe a couple of loveseats, and some upholstered chairs. All that fabric should help with the acoustics, don't you think?" I wrinkled my nose and gazed up at the soaring, twelve-foot high ceiling.

"Some. I think you'll need something on the floors, too. Just area rugs, though. You wouldn't want to cover up this gorgeous hardwood." He ran the toe of his loafer across the honey-colored boards. "Did you have these refinished before you moved in? They're in pretty nice shape."

"I did. And had them put a neutral base coat of paint over all the walls, after they sanded off the stuff that was peeling. Now I just have to decide on colors." I leveled a gaze on his. "I've never had to make these kinds of decisions before.

I went straight from my parents' home, to a college dorm, to Josh's loft." I tucked a strand of hair behind my ear. "My late husband," I clarified."

Heath nodded and lifted his bottle. "To new beginnings, then. I knew you said you'd come here to start over. I just didn't realize how complete and literal a statement that had been."

We clinked bottles and I shot him a shy smile. "How'd your lunch with Scarlett go?"

He barked out a laugh, shaking his head. "She does look like Vivian Leigh, doesn't she? And is probably just as spoiled rotten as Scarlett." As his grin faded, he held my gaze. "So, is that why you came to the shop today? To talk about sofas and side chairs?"

His tone was soft, a rumbling purr. I couldn't help but feel he was not only looking *at* me, but *into* me. A warm flush started in my cheeks and spread quickly south, landing squarely in my core.

I shook my head. "No. I came by to ask you to lunch, so I could apologize for my extreme reactions to your seizures, Heath. The ones I've witnessed." I held up a hand when he began to protest. "No, hear me out. My behavior was childish, irresponsible, and completely inexcusable. Explainable, though." I reached out and caught his hand in mine. "Let's go upstairs. Sit on the gallery. I'll explain."

His grip was warm and reassuring as he followed me through the foyer and up the stairs. It wasn't until we got to my bedroom door that I paused.

"Oh. I forgot. Still no seating out there. Do you mind—"

"You sit on the bed, I'll roll your desk chair in here."

I'd flung the French doors open wide as soon as the sun crested the top of the gallery earlier, allowing whatever afternoon breeze to blow through the house. It was nice, the geographic layout of the Belle Bride. Facing the east, the master bedroom, along with the office, enjoyed the brilliant morning rays. By afternoon, shade kept the rooms, as well as the upper gallery, pleasantly cool.

I crawled up into the center of my King-sized bed and sat cross-legged, my beer cradled there as Heath rounded the corner into the office for the desk chair. As soon as he was seated comfortably, leaning back with his legs crossed at the ankles, I began my sad tale.

By the time I'd described a few of Josh's initial seizures, before we even knew what was wrong with him, Heath leaned forward and placed his beer bottle on the floor. He covered his face with both hands and started slowly shaking his head. He didn't interrupt me. I got the entire story out, right up through the details of the agonizing day I put my husband's body to rest.

I'm not sure when the tears had started. By the time I finished, though, I was drained. Cried out. Finally. I lifted my now-warm beer to my lips and tipped back, draining the bottle into my parched throat. I heard Heath's chair squeak, and the mattress beside me dip.

And then he was holding me. It felt good to be held, his arms strong and steady around me. I lowered my head to his shoulder, breathing in the musky, male goodness of him. His unruly curls tickled my cheek as I burrowed my face into the crook of his neck.

We sat that way a long time, saying nothing, rocking slightly back and forth in a soothing rhythm. Dusk had begun to tint the light outside to umber, slowly merging with the grey-brown bark of the trees in my front yard. Cricket song crept up gradually, as though someone had a dimmer switch on the sound.

I'd almost drifted into a light doze when Heath gripped my shoulders and pushed back to gaze into my eyes.

"There are no words to take away the horrors you've been through, Liv. I can't imagine . . . to be honest, I don't even want to try. It certainly explains your . . . your *extreme reactions* to my seizures. I don't blame you. I understand now. And don't take this the wrong way," he paused to run a finger down my cheek and along my jawline to my ear, his eyes never leaving mine, "but it's a relief. For *me*. Knowing it wasn't me causing you to react that way. My epilepsy."

I shook my head and drank in the warmth, the sincerity in what he was saying, in words as well as with his eyes. "It was never that, Heath. It was all me. I'm sorry if I hurt you—"

He silenced my apology by taking my mouth, soft and yet demanding. Holding my face in his hands, he planted kisses on my lips, my cheeks, my chin, igniting a fire in my belly I couldn't hold back. Didn't want to. When he ran his tongue in small circles on the tender skin under my ear, I shuddered.

"Ticklish?" he growled into my ear. "Or cold?"

"Far from cold," I shot back as I swung my body around, over his, to straddle his lap. It was my turn now.

He smelled of sweat, yet in a good way. A man's hard day of work sweat, mixed with the feral musk that told me he was as turned on as I was. I ravaged his mouth, tasting the yeasty beer on his breath, reveling in the heat and the wetness of our tongue's desperate dance. Combing my fingers into his tousled cap of chocolate curls, the thought suddenly occurred to me. Yes, I was right where I belonged. Where I'd always been meant to be.

Without ever breaking our hungered kiss, his fingers slipped down to unbutton the sleeveless blouse I'd been wearing. Silk sliding free off my shoulders, slithering down heated skin to pool around my hips, a delicious sensation mingling with the anticipation of what would come next. Then his thumbs were circling my taut nipples through the lace of my bra, and I squirmed, rubbing, grinding, myself against him. I wanted more, and I wanted it now.

He was hard and ready, a rock-hard, denim-covered mound beneath me. My hips began an oscillating dance all on their own, the friction against my oh-so-sensitive spot maddening. As my breath came faster, I broke the kiss, resting my forehead against his. It was either that or suffocate, my need for air was so desperate.

Dropping his head back, he groaned, only letting me pleasure myself this way a moment or two longer before he stilled my hips with both hands.

"Not this way, Liv. I want to be inside you."

Lifting me off his lap, he sat me beside him, stood and made quick work of unbuttoning his own shirt. His jeans slid to the floor, then his boxers. Even in the dim light of dusk, the sight of his naked body made my breath catch in my throat. He was a beautiful man, sculpted but not overly cut, broad and strong yet not burly. Chocolate curls covered his body in all the right places, just enough, soft and lush. A hot knot of need coiled deep in my belly.

He reached forward to finish undressing me, and I let him, propping myself back on my hands, reveling in the freeness of relinquishing control. With deft fingers, he unhooked the clasp of my bra between my breasts, then slid the lacy straps back over my shoulders until the garment fell away.

"My God, you are so beautiful," he whispered as he lowered himself to his knees before me.

I thought I knew what was coming next, yet Heath appeared to be in no hurry this evening. Without removing my yoga pants, he simply laid his head on my lap. I felt his back rise and fall, a deep breath that came out on a sigh. The simple, affectionate gesture reached into my chest and squeezed around my heart with an emotion I couldn't ever remember feeling before.

This man wanted not just sex from me. This was way more than a physical act for him. There, on his knees before me, his arms encircling my hips, his entire body relaxed, melting against mine. He was *worshipping* me, as if I were the most special woman he'd ever found.

I'd never been worshipped before. Loved, yes. Valued and respected as a person. As a wife, a mate, a life partner. Still, I'd always played the subordinate role. Always the one to do the worshipping. Not because my husband had insisted on it. So then ... why?

Probably because I'd never considered myself worthy—

You can't truly love someone else until you learn to love yourself.

Delphine's words came back to me, whispered into my brain like a mantra. She was right, of course. I'd simply never realized what was lacking in my life. Before now.

I combed my fingers through Heath's cap of soft curls and he sighed again, a wistful, peaceful sound. When he lifted his gaze to meet mine, there was a mistiness in his eyes. I saw it then, as clearly as if it there were words spelling it out. Emotion, oozing out from a heart as bruised and battered as much, if not more, than my own.

At least Josh's leaving me alone hadn't been deliberate. His illness hadn't been a selfish, deliberate act to hurt me. Not like what Katherine had done to Heath. And God knew how many other people in his life.

"I'm so tired of being alone," he said, his voice thick. "I'm not a person who likes solitude, yet it seems I've been sentenced to a lifetime of it. Until you, Liv. I don't want to put any pressure on you. I'm not asking for promises. I'm just asking for a chance to prove that, epileptic or not, I can make you happy. Even if only for a little while."

I laid a finger on his lips, then slid down onto the floor before him. Face to face, on the same plane. Equal.

"This is how it needs to be between us, Heath. In order to be right. Neither one yielding power over the other. I've been in the subordinate role . . . all of my life, it seems. I don't want to be there anymore. But I also don't want to be the dominant one."

His gaze locked on mine, he nodded, blinking, as though he either didn't understand, or couldn't believe what I'd said. Concern furrowed my brow as I searched his eyes.

"You okay?" I asked.

Another seizure coming on? I prayed not. Not now. This moment between us was too special, too sacred.

He slowly shook his head, a hint of a smile quirking one corner of his lips.

"I'm fine. I'm just wondering if I'm dreaming all of this, or if it's really happening." His lips were soft as he brushed them lightly across mine. Then he pulled back and lifted an eyebrow. "I'm pretty sure I'm not dreaming, because then I'd be asleep. And I couldn't stay asleep long kneeling on this hardwood. It's killing my knees. You really need some throw rugs in here."

I blinked at this blip in mood, then snorted out a laugh. "You're right. Mine too."

We made love on my giant Rice bed in the gathering dark and stillness of the night, and I'd never imagined a more intense experience. Sex was great, but this was something else again. His fingers caressed every inch of my body, gently, as though I were made of glass, or the finest porcelain. Like a china teacup in his shop he didn't want to chip or break.

Instead of the frantic, rapid frenzy the first time we joined, this was languid, lush, decadent. The heat built slowly, steadily, as he progressed from caressing my skin with tentative fingers to lavishing my lips and neck and breasts with his tongue, tasting me, tantalizing every nerve ending in my body. Hovering over me, he made me feel dominated yet adored, all at the same time.

I couldn't keep my own hands still. They explored the strong muscles of his shoulders and back, trailed down corded arms, played across the velvety hair on his chest. The intensity, the excitement of anticipation finally drove me to impatience. I reached down, my fingers closing around him, and he moaned. My hips bucked instinctively up toward him.

"Now, Heath. Take me now," I gasped, no longer able, or wanting, to wait any longer. I wanted to be one with him. One, in every sense of the word.

When he entered me, slowly, agonizingly slow, my entire body began to shudder. I slid my hands down to dig my nails into hard buttocks, pulling him to me, into me. Then he went perfectly still, panting hard into my ear. His control was admirable as I squirmed beneath him.

He paused then, lifting his head, searching for my eyes in the near darkness. A bright moon had risen, illuminating his sweat-slicked skin, with tousled, damp tendrils of hair falling over his brow. His chest heaved against mine, his elbows supporting him on either side of my head. His hands encircled my head on the pillow.

"Liv," he moaned. "Oh, Liv."

When he began to move, hard and fast and furious, he took me with him. Up and up, higher and higher until we crested the summit, together.

Heath

After their first slow, sensual dance, they'd slept a while, then crept downstairs for a snack. No dinner for either of them. And they sure had worked up an appetite.

They'd eaten cold, leftover pizza while sharing the last cold bottle of beer. Curled up on Liv's second-story gallery, his back up against the wall, her snugged up between his legs, they admired an almost perfect, nearly full moon.

"So, has your Soldier Boy made any more appearances?" Heath asked, his fingers trailing lightly over Liv's bare shoulder.

She shivered, then wrapped her arms around her middle. "Not in the last week or so. I think it was my meds. Did I tell you? I quit taking them suddenly and I guess you're not supposed to do that."

"What were you taking?" he asked.

"Anti-depressants. After Josh died . . . well . . ."

"Shhh," Heath hissed into her ear. "No need to explain. It's all behind you now."

When they returned to bed, the passion reignited, and they made love again.

And yes, this was definitely making love, Heath decided. He wasn't quite sure he'd ever truly understood the meaning of the term before now. He thought he'd loved Katherine, yet with her, sex had never been like this. It had been good, passionate, exciting, satisfying. Never, ever like this.

He awoke sometime during the night with Liv in his arms. They were spooned, still naked, covered only by a sheet reflecting the brilliant moonlight spilling over them. One arm curled around her head, the other tossed over her waist, they were as close as two human bodies could get.

Well, almost as close.

Heath thought about the roller coaster of emotions he'd ridden over the past few days. A tumultuous ride, to be sure. To have landed here, with this incredible woman safe in his arms, was well worth the turmoil that had brought him to this moment in time.

Thinking of time, what time was it, anyway? He couldn't see her alarm clock from this angle, and God only knew where his watch and phone were.

Trying his best not to wake her, but desperate for a trip to the john, Heath slipped quietly out of bed and padded barefoot into the bathroom. No need for a light, as the moonlight flooding in through the tall window illuminated the space to near daylight. The trill of crickets from the woods surrounding the house echoed against bare hardwood and plastered walls.

We really do need to get her some rugs in here.

As he headed back into the hall toward the bedroom, another sound drifted in the stairwell. Faint at first, then growing louder, Heath heard a woman crying.

Oh no. No, she can't regret this. She can't.

Hurrying into the bedroom, though, he could see Liv's spill of blonde hair covering her pillow. She was still sound asleep, mouth open and snoring quietly. He froze in the doorway.

The sound was coming from downstairs.

Heath grabbed his boxers and pulled them on, then dug his phone out of his jeans, which were lying on the floor at the foot of the bed. He checked the time.

Two o'clock a.m. Precisely.

He swiped a hand down his face and shook his head to clear it. Had he dreamed it? No, the minute he stepped out into the hallway, he heard it again. The unmistakable sobbing of a woman, and it was coming from the first floor. Somewhere towards the back of the house. Kitchen? Parlor?

By the time he'd crept down the curved staircase, one careful step at a time, he realized the sound didn't really have any source direction. The echo effect was disconcerting, and he wasn't sure which way to go first. It seemed like the sobs were all around him, resonating in the empty foyer.

Almost as though the sound was seeping out of the walls.

That single, ridiculous thought had snagged his brain when a sudden, thunderous hammering on the front door had him staggering back with a muffled shriek.

Bang, bang, bang, bang, bang.

What the holy hell?

Heath slid quickly against one sidewall, where whomever it was outside wouldn't be able to see him through tall, paned windows flanking the heavy oak door. From his angle, he could see no one. If they were right up close to the entryway—

Bang, bang, bang, bang, bang.

For a moment, panic prickled Heath's skin and he was unsure as to what he should do. Answer it? He was unarmed. It could be Liv's weirdo nighttime soldier . . . and he *was* armed, at least from what Liv told him.

If he tried to dial 9-1-1 on his phone, the light from its screen would tell the "visitor" he was there. Who knew what he would do? Break a window . . . Heath's heart raced along with his brain. He had to protect Liv.

One step at a time, he moved backward, toward the small half-bath where he'd found Liv the day he passed out on her. Once hidden there, he could dial for help.

Bang, bang, bang, bang, bang.

Icy fingers of dread climbed up Heath's spine, and his hands were trembling so badly he almost dropped his phone. As he slid around the corner into the tiny bath, he heard an even more dreadful sound.

Footsteps, racing down the stairs. Within seconds he saw Liv's bare feet, slender legs naked beneath the hem of a long tee shirt. Heath couldn't believe what he was seeing. She was running—literally *running*—down the stairs toward the front door.

Before he could step forward, say anything to stop her, Liv stomped to the front door and threw back the deadbolt. She yanked at the door, but it jolted against her when it hit the end of its chain. She let out a growl of fury.

"Damn it, I've had enough of this," she muttered, unlatching the chain and flinging the door open.

Heath lunged forward, intent on putting himself between Liv and whoever it was on the other side. She screeched when he caught her around her waist and pulled her back against him, hard. She recovered quickly, grabbing his wrists and struggling to free herself.

"No! No, this has gone on long enough," she screamed. "You weirdo. You get off my property and stay off! Stay away from my house. This is *my* house now. I'm calling the police."

For a moment, Heath thought Liv was either sleepwalking, or had gone mad. He didn't see anyone on the front steps. She was screeching and waving her arms at . . . nothing.

"Liv . . . Liv, calm down," he purred into her ear. "A dream. You were having a dream."

It still didn't explain the noises he'd heard. The woman crying. The pounding on the door.

Liv wriggled and writhed and finally wrenched herself free. Taking one giant step over the threshold, she raised her arm and pointed to a spot just beyond where his truck was parked behind hers.

"Do you see him? The soldier. Don't you see him?" she screeched.

Heath stepped out next to her, flinging one arm around her shoulders. He needed to calm her down. Get her awake. Break her out of this nightmare—

Then, he saw him too. A sturdily built man, wearing some sort of cap and carrying what looked like a pole—or gun—striding purposefully away from the house. The eerie luminescence of the moon reflected off him, making him seem to glow from within. His form was almost translucent.

Then, by the time he reached the lane in front of the Belle Bride, his form faded to nothing except a patch of moonlight on the pavement.

Chapter Twenty-One

Liv

"So, I'm not crazy, then. This is no delusionary reaction from medication withdrawal. You saw him too."

It was at least the tenth time I'd asked the question since Heath had helped me toss a few things in a duffel bag and bundled me into his truck. After what we'd both experienced, there was no way either of us even considered going back to bed.

Certainly, not in that house.

Now we stood in Heath's kitchen over steaming cups of coffee, facing each other across the counter island. The lovely old grandfather clock in his living room claimed the time as three forty-two. He sighed, bracing his forehead on his hand. Patiently, he repeated what he'd said every time I'd asked ever since his truck's wheels spun us out onto the road at the end of my driveway.

"Yes, I saw him. He was . . . glowing, and not just from the moonlight." He dropped his hand and grabbed my gaze. "I saw him. And then, I didn't."

No matter how many times he said it, a fresh wash of cold fear sent my skin pebbling into gooseflesh. Every time.

"Makes you kind of question your sanity, doesn't it?" I murmured.

He nodded. "I've never been one to believe in the paranormal. Hauntings and all that mumbo jumbo. And I'll be honest—what you were telling me about some Confederate soldier, with you being new here, from the city and all . . . well, these big old houses can be spooky. There's a lot of history in them." He scrubbed his face with both hands. "I just never thought history could infect a house, like vermin. Or termites."

"What makes you put it that way? I mean, there's got to be a logical explanation for all this, doesn't there? Unless we're both losing our minds—"

"No. The soldier . . . it's not all," Heath said, suddenly straightening, remembering. He held up his hand. "There was a woman . . . crying. That's what brought me down the stairs in the first place. Before the pounding on the door even started."

My heart lurched and I slammed both palms down on the counter. "What woman? I've never heard a woman. I've seen a dog, and a horse. And they both glow, like the weird soldier. But no woman."

He waved his hands in the air. "I didn't see her," he clarified. "I *heard* her. At first, I thought she was at the back of the house. Behind it, maybe. By the time I got downstairs, into the foyer, the sound was all around me. These pitiful, heart-wrenching sobs." He shuddered, shaking his head.

Lifting his coffee mug with trembling hands, he paused when it was halfway to his lips. His wide eyes, almost glassy, held steady on mine. His face contorted, as though he was in pain. "The sound was . . . heart-wrenching, Liv. Loud. Echoing. As though the wails were bleeding out from the *walls*."

I wasn't sure if it was relief I felt, knowing Heath had seen my mysterious Soldier Boy, or dread. It was much easier to accept the strange occurrences at the Belle Bride as my overactive imagination. Drug withdrawal hallucinations. Now, it went beyond that.

The soldier. The dog, and the horse. Now, the sobs of some unseen woman.

Side effects from drug withdrawal are on thing. Mass

hallucinations are more difficult to explain.

"Bitsy told me there was some legend about the place, but she never got the chance to tell me what it was. Edwards, though, he swears there's no record of *ghoulish activity*. It's what they call it. I went to see him, you know. I could cancel my contract if there were some record—"

Fury began to simmer in my chest, fueled by adrenalin and quickly edging out the fear. I'd sunk a good chunk of my savings into buying that house, damn it. This was going to be my new start. My fresh, new beginning. And tonight, not even a month after I'd moved in, I didn't feel safe sleeping there.

Heath set down his cup and skirted the counter to wrap his arms around me.

"Shhh. We'll get to the bottom of this, Liv. You're right. There has to be some sort of logical explanation. And if there isn't, we'll get you out of your contract. I promise you that. I have a good attorney in Birmingham."

The tension drained out of me as I melted against him, relaxing against the warm strength of his body. Safe. I was safe here, with Heath. The tears came then.

"Did you ever hear this legend Bitsy mentioned? About the Belle Bride?" I choked out. "She acted like it was some big secret, and she was about to tell me when Benjamin shuffled out and interrupted us." I pushed back and looked up into his eyes. "He creeps me out, by the way. He was watching me, the other morning, you know."

Instant concern hardened Heath's features. "What do you mean, watching you?"

I pushed away and began to pace in his kitchen, from the cooktop to the end of the island and back. Wringing my hands, I began to babble.

"That night, I'd heard the dog again. Scratching at the back door. When I went to shoo him away, I heard hoof beats, and this horse comes careening around the side of the barn. A white horse. Blindingly white, just like the dog. The two of them started romping around together. Like they know each other. And they were both just like the soldier. All glowing and kind of see-through—

"Tell me about Benjamin," Heath cut in, his voice stern. "When was Benjamin watching you? Where?"

I stopped pacing and froze in place when I saw the stiffened stance Heath had taken. Feet set wide, fists balled at his sides, fire sparked from his eyes.

"Why are you so mad? You told me Benjamin is harmless."

He whooshed out a breath and rubbed the back of his neck. "I've always thought he was. But he's mentioned you, to me, more than once. Wants to know when we're going back out to your house for deliveries." Heath paused and reached out to lay a hand on my shoulder. "He's a simpleton, true. He's still a full-grown man, Liv. With all the same hormones running through any man's body."

I shuddered at the thought of Benjamin, the way he was looking at me that day. *Hungrily.*

"I know."

I told him, then, about the morning I'd been checking the fence, and had the feeling I was being watched. The rustling in the woods. Then Ben admitting he'd been watching me.

Heath gathered me to him, yet his muscles were rigid, his voice tight. "I guess I'm going to have to have a talk with Robert. Their property butts right up to the Belle Bride. I don't like that Benjamin could be watching you, stalking you, without ever leaving his parents' land. Without breaking the law in any way."

"Neither do I."

Such a mistake I'd made, I thought. Buying the Belle Bride, on impulse, without doing my homework, had been such a dumb move.

"What am I going to do, Heath? What should I do?" I croaked.

He smoothed a hand down my hair. "We'll go, together, to talk to the Warrens. We'll find out about this silly legend, and I'll make it clear Benjamin is to steer clear of you. Tomorrow, okay?"

The grandfather clock chose that moment to bong out four times, making both of us jump.

"Don't you mean today?"

Heath

Liv tried to convince him it would be more proper to call first, find out if the Warrens were going to be home. Heath decided a surprise visit might be more effective. Lend it more credence. In regards to the legend, it wouldn't give them time to filter their story.

In regards to Benjamin, well, there just wasn't any softening the awkwardness of that situation.

It wasn't so far a drive. If they weren't home, they'd just come back later.

When they pulled up to the quaint cottage, Heath took note of Robert's old blue pickup under the carport. At least he was there. He would much rather speak of the Benjamin matter with Robert present, and not just Bitsy. That would go beyond awkward.

Who was he fooling? The Benjamin matter was going to be uncomfortable either way. Especially if Benjamin was home. And where else would he be? Heath didn't have any work for him today—the shop was closed on Sundays.

Maybe he should rethink this part of the discussion. He could revisit the subject when he knew Ben wasn't at home, but was in his shop, heaving furniture around. Liv would be safe until he did that anyway, he decided. She would be staying with him.

His jaw tightened when he heard the heavy footfalls following the echo of the bell. The door swung open, and there stood Benjamin. All six-foot-four or five of him, barefoot and in baggy overalls.

Heath felt Liv tense and inch closer to him.

"Hey, Ben. I hope we haven't come at a bad time. Liv and I would like to speak with your parents. About some local history," he added quickly.

Ben's face lit up, his eyes transforming from their usual bland, dullness to Christmas morning.

"Hi there, Mr. Barrow. Did you need me today? Is it why you come by?" Heath noted that although the big man addressed him, his eyes never left the lady at his side. "Mornin', Miss Larson." Unabashedly, he licked his thick lips.

Heath took a deep breath and tried to tamp down the urge to punch him. Dimwit, he thought. Ben hadn't heard a word he'd said. He wasn't listening. He was too focused on Liv.

"I want to see your parents, Ben. About some legend. About the Belle Bride." Heath cleared his throat and scuffed one boot on the boards of the porch when Benjamin just stood there. "Your parents, Ben. Are they home?"

Like a man blinking awake from a dream—and Heath didn't even want to think about what kind of dream—Ben jolted and glanced back over his shoulder.

"Uh, yeah. They're here. Come on in."

Heath draped his arm around Liv as they stepped over the threshold, then stood awkwardly in the museum-like foyer as Ben hollered, "Momma! Papa, we got company."

Bitsy hurried out from the side hallway, looking every bit the country bumpkin homemaker she was. A red plaid shirt topped faded jeans, rolled up to mid-calf. She, too, was barefoot. She greeted them with a warm, welcoming smile.

"Well, hi there, you two. Didn't expect company this mornin'. It's not a problem, though. No, not at all. Come on in. Some lemonade? Coffee. It's early yet. Can I brew you some coffee?"

Heath pulled Liv in closer to his side, felt the tenseness in her body. Benjamin hadn't budged, just stood just a few feet from them, his eyes and his smile all on Liv. Heath squared his shoulders.

Stiffly, Heath nodded. "I'll take coffee. Liv and I are on a mission today, Bitsy. She said you mentioned there was a legend about her house the other day . . . the Belle Bride. You never finished telling her about it."

Tiny lines formed between Bitsy's straggly eyebrows as she gazed up at Heath. "Well, Mr. Barrow, you've lived in Camellia about as long as I can remember. Surely, you've heard the story about the Belle."

Heath sighed. He'd grown up in Camellia, but tended to avoid wasting his time paying attention to the stories he considered nothing more than gossip. Fabrications to enhance the town's miniscule tourist appeal. Besides, even though he loved antiques and old things, history hadn't been his favorite subject. Most of history told the stories of war. Heath preferred to cherish the things that had survived the turmoil.

Bitsy was still staring at him as though he didn't have any more sense than her gigantic stepson.

Liv stepped forward. "Well even if Heath does know the legend, I'd like to hear your version of it, Bitsy." She motioned to the hall around them, overflowing with visual fragments of the past. "You seem to be the history expert in these parts."

Her face brightening into her broad smile once again, she lifted a hand to lay on Liv's arm. "That might well be true, Ms. Larson. Y'all come on in and I'll get us some coffee."

Fifteen minutes later Heath and Liv sat at the Warren's patio table. Robert was in his usual spot, rocking gently, eyes intent on the morning paper. Bitsy had poured them thick, black coffee and set a delicate china plate on the table bearing a mound of sugar cookies.

"By the way," she said as she fussed with cream in her coffee, "don't let me forget. I done got you a housewarming present for your new home." She beamed proudly. "Just finished wrapping it up all real pretty this mornin'."

She sat, plucked a cookie off the plate and set it on a napkin beside her mug. Then, dusting sugar off her hands, she met Heath's gaze.

"Now, what is it you want to know about the Belle?"

Heath sipped his coffee and fought to suppress a grimace. It was hot coffee, alright. But was it just strong or was it three days old? He forced a swallow and said, "I've heard rumors here and there about Liv's house, Bitsy. I don't pay rumor much mind. I do know it's been empty most of my life, off and on. Doesn't seem like folks hang onto it too long. Why is that?"

Bitsy pulled a face. "A very good question, Mr. Barrow. I don't rightly know the reason myself. Not for certain, anyways." She lifted her mug and rested her elbows on the tabletop.

"You said there was a legend," Liv prodded. "What's the legend, Bitsy?"

Twenty-Two

Liv

I sat in wide-eyed amazement as Bitsy began her story with the words, "You know you're sitting on the very piece of land where the main plantation house was, don't ya?"

Blinking, I shook my head. "Uh, no. Had no idea. You mean, the Belle wasn't the main house? There was one even bigger?"

Bitsy made a shooing motion with one hand as she lifted a cookie to her mouth with the other. "Oh, shoot, the Belle is an outhouse compared to the Bienvenue. No slight to your house, Ms. Larson," she added quickly, "but it just ain't nearly as grand as the Belle Bienvenue was. From what folks say." She took a bite, nodding appreciatively. "These just come outta the oven, kids. Get ya one while they're still warm."

Over the next half-hour, Bitsy explained the original plantation house, owned by a wealthy attorney from Birmingham, was destroyed during Wilson's Raid during the final months of the Civil War.

"That spring, they come through here like a plague of locusts, them damn Yankees," Bitsy said. She was oblivious to her implied insult to me until Robert looked up over his readers and kicked the leg of her chair.

"Manners, Betty," he growled.

Her eyes flew open wide and she covered her mouth with one hand. "Oh, I'm sorry, Ms. Larson. I done forgot you was from up north." She paused, shrugging. "That's what happened, though. The Union soldiers cut them a path from Gravelly Springs south, clear through the state. They was headed for the ironworks, you see. Wiped out every one in their path, along with whatever else. That included the Bienvenue. Fact is, nobody really knows why they left the Belle Bride standing."

Heath set his mug down on the glass tabletop with a click. "I knew Wilson's Raid went through near here. And I'd heard of the Bienvenue, but didn't realize—"

"Well, that rich lawyer, he had him a daughter, see. An only child. And she married a staunch supporter of the Confederacy. The Belle Bride was a wedding gift to them. Shame they never got to spend much time in it," Bitsy said, shaking her head.

"What happened?" Heath's and my question rang out together as if we'd rehearsed it.

"Well, he went off to war right after they was married. Never come home. Alive, anyway." Bitsy turned toward Robert. "You want a cookie, Robert? They're still warm."

Robert grunted and shook his head. Bitsy continued her tale.

"Her soldier man died at the Battle of Decatur. The family was lucky to recover his body. Buried him somewhere . . . nobody's quite sure where. If there'd been a marker, you see, the Yankees woulda yanked it outta the ground and smashed it when they came through." She set her lips into a grim line and tipped up her chin. "Everything. They came through and just wiped out everything."

"What happened to the daughter . . . his bride?" I asked. "Did she survive the raid?"

Bitsy slid forward until she was perched on the edge of her chair. "Legend has it she fled with her family and servants just ahead of the Yankee troops. It's said she was with child when her husband went off to war. She done had the child, then she came back. After the war. Lived there, with the child. At the Belle Bride. But not for very long. She died only a few years later."

"From what?" Heath asked.

Bitsy scowled and lifted her gaze to the patio's ceiling. "What was it they used to call it, Robert? Melon . . . something —"

"Melancholy. Now they call it depression. Now they got pills for it," Robert murmured and turned a page of his paper.

Yeah, I thought, *but those nifty little pills aren't as helpful —or as harmless—as they're supposed to be.*

Nodding vigorously, Bitsy added, "What she really died of, I figure, was a broken heart." She shook her head sadly. "That house you bought, Ms. Larson. There's a lot of sad hangin' over it. I figure it's why nobody stays there long. The Belle Bride is . . . cursed, sort of."

I tried to ignore the lead blanket that had just draped itself, invisibly, silently, over my shoulders. So, I'd bought a house the locals considered cursed. Ironically, the woman who'd lived there—*died there*—had suffered the same emotional wound I had. She'd been a widow. A mourning dove.

Lovely. Why hadn't I done more research? Too many coincidences here. Was that what had drawn me to this house? Did I somehow sense the widow's pain? Had it mysteriously seeped into the very structure of the building?

Did I feel a strange camaraderie with her?

The notion chilled the blood in my veins. Still, I wasn't about to stop digging into the house's history now. I leaned forward anxiously, almost afraid to ask the question bubbling up in my chest.

"Bitsy, what was her family . . . the plantation owner's

name?" I asked.

Her eyebrows drew together again. "Well, they was just about the oldest family in the area. 'Sides mine." She nodded and pressed her lips together, as if the fact provided me with the answer to my question.

"And that was?" Heath asked. I could hear the slight tinge of impatience in his tone, and I laid a hand on his arm.

Bitsy dropped back in her chair and folded her arms across her chest. Scowling at Heath, she snapped, "Heath Barrow, don't you tell me you don't know a thing about the heritage of the foundation families in this town. You grew up here. I woulda thought your own momma woulda taught you better than that—"

She jumped when again, Robert's heavy boot rapped against the leg of her chair, this time shifting it sideways an inch or two. Glancing back, she shrank a bit as he growled,

"Manners, Elizabeth."

Bitsy shifted in her seat, closed her eyes, and huffed out a breath. "Mr. Barrow, surely you're not going to tell me you've never heard of the Bernard family. They go back in this county almost two hundred years."

Bernard. Tendrils of electricity began crawling up the back of my neck at the mention of the name, like the legs of an errant spider. It couldn't be. This was just too freaking weird. Could he have been an ancestor of Samuel Bernard? The last man to own the Belle Bride in 1980?

The man who'd owned my piece of hair work jewelry?

Heath's brow knitted and he tipped his head. "I've sold a fair number of pieces to folks with that name over the years, but I don't know any of them personally. I never realized the family went back so far."

I swallowed hard, and set my cup down before I dropped

it. It hit the glass hard and clattered a little. Heath slid me a glance and, sensing my tension, curled his fingers around my wrist.

"What is it, Liv? Is something wrong?" he asked quietly.

I kept my gaze riveted on our hostess. "Bitsy, can you tell me the name of the woman . . . the *bride* of Belle Bride? The daughter of this attorney . . . the one he built the house for?"

"Surely can," she said with a snip in her tone. Lifting her chin, she said, "And if you ask Mrs. Edington down at the library, she can pull you up all sorts of records on the family. They do go back that far. There's a whole record on some sort of film . . . tiny film . . ." She scrunched up her face and turned toward her husband. "Robert, what is it they call that?"

"Micro fish," Robert grumbled. "Or some such thing."

Bitsy screwed up her face. "Got no idea what fish've got to do with it. Anyway, Mrs. Edington, she can get it all on her computer now. You just need to go ask her about it."

I rubbed my arms as a sudden chill had my skin pebbling.

"I will do that, Bitsy. I really will. I'm very interested in the history of the Belle. The bride's name . . ."

"Emma. Emma Bernard married Daniel Ruffin in the spring of 1861. Just a few days before the Battle of Fort Sumter." She lifted a napkin to pat her lips primly. Raising an eyebrow, she added, "We done won that first one, by the way," with a cocky twist of her head.

I leaned into Heath and his arm came around me as the room began to spin. I was trembling all over, and the whir of blood in my ears dulled all sound. For a moment, I was sure I was going to faint.

"Liv, are you alright? What's wrong?" he asked. Placing a finger under my chin, he turned me to face him. "My God, you're as pale as death."

"I . . . I think I need to go now. I'm not feeling very well—"

"Oh, my, Ms. Larson. What's come over you? Can I get you some water, maybe?" Bitsy leapt up and skirted the table toward me.

Heath helped me to my feet. "She's okay. Just hasn't been sleeping well lately," he told her. "I'd better get her home."

"She sure does look poorly of a sudden," she crooned, earnest concern coloring her words.

With Heath supporting my left side and Bitsy clamped onto my right elbow, we headed toward the patio door. We were only a few steps from the threshold when I looked up, froze and shrieked. Benjamin's gigantic form stepped out, blocking the doorway. I hadn't heard his heavy Bigfoot stomping. Had no idea how long he'd been standing there.

"Any more of them cookies left, Momma?"

Heath

Bitsy helped Heath hoist a limp and weak Liv up into the front seat of his truck. He had no idea what had suddenly come over her, but now had a clear understanding of how *she* must feel when his epilepsy caused *him* to zone out. Helpless. Confused, concerned, and helpless.

"Ya'll let us know if there's anything else we can do to help now, ya hear?" Bitsy said as Heath fired the engine.

He could see Benjamin watching intently from the front steps. *Damn,* he thought. *I never did get to address that part of the situation.* Liv honestly looked like she might faint on him at any minute, and he was sure having Ben staring at her only made things worse.

"I'll do that, Bitsy," he called as he backed the truck out onto the road. Then he turned to Liv, who was leaning heavily against the passenger door, her head propped on her hand. "What's wrong, Liv? What happened to you back there?"

She sucked in a stuttered breath before shifting to meet his eyes. "Heath, my soldier. My Confederate soldier . . . he talks to me. He tells me he's come home from war. He calls me . . . Emma."

Heath felt a chill run down his back. Shifting his gaze between Liv and the road, he stammered, "Well, surely . . . surely, that's a coincidence, right? You must have seen the name somewhere. At the museum. Or the library. When you went there to research the pin you bought, right?"

Liv had closed her eyes and was shaking her head. "I never found out anything about a woman named Emma. Your sister showed me the auction record. The pin was part of the estate of a man named Samuel Bernard."

Heath blinked. Wow, small world, he thought. But not really. Bitsy had said that family was one of the oldest ones in these parts. So why should the fact upset Liv so?

Liv continued. "The librarian . . . Mrs. Edington? She told me she knew this Bernard man. She worked for him years ago." She slid him a watery gaze. "Heath, Samuel Bernard owned the Belle Bride at one time."

Now the chill climbed around from his back to clench at his insides. He slammed on the brakes and skidded the big Ram pickup onto the gravel on the side of the road. Shifting in his seat to face her, he kept his voice level, calm.

"Okay, so the house stayed in the family. Until when? How long ago did this Bernard guy own the house?"

She had wrapped her arms around her middle as if she were freezing, even though it was a warm, humid May morning. Her hand was shaking violently as Liv lifted a fist to her mouth. Eyes wide, panicked, and shining with unshed tears, she looked positively spooked.

As if she'd seen a ghost, he thought wryly. Heath was beginning to wonder if maybe she had. Maybe they both had.

"Samuel Bernard sold the Belle Bride—or donated it—to the First National Bank of Birmingham in 1980. September 29th of 1980." Her voice was soft, quivering.

Heath raked a hand through his hair, his mind buzzing. Okay, so there were a few coincidences. The same man who owned the pin she bought had owned the Belle Bride. She'd also imagined this phantom soldier calling her Emma, the name of the original bride of the house. Surely, she'd come across the name somewhere and—"

"Heath, I can tell what you're thinking. I'm making a big deal over nothing here, right? Coincidences. Serendipity. Still, there's one more piece to the puzzle you don't know yet." She chewed on her knuckle, locking her gaze on his. "I was born that year, Heath. Same year, same day as Samuel Bernard sold the Belle Bride. My birthday is September 29, 1980."

"You're coming home with me. Staying at my place for a while," Heath said evenly as he pulled the truck back onto the road. It had taken several minutes for his heart to stop somersaulting in his chest after this last revelation. Too many connections, he thought. The situation had gone way beyond the definition of coincidence.

And there was just way too much weird shit happening at the Belle Bride for him to even consider leaving Liv alone there.

Liv nodded numbly, still chewing on one knuckle and staring straight ahead.

"Do you need to stop and get some more things?" Heath asked. "You didn't bring much with you last night." They had to drive right past the Belle Bride to get into town. To get to his place. Better to take care of that right now, while they were together. In daylight.

"Yeah," she answered weakly. "You'll come inside with me though, right?"

"Of course."

As they pulled up to the driveway Heath spotted the FedEx truck pulled alongside the road. A young man in a navy-blue shirt slashed with the purple company logo was striding back from the entryway to his vehicle. He paused when Heath rolled to a stop.

"Mornin'. Left you a package at the door." He touched the brim of his matching ball cap before leaping into the open cab of the boxy delivery van.

Heath glanced over at Liv, whose eyebrows had drawn together.

"You expecting something?" he asked.

She tipped her head, then suddenly brightened. "Oh.

Yeah. That's from Delphine. My friend in New York. I didn't think it would get here so quickly."

Heath pulled the rest of way up the drive and turned off the engine. A small, white box bearing FedEx's purple and white banner was leaning against the front door. Skirting the front fender, he opened Liv's door and asked, "A gift for your new home?"

Liv shook her head as she climbed down. "Nope. But hopefully, something that will tell me where home really is."

Twenty-Three

Liv

With my brain clouded by some kind of emotional fog, I lugged my travel bag and cosmetic case out of the closet and began tossing things in. I heard a tiny part of me—the independent, stubborn, emotionally armored part that had carried me down here—screaming from the back of my mind: *Don't give up. Don't move in with this man you hardly know so quickly. Stay the course.*

The bigger, more logical part bitch-slapped Ms. Tough Chick and told her to shut the hell up.

I needed some time away from this house with all the "sadness hangin' over it," as Bitsy had described. Sadness was the last thing I needed more of right now. Besides, I wasn't *moving in* with Heath. I was staying with a friend for a few days until I got my head wrapped around this thing. Until I could investigate the myriad of "coincidences" we'd discovered this morning.

Decide what I was going to do about the plantation-style, white elephant I'd spent a huge chunk of my savings on.

Heath wandered about the bedroom, hands shoved in his pockets, watching me sort through my clothes. I could sense his unease, and although he didn't push me, perceived his unspoken intention: *hurry up.*

I selected each item of clothing carefully, folded each one, and rolling it into a wrinkle-averting tube before tucking it into my sturdy TravelPro. Focus on the here and now, I told myself. Be present. It was the only way I could stay calm.

Heath scanned the room, the beautiful new Rice Bed, the armoire, the ornate lines of the Astral lamp on the chest beside my bed. Then he strolled toward the door leading out to the gallery, gazing out over the front lawn.

"It's such a shame. I know how much you'd had your heart set on this house. But until we figure out what's going on here, I'll feel much better with you at my place," he asserted.

It was his tone more than his words prickling my pride. I whirled on him.

"Don't make this sound like you're whisking off the helpless little lady to take care of her, Heath. I'm not made that way. Never have been," I snapped. "And I'm not about to accept the role now. I appreciate your offer to put me up for a few days, but—"

"Hey, hey, don't be like that," he murmured, coming to me and folding me against him. "I just want what's best for you, Liv. I don't mean to make you feel as if I'm trying to control you." He tipped up my chin and gazed deep into my eyes. "I'm trying to protect you. Is that so bad?"

A small corner of my heart melted. His eyes, those chocolate-caramel pools of sincerity, said more than his words. And what I saw there went beyond concern for a friend. Way beyond.

The tiny, independent Liv shifted uncomfortably in the back of my mind, readjusting her armor and lifting her shield. This was all happening way too fast. I heard warning bells going off in my head, and heard the door to my heart slam shut.

No. The slamming door wasn't in my imagination. I felt Heath stiffen as he glanced over the top of my head.

"Did you leave the front door ajar?" he asked in a hushed voice.

I shook my head and turned in his arms, not wanting to

leave the warm security of his embrace.

"No. I locked it behind us. That sounded like it came from somewhere inside the house."

A second later, from out in the hallway, we heard the knob for my office door squeak. I'd left it closed. Now it whined on its hinges as it opened of its own accord.

Heath stepped away from me. "You must have a window open somewhere," he said as he headed for the hallway.

That's when the cold swept in.

I knew we both felt it, because he jerked to a halt and glanced back over his shoulder. "Do you feel that?" he asked. His breath came out in visible puffs of steam.

It was nearly noon on a balmy spring day. The temperature on Heath's dashboard when we'd come in said it was eighty-five degrees. What the hell?

The sheen of sweat already covering my skin turned icy, and again, tendrils of fear began slithering up my spine. I rubbed my arms.

"How much longer? You almost ready?" Heath asked, his voice tight.

"My laptop. I just need to grab my laptop. It's in my office," I said, my voice unsteady.

He motioned for me to follow him. "We'll go in together."

I latched onto Heath's arm and clung close beside him into the hallway.

The office door was, in fact, standing wide open. Late morning bands of sunlight glinted off the shiny edge of my mahogany desk. My laptop lay closed on the leather-covered surface, right next to my new desktop monitor.

And through the window leading to the upper gallery,

I could see a man standing near the railing. His back was towards us. His wrinkled uniform was grey.

I sucked in on a gasp and froze in the doorway. "Do you see him?" I whispered.

Heath's entire body had gone stiff beside me. He nodded slowly. "I see him." He patted my hand that clutched his bicep. "You stay right here. I'll get your laptop."

The cold persisted, and Heath's words hung on the air in a wispy mist. I wrapped my arms around myself as a violent shudder racked my body, watching as he crept silently into the room. The form of the soldier seemed more solid now than ever before—I couldn't see through him at all. With a jolt of terror, I caught sight of the bayonet glinting in the sunlight atop the gun propped on the gallery railing beside him.

Heath succeeded in sliding the thin MacBook off my desk without making a sound, then slid it under his arm as he backed toward the doorway. I stepped aside to let him through. The soldier hadn't moved, yet hadn't disappeared either.

His strong fingers closing on my upper arm, Heath whispered, "Grab your bags. Let's get the hell out of here."

We were halfway to my bedroom door when I stopped short. "The brooch, Heath. I need to get the brooch." It had been on my desk, cradled in its velvet pouch, on the opposite side from my laptop.

Heath's eyes widened and he shook his head. "I'm not going back in there. Leave the damned brooch."

In that moment, the office door slammed shut, violently, echoing so loudly in the hall I covered my ears and stifled a scream. Heath shoved the laptop into my hands and strode past me into the bedroom, snatching up my suitcase and cosmetic bag. Together we crested the curved staircase.

And then again, we froze. Weeping—a woman's pitiful, nearly hysterical sobs rose to our ears from the lower level.

Heath had told me he'd heard a woman crying last night. This time, I could hear her too.

Fear turned my entire body to a block of stone. I couldn't move down another step, towards that awful sound of visceral pain echoing from the ground floor. Yet behind me, I knew, the soldier still stood sentry on the upper gallery. My knees wobbled and gave way. I slumped against the railing, sinking to sit on the top step.

Heath shoved the smaller bag under one arm to free a hand, then grabbed my arm and yanked me to my feet. "We have to get out of here. Now," he hissed, the steam from his breath curling from his lips. "Come on, Liv. I can't carry both you and your stuff."

With gargantuan effort, I stumbled to my feet, clinging desperately to Heath's arm. One step at a time, we descended the newly polished steps. As we did, the women's wailing escalated. I covered one ear with my free hand and pressed the other to Heath's shoulder to try to deaden the sound.

It was no use. The echoing sobs, just as Heath had described, seemed to seep out from the very walls of the house. Sadness, a deep, heart-rending grief wrapped itself around me, squeezing my heart until I felt tears streaming down my face. By the time we reached the foyer, the wail had transformed into a howl.

A dog's howl. Coming from behind the house.

We left the front door standing wide open as we stumbled down the steps. Heath tossed my bags into the bed of his truck and yanked open the passenger door, shoving me in. As he hurried around to the driver's side, I saw him steal a glance towards the upper gallery. I followed his gaze.

The soldier was gone.

Heath

Heath had always considered himself a sensible, well-grounded man. He had built his life, and his business, trusting common sense and logic to guide his way. It had worked out well for him thus far. Except for his debacle of a marriage—the one time he'd indulged in a fantasy. He hadn't planned on making the same mistake again.

Since Olivia Larson waltzed into his life, all bets were off.

She'd not only swept him off his proverbial feet, as well as his *actual* feet. She'd also introduced all sorts of wild weirdness into his sleepy, predictable country life. Leave it to a city girl . . .

Yet Liv didn't fit that mold. Everything about her screamed down-to-earth, sweet Southern lady. Yeah, she was some sort of software guru, and made her living doing something more complicated than baking cornbread, but underneath she was . . . genuine. Caring. Sentimental.

And, whether she liked it or not, vulnerable. That aspect of her personality brought out the valiant gentleman in him. Made him want to protect her.

The only way he knew how to shield her from the strange phenomenon surrounding the Belle Bride was to get her away from it.

He gunned the gas and spun out of her driveway as if his tailgate was on fire, his heart hammering in his chest. What the holy hell was going on in her house? Had Bitsy's relating of the sad legend surrounding the Belle Bride that morning gotten to them both, fired up their imaginations?

The logical, sensible part of him wanted to believe just that. He didn't believe in aliens, vampires, or ghosts. At least, not until this morning.

After he'd put a good three miles between them and the house, he glanced over at Liv, who hadn't made a sound since they'd screeched out onto the road. She was sitting stiffly, staring straight ahead, clutching her laptop to her chest. Her silky, straight hair was tumbled and tangled, sticking out in clumps at the back of her head. Tears were streaming silently down her face.

He reached over to touch her arm and she lurched and screamed.

"Geez, Liv. Calm down. It's me. Just me. We got out. We're safe now," he crooned.

When she met his eyes, hers were Anime wide and round. The thought crossed his mind: Is she in shock? Should I take her to the clinic?

Seconds later she shook herself out of it. Laying her laptop on the seat between them, she shifted in her seat, ground her knuckles into her eyes. He stroked gentle fingers down her arm. The goosebumps had not yet subsided.

Blowing out a breath, she said, "I wish it wasn't Sunday. The library is closed today, isn't it? I need to go talk to Mrs. Edington again. Get her to pull up those records for me."

Heath pressed his lips together. "Yup. Closed. Today and tomorrow." He could see her shoulders droop, and added, "I know where the Edington's farm is, Liv. I can take you there. If you want."

She straightened hopefully. "Could you? Right now?"

Twenty minutes later, Heath pulled his truck onto a long lane dividing two lush pastures edged with white, post-and-rail fencing. Halfway down the stretch, an ornate iron gate secured the property. Heath rolled down his window and pressed a red button on the speaker box just outside.

A few seconds passed before a squawk and static preceded a male voice coming through.

"Yes?"

"Clyde, this is Heath Barrow. I hate to bother you on a Sunday, but I was wondering if we might speak to Florence for a few moments. It's important," Heath said.

Almost immediately, the voice boomed through the box. "Heath! Glad you're here. I'll buzz you through."

"Wow," Liv said, staring at Heath. "I guess pretty little Scarlett grew up on Tara for real."

Heath shot her a lopsided grin. "Yeah, the librarian thing is sort of a hobby for the Edington women, I think. Clyde made his fortune in the stock market—both kinds. Shares *and* cattle."

The Edington's farmhouse—if one could downgrade it to that description—was more of a sprawling, country manor. Two levels were punctuated by a dozen or more windows, it seemed, lining the wraparound porch and peaked, second-floor gable. A brick chimney anchored the left side of the house, while the right featured a hexagonal bump-out linking both stories. An elegant stained glass oval graced the center of the peak, framed in iron scrollwork.

Liv's initial "Wow" reaction escalated to "Holy crap. This *is* Tara."

Heath pulled his truck onto the paved pad in front of an attached, four-bay garage and parked. "Not Tara. Not nearly as old. Clyde built this house for Florence just a few years ago. It's vintage-*new*."

"A repro," Liv murmured. "What I should have looked for. Or built. No chance for any old tragedy staining this foundation."

One half of the double front entry door swung open before they'd even reached the top step. Standing there, dressed in a fluttery pink dress with her dark hair tumbling down over her shoulders, was Ruthie Edington.

Heath swallowed the lump of embarrassment that

threatened to gag him. Growing up in Camellia, he'd been friendly with the Edingtons almost all of his life. Spent countless hours in the library, begging Florence's help to finish a last-minute research paper. Sat in the same pew with Ruthie, her parents, her grandparents at church. Before he'd quit going. He almost couldn't believe he'd had the gall, the gumption to ask their little Ruthie to lunch the other day with thoughts of—

"Good morning, Heath. Ms. Larson. What brings you folks out this way on a Sunday morning?" Ruthie glanced down at the dainty watch on her left wrist. Now, there was no missing the sparkle of the formidable-sized rock adorning her ring finger. "Or afternoon by now, I should say. Come on in."

Heath swallowed again and placed his hand at the small of Liv's back. "Thank you, Ruthie. Is your grandmother busy?"

Ruthie ushered them in and through their gigantic sitting room, with the massive brick hearth anchoring the wall. Just beyond, a wide hallway lined with gleaming, wide oak boards led to what Heath knew they called their family room: a combination kitchen, dining, and sitting area that spanned the entire width of the building.

He'd been here a few times since they built the house. In fact, some of the classic, antique pieces dotting the room here and there had come from his shop. The architectural design never ceased to impress him.

Florence was taking something out of the massive oven —one of two—that smelled like heaven with vanilla and cinnamon candles burning on every cloud. She straightened and turned to greet them, a huge smile brightening her wizened features.

"Well isn't this a nice surprise," she exclaimed. "I was just saying to Ruthie, it's such a shame we went to the trouble to bake this big old sour cream coffee cake and it's just us three. Heath Barrow, don't tell me you didn't smell it baking from out there on the highway." She grinned.

The tension eased out of Heath's shoulders a bit and he said, "No, ma'am. But I sure wouldn't mind helping you folks get rid of it."

Twenty-Four

Liv

The grandeur of the Edington's home—their warm, welcoming hospitality, and the comforting scent of coffee cake on the air—laid a blanket of balm over the terrifying morning I'd experienced. *We'd* experienced. I was glad Heath had brought me here, and not just for the information I hoped I could glean from Florence's experience. I accepted the coffee and slice of warm cinnamon cake Ruthie handed me and settled next to Heath at their long, trestle table.

"So, what brings you folks out this way?" Florence echoed her granddaughter's question as she joined us.

When I didn't say anything right away, Heath cleared his throat and shot me a glance. "Liv here was wondering if she might bother you with some questions about local history, Florence. I know it's your day off, and we hate to bother you on a Sunday, but Liv was real anxious—"

"I've discovered a couple of odd coincidences since I moved into the Belle Bride, Ms. Edington. Florence," I corrected when she scowled at me over her coffee cup. "Remember the pin I brought to show you the other day?"

Florence set down her cup and nodded. "The piece Samuel Bernard owned. I remember." Her face had drawn to serious, yet I could read no other reaction.

"Didn't you work for him at one time, Grammy?" Ruthie asked, her forkful of cake poised halfway to her mouth.

"Long time ago, Ruthie. You were no more'n a baby,"

Florence confirmed.

I slid Heath a glance for courage, and he nodded almost imperceptibly. I plowed on. "Well, I wonder how well you knew Mr. Bernard. I mean to say, his family. It seems," I paused to take a deep breath, "It seems I've discovered that Mr. Bernard was a deed owner of the Belle Bride. My house. At one time."

Florence's unkempt white eyebrows lifted, but she kept her gaze down on her cake. "That's true, I believe. In fact, we discussed this the other day."

"Did you know him when he owned it?" I asked hopefully.

Still avoiding eye contact, she shook her head slowly side to side. "As I told you before, Ms. Larson, Mr. Bernard no longer owned the Belle Bride when I worked for him."

I huffed out a breath. Damn. I'd so hoped to speak to somebody else who'd been in the house, who might know more about the strange happenings there.

"Did he ever talk to you about the house?" I asked, probing. I could see I was overstepping the older woman's comfort zone, as she set down her fork and folded her hands under her chin, elbows resting on the table. She refused to meet my eyes.

The former relaxed warmth in the room had suddenly drained away, leaving a silent chill in its wake.

When Florence finally did raise her gaze to mine, there was a sternness there. A closed off look. "Mr. Bernard was a very private person, Ms. Larson. He didn't really share much about any of his business dealings, nor his family life with anyone. And whatever he did share with me, he trusted me not to make public knowledge."

Whoa, I thought. If this doesn't smell like a scandal, I don't know what does. Of course, if Bernard had a financial interest in the house, he wouldn't want any rumors of *ghoulish activity* spread around. Still, it didn't make any sense. From what she was saying, by the time Florence worked for him, he'd already sold the house.

Or given it away.

Florence's husband, who'd been uncomfortably silent throughout the interchange, suddenly pushed his empty cake plate away from him. "What time is it we're supposed to help set up for the church picnic?" he asked, his voice tight. He made a show of checking his watch.

"Two o'clock, Grampa," Ruthie offered in a small voice as she rose to clear away his plate and cup. "We have time."

Panic began to bloom in my chest like wildfire. The last thing I wanted to do was to alienate one of the few people who had known, actually *known* Samuel Bernard. I sipped my coffee and switched gears.

"The cake is out of this world, Florence. I'd love to have the recipe, if it's not a secret family one," I said, forking up another mouthful.

Her shoulders softened and a shy smile eased her features. "I'd love to share it. Come on in to the library on Tuesday and I'll have a copy of it printed out for you."

By the time they saw us to the door, the relaxed, congenial atmosphere had returned to the Edington house. Clyde pumped Heath's hand and asked him to let him know the next time he snagged a treasure at auction. Ruthie squeezed my fingers, then reached up to plant a demure kiss on Heath's cheek. Florence offered her hand to me easily enough, but her gaze was guarded.

"Florence, one more thing," I added as we stepped out the door. "Bitsy . . . you know, Betty . . . Warren? She told me you had access to some old records on plantations in the area. The families that owned them. Used to be on microfiche, but she says you can get them online. Can you?"

Again, Florence, after an initial bowing up, seemed to relax a bit, retreating into her area of expertise. One she felt comfortable discussing. "Yes, I can. There's a big database at the University of North Carolina where they digitized all the old Plantation records. What is it you're looking for?"

"I'd like what you can find about the Bernard family. Way back," I added quickly, holding up a hand when I saw her eyebrow quirk. "Back when they owned the Belle Bienvenue. Back in the 1800s."

Heath

Liv seemed much more relaxed, more upbeat by the time they pulled into Heath's driveway. He'd stopped in town, made her sit down and order a meal at Nan's Diner. Even after the sweet treat they'd enjoyed at the Edington's, he knew he needed to get some real food into her. The trauma of the day had taken its toll on both of them.

After a bowl of Nan's special homemade chicken stew, along with a chunk of good, fresh cornbread, she had more color in her cheeks. Heath breathed a little easier to see it.

He helped her carry in her things, and pushed the limited contents of his oversized closet to one side.

"Plenty of room in here to hang whatever you need."

Then he quickly condensed the contents of two drawers in his bureau—one for underwear, one for socks—into one.

"Second drawer from the top is all yours, too, Liv," he said. "If you need more room, just let me know—"

"Stop." She stood in the doorway of his bedroom with one palm outstretched. "Stop, Heath. I'm not moving in. I'm just bunking here for a few days. Until I get my feet under me again. If you'd rather I move into your guest room—"

"No," he barked, "*you* stop." He crossed the few feet between them to fold her against him. "We're more than just friends, Olivia Larson, and you know it. You may not be quite ready to accept the fact yet, but it's gospel. You'd better start getting used to it."

Her initial stiffness eased, bit by bit, until she molded herself against him. "I'm just so confused, Heath. So much has gone wrong with this move. There's so much I don't understand."

He smoothed a hand down over her hair. "I know, babe. I also know this: You're here in Camellia for a reason. Of that much, I'm completely sure. I can't explain how, or why. This . . . us . . . we're more than a coincidence. You didn't just throw a dart at the map to land here in Camellia, Alabama."

She dropped her head back, blinking. A whimsical smile lit up her features. "How did you know?"

"Know what?" he asked, confused.

"That I ended up here from throwing a dart at a map?"

"You're kidding, right?" he said with a quirky grin.

When she shook her head slowly without saying another word, his shoulders lifted and dropped on a deep breath. Tipping his head forward until their brows met, he closed his eyes and said, "Well, then."

They spent the rest of the afternoon enjoying a balmy breeze under his arbor that made the wisteria blooms dance and sway. He spoke of his family, and his childhood in the sleepy town of Camellia. How his epilepsy had made him a kind of outcast in school, and so, he'd embraced the role of loner. His life had revolved around family, and building his hobby of cruising yard sales and estate sales into a business. Gradually, his parents and siblings dispersed to distant towns to continue their lives.

Except Cynthia. She'd stayed in Birmingham, and so, remained his closest confidante.

"I got lonely. I suppose it's only natural. Cynthia has her own life, a live-in significant other who she's been with now for over a decade. So, one night I took a chance, and asked out the daughter of one of the dealers I worked with. Kathleen grew up in Birmingham, and had just come back from Atlanta, from Emory. Had her a fancy business degree and a lot of ambition. I love the antiques business . . . the treasure hunt part. What I needed someone who could help me manage it. And a companion. I thought for sure we were a match made in heaven." He sighed wistfully. "Didn't work out quite the way I'd planned."

"The epilepsy, and her love of city life," she said with a sad smile. "That's why she left you, Heath. It wasn't you, or anything about you."

"You're probably right." He straightened and bristled. "And being a country boy, *and* epilepsy—they're both *part* of who I am. I'll never choose to live in the city. And I'm not crazy about my condition, nor can I control it. That's just the way it is."

She came to him then and laid her head on his shoulder. "It scared me at first. I'll admit that. Josh . . . his cancer. The symptoms started just like your seizures do. I didn't have time to adjust or brace myself when Josh got sick. I couldn't do anything except cope with one day at a time. Before I knew it, he didn't know who I was. And then, he was gone. I was alone."

"Oh, Liv. I'm so sorry."

He held her, rocking her gently as he breathed in the scent of her, buried his face in her hair. He finally understood why she'd reacted so coldly. Run out on him in a seemingly heartless gesture. Liv had been reacting on instinct. From a learned response. A sad, tragically learned lesson. Protecting a wound still raw inside her heart.

He opened a bottle of wine about three o'clock, and by six, it was gone. They were both feeling languid and very familiar. Very comfortable with each other. He'd settled in the wicker rocker at the end of his porch, and she was sitting on the floor, on a pillow he'd dragged out from the sofa. Her head rested in his lap.

As the afternoon shadows grew long in Heath's backyard, they sat in a quiet, companionable silence for a long time. For a while Heath wondered if Liv had fallen asleep as he stroked his hands over her hand and down her back. She'd relaxed completely now, and the rise and fall of her shoulders was even and steady. Finally, she stirred, lifting her head with dazed, sleepy eyes. She searched his face.

"You know what my biggest problem is, Heath? I mean, losing my husband, the way I did, well, it was horrible. Yet now I don't think it wasn't the beginning of this . . . this identity crisis I've been going through. Hell, when I think about it, I've been going through that all of my life." She clambered to her knees, yawned and stretched.

"What do you mean?" Heath asked. "You said your foster parents were good to you."

She shimmied up to snug her body between his knees, then wrapped her arms around his waist and laid her cheek against his chest.

"Heath, I don't know who I am. Who I'm supposed to be. My friend, Delphine, she works in a DNA lab that specializes in ancestry analysis. She's been trying to convince me to do the analysis for years. Says I'm suffering from a lack of what she calls *cultural identity*."

"So, why haven't you? At least then you'd have some idea of where your family came from. Maybe you're not really a native New Englander. Maybe it's why you never felt at home there," Heath murmured. "You might even find out who your birth mother is. I think there's a way to unlock those records now—"

"No," Liv snapped, pushing up to her feet. "That's a road I definitely don't want to go down." She strode away from him, to the edge of the patio, and leaned up against one of the arbor posts. With her arms crossed, her back to him, she grumbled, "My mother didn't want me then, and most certainly wouldn't want to hear from me now. She was only fifteen, Heath. A kid. She never even held me, my parents said. Popped me out and walked away."

Heath jumped up and went to her, wrapped himself

around her and laid his cheek against her neck. "Young people make mistakes, Liv. If she didn't want you, you're lucky to be standing here at all. She could have gotten rid of you before you ever took a breath. And if she was only a kid, who knows what kind of life you would have had?"

She sighed. "So. I'm a mistake. That's my cultural identity."

He turned her to face him. "You are not a mistake. You are a beautiful, intelligent, vibrant human being. You're independent and courageous, yet generous and tender in here." He tapped her chest with his fist, gazing deep into her eyes. "You're a woman who has set my heart on fire. And one, I hope, who will someday care for me in the same way."

Her beautiful blue eyes filled and her lip trembled. "Del said it best, Heath. *You can't love somebody else until you learn to love yourself first.* In order for me to love myself, I need to know who that person is. I'm not *just* the adopted daughter of a nice couple from Boston. Not *just* the wife—the widow—of an esteemed Manhattan attorney. More than a geeky creative whose palette is a keyboard." A tear slipped out and trickled down her cheek. Stubbornly, she ignored it and kept her eyes riveted on his.

He gripped both of her shoulders and gave her little shake. "Do the DNA test, Liv. Find out what you can . . . you don't have to find *her*, physically, to get a grip on your familial background." He stroked the tear away with his thumb. "I don't know much about the process, Liv. I do know a lot of people are doing it, and I know in some way, for some reason, it makes them feel more complete. More whole."

Liv squeezed her eyes shut and nodded. "That's what Del says. It's why she sent me the kit." Her lids fluttered open and she glanced toward the kitchen. "Where did we put the FedEx package, anyway? We brought it with us, right?"

Heath ran his fingers along her jawline, nodding. "I put it

in the bathroom. I had no idea how those things work . . . what kind of sample you needed to collect." His lips quivered into an embarrassed smile.

She giggled and covered her face with one hand. "Just a few skin cells off the inside of my cheek, is all. They sent a swab."

He bent to cover her mouth with his, reveling in the smell of her, the heady exhilaration of her submission when she opened her lips to him. It felt right. This all, somehow, felt like it was the way it was supposed to be.

When he broke the kiss, he nipped her lower lip before flashing a devilish grin. "Better brush your teeth and use some mouthwash before you do the cheek swab," he said, "or the results will come back showing you and I are somehow related."

Liv dropped her head back and smiled. "In the morning. We can't mail the thing until tomorrow anyway. Tonight," she combed her fingers into his hair, "tonight, Mr. Heath Barrow, I want you and I to indulge in a little more interesting kind of fluid exchange. If you don't mind." She waggled her eyebrows, and Heath's heart squeezed.

God, I love this woman. The thought shocked him, yet felt strangely familiar. He'd known, deep inside, he'd fall in love with this city girl the minute she'd strolled into his shop that morning. Slurping on her cup of cold coffee.

For better, or for worse.

Twenty-Five

Liv

Over the next few days, time slowed to a snail's pace. I was living in limbo. Literally. I'd sent the DNA kit back to Delphine, who'd assured me even though test results usually took six to eight weeks, my sample wouldn't take that long— she would push it through as a rush. Still, I shouldn't expect any kind of answer for at least two or three days, a week at most.

On Tuesday, I went in to visit Florence at the library. She handed me a folded sheet of paper containing the recipe for her coveted sour cream coffee cake. Then she patiently explained that procuring the records from the Antebellum Plantation Database I'd asked for would take a few days.

"I should have whatever they can find by Friday," she said as she wrote down my cell number. "It could be up to fifty pages, you know," she added, studying me over her readers. "The library gets ten cents a page."

Aside from going back with Heath to retrieve my own vehicle, we steered clear of the Belle Bride. Another situation in limbo. I owned a big, old plantation home, yet was afraid to live in it. What I was going to do about that, I tried to push to the back of my mind.

Talk about an identity crisis. Now I not only didn't know who I really was or where I came from, but I was, essentially, homeless.

So, I threw myself into my work. Heath cleared a spot for me in a corner of his shop, and let me set up my laptop on one of his vintage roll top desks. I began work on his website. It was comforting, familiar to be back in my element.

We fell into a kind of routine—living in the same house, working in the same space every day. Heath greeted me each morning with a hot cup of coffee, a smile, and a kiss. We ate lunch together at Nan's Diner. In the evening, we shared wine as we sat on his lovely patio, watching each day fade away into night.

It only took a few days for the walls to start closing in around me.

"I can't believe how much easier it is to find things on the site now," Heath said, peering over my shoulder. It was early Friday afternoon, and I was putting the finishing touches on the navigation bar for the HH website. He kissed the top of my head and gave me a little squeeze. "The business is going to bloom like crazy now. We make a fantastic team, Liv."

I bristled. "You do realize, once I'm finished with your site, I do have other clients. My *own* business. Eventually, I'll have a place of my own again. I won't always be here, huddled in a borrowed corner of your shop." I shot him a level gaze. "I'm not all yours."

There was a long pause before he swiveled my chair around and crouched down beside me. "Hey. I understand you want to maintain your autonomy. I get that. Still, haven't you been happy these past few days, Liv? Living with me? Spending your days with me?" He tucked a strand of hair behind my ear. "And nights?" he added with a mischievous grin.

I sighed and closed my eyes. "I can't tell you how much I appreciate your putting me up the past week, Heath. You've been very supportive. Very kind. I guess, if it hadn't been for you, I'd be on my way back to New York by now."

He blinked and started as if I'd slapped him. "Don't say that. I know it's not what you really want. You told me that.

You said you didn't feel at home there anymore—"

"I don't feel at home anywhere, Heath. I'm a homeless, mongrel bitch who's using her body and her laptop to keep a roof over her head and food in her belly." Anger, resentment surged up in my chest so fast it took me by surprise.

It wasn't Heath's fault I was in this position. It was nobody's fault except my own. Regardless, the helplessness I was feeling had reached a peak. My self-esteem, a new low. He just happened to be the only, unlucky one I could vent on.

"Whoa, whoa, Liv. Baby, don't say that," he rose, pulling me to my feet. But when he went to wrap his arms around me, I spun away.

"I'm not your baby, Heath. I'm not *anybody's* baby." I started pacing, back and forth from the reception counter and back to my temporary corner nook. "That's part of the problem. Don't you see? I made a huge mistake coming here to Alabama. Spent a good chunk of my savings on a house that's cursed. I have nowhere to live, nowhere to work . . . and besides you, I don't know anybody. I'm all alone in the middle of nowhere."

Heath stood stiffly, watching me pace, listening to me rant, a pained and almost panicked expression contorting his features. A flash of guilt shot through me. I hoped my tantrum didn't trigger another one of his seizures. Wonderful. A fresh, new worry to heap itself on top of desperation, on top of a torturous, aching loneliness twisting my stomach into a writhing knot.

Steeling myself, I decided I couldn't worry about Heath right now. I barely had enough strength to stay afloat in the sea of warring emotions inside my own head. After several long, uncomfortable moments of silence, I grabbed my purse.

"I need some air," I mumbled as I headed for the door.

"Liv?" The pain in Heath's tone broke through my haze of

despair. I stopped, but did not turn to face him. "I love you."

I squeezed my eyes shut, swallowing the ball of tears threatening to overtake me. After sucking in a shaky breath, I choked out, "How can you possibly love me? You don't even know who I am."

I burst out onto the street, the late morning sun blinding me. I'd head to the library, I thought. It was Friday. Florence said she would have those records for me today. Maybe she hadn't had time to call me yet to let me know.

When the lyrical notes of Beethoven's Bagatelle began drifting out form inside my purse, I thought, *There's Florence calling me now.*

No. The caller ID read *Delphine.*

Del's warm, familiar voice wafted into my ear. "Olivia darling? I've got some preliminary test results for you."

I stopped walking. Breathing. Thinking. Did I want to know what Del was going to tell me? Was it going to help me in my present situation? Or just make things worse?

After a deep breath, I said, "Well?"

"These are just the preliminaries, now Liv. I'll have more detailed information for you soon," She paused. "It's almost noon here. Little chance I'll get the rest today. I have to admit, what I see so far surprises me." Del's voice was smooth and even. She didn't sound surprised, or excited.

Of course, this is what she did for a living. She was in her technical persona. Her comfort zone.

"What, Del? What do they show?"

"Well, we know you were born in a Boston hospital, right? UMass, I think you said. If your mother was local to New England, chances are very good there would be a lot of Irish in your background. English, too. That's what I expected to find. Instead, it seems you're more than fifty percent French, and the rest is . . . Scottish."

I blinked. French and Scottish. "Okay, so what does *that* mean?"

"It still means you may well be a native New Englander. Lots of French Canadians migrated into New England in the late 1800s. All the industrialized areas, including New York. We'll know more when the rest of the results come through." She paused, then added, "Manhattan may be the home you've been looking for all along."

After ending the call, I felt numb and more than a little disappointed. I really didn't know any more than I had before. And the thought I really did have roots . . . at least genetically, in the place I'd run away from was unsettling.

If New England truly was my home, why had I felt so certain, when I'd found the Belle Bride here in Camellia, that this was where I belonged?

I was relieved to see Florence sitting at her desk, readers slid halfway down her nose, when I came into the library. She glanced up as I approached and her face brightened.

"Oh, Liv. I was just going to call you. I have those records you were asking about. They came through about a half-hour ago," she said, evening the stack of papers she'd been studying. "Only twenty-two pages, but hopefully they will contain at least some of the information you're looking for."

I spent the next three hours bent over pages of tiny print, some of it blurred, some completely illegible. Apparently, preservation of documents has come a long way in the past however many years. I was grateful; at least, they'd been saved. Scanned to microfiche sometime in the twentieth century, and then digitized within the last couple of decades.

For the most part, the records on the Belle Bride provided me with few bits of information I didn't already know. There were lots of dates and names, clippings from newspaper articles. It took me hours, literally, to stumble on pay dirt. My blood chilled to ice in my veins when I came across a biographical note on the family who'd originally owned the Belle Bienvenue. The family that had built the Belle Bride.

RECORDS OF ANTE-BELLUM SOUTHERN PLANTATIONS FROM THE REVOLUTION THROUGH THE CIVIL WAR.

Series H

Selections from the

Southern Historical Collection, Manuscripts Department,

Library of the University of North Carolina at Chapel Hill

Part 7: Alabama

Biographical Note

Adam Bernard (1825-1886), a lawyer from Birmingham who became chief justice of the Alabama Supreme Court, was married to Olivia Kirkland in 1845 and settled in Camellia where her family's home, Belle Bienvenue, was located. Bernard's only child, a daughter, Emma, married Daniel Ruffin (1840-1863), a renowned horseman and soldier who trained cavalry mounts for the Confederate army. Bernard built and gifted the couple with a smaller version of the Bienvenue, the Belle Bride, along with a fine albino stallion and a valued walker hound sire. Emma and Daniel had one child, Adalene, who outlived both of her parents to marry Alastair Brodie in 1883.

Heath

After Liv stormed out of the shop, Heath stood there for a long moment, staring after her. An old, familiar ache began deep in his chest. Damned fool, he'd done it again. Fallen in love with a city girl who was untouchable, unreachable, and incapable of returning the kind of love he offered.

Another one who was most likely making plans right now for her return trip to Manhattan.

He combed shaking fingers through his hair and stumbled to his desk. A twitch started in the corner of his left eye, and he swore. At least, he thought grimly, it hadn't been the epilepsy that had driven Liv away from him. Sentenced him, again, to a life of solitude. Not this time.

Liv didn't return to Heath's shop until almost closing time. To retrieve her laptop, he thought. She didn't say anything to him as she slipped through the door and headed for her corner desk. She had a thick, manila envelope tucked under one arm.

Probably real estate contract papers, he thought. She's probably been busy putting her house back on the market.

"Liv? You okay?" he asked.

She slid him a glance, her face impassive. "I'm fine. Sorry . . . I've been at the library. Florence got me the records on my house."

"And?" he asked. "Any answers there?"

She sighed, plopping the manila envelope down on the desk. "Maybe. Some more eerie coincidences, I figure." Maddeningly, she didn't elaborate.

They drove home in an uncomfortable silence. There were so many questions Heath wanted to ask. So much he wanted to say. Still, he didn't want to push her. God knew, the last thing he wanted to do was to drive her any further away than she'd already drifted.

She was slipping away from him, like sand through his fingers. The thought slashed at his heart with razor-sharp swipes. How could he have allowed this to happen to him, again? How could he have been so blind?

Grimly, he admitted that part of him knew—when it came to Liv Larson, he'd simply had no choice in the matter. She stepped into his shop one morning six weeks ago and walked out with his heart.

"I've got some steaks in the fridge," he said as they pulled in his driveway. "I'll grill them up for us."

She nodded but didn't say a word as she gathered her things and climbed out of his truck before he'd even had a chance to open her door.

Heath seasoned the rib eyes, tossed a simple salad, and opened a bottle of Cabernet while Liv holed up in his bedroom. He'd heard the shower go off a half-hour ago, and wondered what she was doing in there all this time. Probably packing, he mused. Gathering all her things to make a quick getaway first thing in the morning.

Maybe so. But one thing he knew for sure: He had her for at least one, last night. One more night to persuade her to stay. Convince her that his feelings for her were genuine, no matter who she was or where she came from. He didn't care about any of that. He loved her, dammit. And by God, he was going to give winning her heart his best shot.

When Liv finally crept out of his bedroom, she was wearing her customary loungewear: pull-on shorts and a long tee shirt. This one was whimsical, striped in bright pink with Gandhi's famous words emblazoned on the front.

Where There is Love, There is Life.

Does her choice indicate a lighter mood, he wondered? Or has she just run out of clean clothes to wear?

She shuffled into the kitchen barefoot, and smiled shyly up at him from under her curtain of damp, golden hair. Heath thought for sure his heart was going to tear open, right then, right there, and bleed out on the spot. He managed a watery smile.

"Hey," she said. "You cook. A man who cooks." Her gaze swept over the counter, where the steaks lay waiting under plastic wrap for their trip to the grill. The salad. The open bottle of Fox Run Cabernet with two glasses, one empty, one nearly so. Sighing, she lifted the empty glass. "I'll take some, please."

He pulled the stopper free and poured, refilling his own glass too. "I figured you might like this wine," he said. "It's from a New York winery. A little taste of home."

She laid her hand over his. "Stop, Heath. I don't have a home. Not yet. I'm still searching for one."

It took two, long swallows of his wine before he mustered the courage to ask, "Does this mean I'm not out of the picture yet?"

He locked gazes with her, and those blue, Anime eyes shone with unshed tears. "No. You're the only anchor that's kept me stable these past few weeks. Since I got here. I'm not about to let go. Not just yet." She set down her wine glass and glided around the counter toward him. "Don't give up on me, Heath. Please, don't let me go."

He'd barely gotten his wine glass set back down on the counter when she engulfed him. There was really no other word for it, Heath thought, as her mouth covered his and her fingers raked into his hair. She tasted like minty toothpaste and sin. Pressing the entire length of her body to his, she pushed until he lost his balance and staggered back a step. She walked him backwards until he collided with the refrigerator.

It was as though she was trying to insinuate herself,

her entire being into his. Hungry mouth over his, her tongue invaded in a desperate, not-so-gentle dance. He could feel the stiff nubs of her nipples through the cloth of her shirt and his. Her fingers ran over him, everywhere, stroking, kneading, pleading. Demanding.

She bit his lower lip, and he growled. Instantly rock hard, Heath grabbed her soft round bottom with both hands and lifted her. Her legs wrapped around his waist in a vise grip.

Breathless, between feral kisses, he gasped, "You don't want to eat first?"

He felt her lips curve up in a devilish smile. "Yes, I do."

Somehow, he knew it wasn't steak and salad she was hungry for.

Chapter Twenty-Six

Liv

Like a loose balloon in the park, I thought. On a windy day. It described exactly how I'd been feeling lately. Longer than lately. For most of my life. I didn't want to feel that way anymore.

I longed to be tethered. Not tied up in bondage or anything like that, but joined, *really joined*, to another human being. Heart, mind, body, soul. Heath's words had spun around in my head all afternoon.

. . . you're here for a reason. Of that much, I'm completely sure. I can't explain how, or why. This . . . us . . . we're more than a coincidence.

Did I believe him? I wanted to. Soon, hopefully, I would know for sure. For now, I wanted what Heath was offering.

He carried me to his bedroom as I clung to him, my body ravenously hungry, and my heart soft and malleable. I loved the smell of him, the tickle of his chocolate brown curls on my cheek. The way his heartbeat thudded against my chest, his hot breath coming fast on my neck. The way his big, strong hands cupped my bottom, squeezing and molding me to him.

Tonight, I wanted us to be one in every conceivable sense of the word. I wanted—needed, to feel complete. Heath seemed willing, so . . .

I'd never made love quite like this before—I'd always been more the beta partner. More passive than aggressive. Oh, I was willing to give as good as I got. But tonight, I was too hungry, too desperate to wait for cues. For tonight's dance, I would lead.

We crashed down on his bed and I rolled him under me, tearing at his shirt, the buttons flying everywhere. I descended on him with lips and tongue and teeth, his mouth, his neck, his earlobe. His hands ran up and down my back, into my hair, as his moans fired my fury.

I slid down, working my way across his chest, kissing, licking, nipping. I was panting now, too, and wild and dizzy with passion. When I got to the waistband of his jeans, I gave it a tug.

"Get them off, Heath. Get them out of my way. I want to taste you all over."

He groaned and immediately complied. Within seconds, there he was. Every gorgeous, masculine inch of him, lying there beneath me, before me. His eyes locked on mine.

"Liv, let me please you first. I don't know how long I can —"

I didn't give him the chance to finish the sentence before I was on him, around him, fingers, lips, tongue. He groaned and scratched at the coverlet beneath us, fisting it in his hands. When I'd stroked and teased and tasted until his body quivered, I stopped.

I looked up. "Are you okay?" I needed to be sure it was pleasure and not a seizure gripping him. He cupped my face in his hands, hair wild, pupils blown and dark, panting.

"Never better. But almost there." He was breathless, desperate, pleading.

In the next moment, he'd flipped me under him. "My turn," he growled.

Bruises, I thought. I'll have bruises from all the places on my breasts, my belly, my thighs where he sucked and suckled and nibbled playfully with his teeth. Love bruises. He was marking me, as I had him.

I shattered within seconds after his tongue slithered up the inside of my thigh and hit its target.

There was no interlude, no time to catch my breath. In one swift move, he was above me, on me, plunging into me. He took me, joining us with one rapid, hard thrust that stole my breath and made my muscles quiver. Then he stilled for one, breathless moment. Pain sharpened my senses when he yanked my head back, his fingers wound in my hair.

Dark, wet tendrils hung around his face as he hovered over me, sweat trickling off the ends to tickle my skin. When he spoke, his words came out gruff, punctuated by panting that heaved his chest.

"Do you want me, Olivia Larson? All of me? Heart, mind, body, soul—"

I dug my nails hard into the flesh of his buttocks and bucked beneath him. "Yes. Take me, Heath. Ravage me, hold me, keep me. Take me up with you."

And he did.

I barely heard it, Beethoven's Bagatelle singing from inside my purse out in the kitchen. It might be Del with more news, I thought lazily. I'll call her back. I didn't want to move, to end this precious, soul-soaking moment. Our ragged breaths had barely subsided, and we were still joined.

Still joined, I thought with a clutching in my belly. I squeezed my eyes shut. Still joined, skin to skin, with nothing separating us. No protection.

Tonight, we really had exchanged some serious body fluids.

Heath propped himself up and gazed down at me, brushing the hair back off my face. "I didn't hurt you, did I?"

I shook my head. "You gave as good as you got," I murmured. "But you gave me . . . everything."

He blinked, confused. When realization dawned, he groaned, squeezing his eyes shut as he dropped his forehead to rest on mine. "I'm sorry. I got caught up. You were wild and feral and my brain shut down . . ." He lifted his head studied my eyes. "I love you, Liv. No matter what. I will always love you—"

Again, Beethoven's Bagatelle. I huffed out a breath. "I'd better get that," I mumbled. "Del said she'd call if she got the rest of the results. And trust me, if it's her? She won't give up until I answer."

Sure enough, it was Del. I stood in the kitchen wearing only my tee shirt when I called her back. Her agitated voice rattled into my ear the minute she picked up. She didn't even bother to say hello.

"Liv, you're not going to believe this. I can't believe it myself. It's just freaking weird, it is."

"I take it you got the rest of my ancestry panel?" I cut in. "Or, wait, no . . . you just saw a spaceship land on the top of Trump Tower."

Del snorted. "Yeah. Possible, but no. Sorry. Ancestry panel. The lab couldn't hone it down to single alleles. Not yet, anyway. We did get some pretty close matches on the genomes. Three family lines. I've got names—three surnames. And their origins." She paused and blew out a breath. "I can't believe it, Liv. They're all from the South. Mississippi, Louisiana, and Alabama."

My knees went to jelly and I plopped down onto the counter stool. Good thing it was there or I'd have hit the floor like a brick. I swallowed and then choked out, "I was born in Boston."

"Doesn't matter where you were born, Liv. Your mother, and most likely your father too, their families, were from down there. Somewhere within a few hundred miles, most likely, of where your dart landed on that blasted map."

My heart was slamming against my ribs and I felt suddenly lightheaded. I propped my head against my palm as I asked, "What are the names, Del? The surnames?"

I heard paper rustling before her next words. "Bernard, Martin, and Willard."

The phone slid from my hand and clattered onto the countertop. As I melted off the stool, the world whirling around me, the last thing I remembered was the sensation of warm, strong arms encircling my waist.

Heath

A towel wrapped around his waist after his shower, Heath followed the sound of Liv's voice out into the kitchen. She was holding her head as if she'd gotten some horrific news, yet was speaking so quietly he couldn't make out the words. He froze in the hallway, uncertain. Should he creep back into the bedroom until she was through? Respect her privacy?

Before he could decide, he saw the phone drop from her hand. He sprinted three, long strides to catch her before her head hit his ceramic tile floor.

She came to almost immediately after he laid her on his sofa. He was crouched over her when her lashes fluttered, her eyes darting wildly about for a moment before they found his face. Then she blinked and reached for him.

"Oh, Heath. I can't believe it. The tests show I'm from here. My family lines are from the South." She hugged his neck.

He pulled back and squinted at her. "You're not a Barrow, are you?" he asked, one brow cocked. "Or an Anderson? That's my mother's maiden name."

She shook her head. "Nope. But I might be a Bernard." A sudden flash of urgency tensed her body. Grabbing his arms, her eyes riveted his as she blurted, "The brooch, Heath. I need to send the brooch to New York."

Heath, now totally confused, shook his head as if to clear it. "What are you talking about, Liv? What does the brooch have to do with—"

"The brooch belonged to Samuel Bernard. It could have been, *must have been* a family heirloom of some kind." The words tumbled out so fast Heath had a hard time keeping up. He still didn't understand what some piece of jewelry had to do with all this.

"Why would you send it to New York, Liv? I thought you said Cynthia bought it down here somewhere. An estate sale, right?"

Liv was scrambling to her feet. "Yes. But there's hair under the glass, Heath."

He stared at her, baffled.

She scurried to the counter and grabbed her purse, digging through it wildly. It was in here, safe in its little bag . . . "

Frustrated, she dumped the contents onto the Corian. Her wallet, pens, a tin of breath mints, keys, and a few loose dollar bills tumbled out. A tube of lipstick rolled to the edge and clattered to the floor.

"It's not here," she squeaked. "Where is it? Where did I leave it?" Panic filled her eyes. Heath gripped her shoulders.

"Calm down, Liv, or you're going to pass out again," he soothed.

Then she froze, locking her eyes on his. "It's at the Belle Bride. I left it on my desk, in my office, at the Bride. We have to go get it. Now."

He tried to talk her out of it, but there was no reasoning with this woman once she set her mind on something. Fifteen minutes later they were both dressed and climbing into his truck as dusk draped itself over his dooryard. In the distance, Heath caught sight of a flash of lightning. Twenty seconds later, the rumble of thunder followed.

"Storm's rolling in, Liv. We've got to make this fast. It's only a few miles away." He shot her a glance. "Can't this wait until morning?"

She only shook her head vehemently and held up one finger. The phone was pressed to her ear again.

"Del, hair. Didn't you say you could test hair for DNA?"

Twenty-Seven

Liv

I was practically vibrating out of my skin on the short drive to the Belle Bride. I'd already pulled out the keys, and they were imprinting sweaty ridges on my palm. Heath shot me a look and said, "I don't think you'll need those. We left the door swinging on its hinges, remember?"

My belly turned over on itself. The house was unlocked. What if someone went inside? What if the brooch was gone?

The air whooshed out of me as Heath skidded up to the front steps. The heavy, oak door was closed, seemingly latched.

"Blew shut, probably," he muttered, scowling. A flash of lightning lit up the yard, making me jump.

"I'll only be a minute," I said as I slid out of the truck before Heath had even killed the engine. I heard his door slam behind me.

At the edge of my vision, before the sudden light faded, I caught a glimpse of movement. A large, dark form, moving clumsily off toward the woods. Ignoring the jolt of fear, along with the eerie sensation of being watched, I ran up the steps.

"You're not going in there alone, Olivia."

Secretly, I breathed a sigh of relief.

The doorknob turned easily. Closed, but not locked. Blown shut by the wind, as Heath had said. I stepped over the threshold and stopped, listening. The distant rumble of thunder was all I heard, then Heath's shoes hitting the hardwood behind me.

No crying women. No barking dog. No thundering hoof beats. Although I was fairly certain I now understood why those shadows of the past still permeated this house. Along with the sadness. The deep, heart-hollowing sadness. I headed up the stairs, Heath close on my heels.

When I reached the top of the stairs, my office door stood closed, as I had left it. I paused, my hand hovering over the knob. Heath reached my side and whispered, "Wait. Let me," before reaching down to open the door.

He hit the wall switch, and light flooded the room from the new ceiling fixture I'd had installed only days before leaving the house. We stood blinking for a moment, allowing our eyes to adjust. I scanned the room. There was no soldier.

Air whooshed out of my lungs in relief when I spotted it. There, on the corner of my desk blotter lay the velvet bag containing the hair work brooch. I surged forward and snatched it up, feeling frantically for its contents. The now-familiar, oval shape settled my tumbling heart. It still made my palm tingle, imparting a strange warmth when I held it.

This was my key, I thought. The key to unlock the mystery of my past.

Through the windows, I saw another flash of lightning light up the entire front yard. This time, the thunder followed only seconds behind it. Heath grabbed my arm, and I could feel he was trembling violently.

"Come on, Liv. We've got to go." Leaving the lights on, the door open, he hauled me to the head of the stairs and we barreled down them. As we raced down the porch steps, the first, fat drops of rain began to pelt us.

Heath yanked open his passenger door and was in the process of hoisting me in when the next lightning strike sparked in the air around us. Close. Too close. I screamed as the hair on my arms stood up, and I felt Heath's grip on me loosen and fall away.

The thunder was almost immediate, a huge boom that shook the truck, loud, deafening, painful to my ears. Then, darkness. Darker than before. For a moment, I was blind, deaf.

I screamed his name, but he wasn't there. The truck door stood open, and Heath was no longer beside me. With another flash of lightning, the sky opened up, but not before I saw him. Heath was sprawled on the ground beside the truck, his body twisted at an awkward angle, his limbs twitching violently. He was in the grip of another grand mal seizure.

"No, no, no, no, no," I wailed, sliding out onto the ground beside him. Lashing rain soaked me immediately to the skin, icy and unforgiving. It was soaking him too, and he lay on his back. I realized if I didn't protect his face, he might drown.

I bent over him, using my body to shield his face as the rain obliterated the world around me, all sound, all sight. My stomach twisted and turned each time another spasm overtook him, and I was glad I couldn't see his face. The helpless, whimpering noises escaping him as his chest heaved at a frantic pace under me tore at my heart. His hands flailed around us, stiff, twisted fingers tangling in my soaked hair.

Then, suddenly, the rain stopped, and a warm, heavy weight settled over us both. Panic rose in my throat but before I could scream, I heard a familiar voice against my right ear.

"I'll get you both inside, Miss Larson. You just wrap your arms around Mr. Barrow, and I'll carry you both outta this rain."

Benjamin. I heard the rustle of fabric, and then he had bundled us, Heath and I together, in some kind of huge tarp. He only grunted once as he lifted us, one clumsily wrapped package. And then, we were floating. The rain made a rattling, tapping sound as it bounced off whatever it was Ben had used to cover us.

Abruptly, the rain ceased, and I heard the door slam. Slowly, we drifted down until we settled onto hardwood. My foyer floor. The minute I felt his grip relax, I threw back the crackly covering and struggled free, a new kind of terror washing over me.

It must have been Benjamin I'd seen, the large, dark shape slipping into the woods beside the house. What was he doing creeping around my yard in the middle of the night?

It was pitch black, and I could hear his heavy footfalls yet could not see him. In the next moment, a light flared and he stood over us, monstrous, water streaming down off his long, dark hair. In one hand, he held a camping lantern. I threw an arm protectively over Heath.

His body was cool and still beneath me. He had stopped convulsing, but was unresponsive. I felt for his pulse, which was weak and rapid under icy skin.

My voice was tight, trembling as I sputtered, "Mr. Barrow is sick, Benjamin. He needs help. A doctor. Hospital. Don't hurt us, please."

A quizzical look came over Ben's face. "I would never hurt you, Miss Larson. You nor Mr. Barrow." He stepped closer, studying Heath's face impassively. "Is he sleeping, Miss Larson?"

"No, not sleeping, Benjamin. Heath is unconscious. We need to get him to the hospital. My phone . . . " I reached into the back pocket of my jeans where I'd slid my phone after my call to Del on the way over. Even before I hit the button, I knew the screen would remain black. The phone was as drenched as I was.

I choked on a sob. Running my hands down Heath's body, I did not feel his phone on him anywhere.

"Aw, don't cry, Miss Larson. We'll get Mr. Barrow to the hospital. I'll go get Pa. He'll drive him." He turned toward the door, the lantern swinging wildly, casting crazy shadows over the walls and floor.

"Benjamin, no. There's no time for that. Heath . . . Mr. Barrow has a cell phone. Like this one." I held up mine. "It's in his truck, Ben. Can you get it?"

The big man lowered the lantern carefully to the floor, then turned toward the door. "Don't let it get wet," I called after him as he slung it open and disappeared into the darkness.

I sat cross-legged on the floor beside Heath's prone body, shivering and crying quietly while we waited for the ambulance to arrive. With Ben's help, we had wrapped his gigantic rain cloak—the "tarp" he'd used to carry us inside—in an attempt to keep Heath's body temperature stable. Almost twenty minutes had elapsed since Heath's seizure ended and he'd gone deathly still.

Benjamin stood awkwardly near the front window, watching for flashing lights.

"Ben? Why were you here? In the woods by my house again?" I asked gently.

He turned to look at me, embarrassment causing color to rise in his pallid cheeks. "I come here at night a lots o'times, Miss Larson. I like to watch the dog and the horse play."

So, he can see them too, I thought.

"What about the soldier, Ben? Do ever see the soldier? The man wearing a uniform and carrying a long gun."

He nodded. "He comes here a lot," Ben said. "He don't talk to me, though. Just bangs on the door and then goes away. I followed him once. I know where he goes."

Heath

When Heath opened his eyes, he was lying in a strange, hard bed, propped up by pillows. Dim light filtered in through a wall of glass nearby, and a strange beeping sound punctuated the silence. He struggled to sit up, then stilled when a jab of sharp pain shot up his right arm. Glancing down, he saw the IV needle taped to his hand.

He was in the hospital. Shit and damn. What had happened to him *this* time?

Immediately, he heard Liv's voice beside him. "Lie back, Heath. You're going to be okay. You had another seizure. A bad one . . . the lightning." She was bending over him, her hair a tangled mass of spun gold around her face. He felt her fingers stroke his cheek. "I thought I was going to lose you, too. Dammit, Heath. I'm not letting go of you." She intertwined her fingers with those of his free hand. "Not letting you go. Ever."

Twenty-Eight

Liv

Over the next few days, when I wasn't in the hospital visiting Heath, I kept busy. They wanted to keep him for tests to be sure it was only the epilepsy, and nothing more serious, that had taken him down yet again. Against his protests, I had insisted he stay.

"I have to know, Heath. We *both* have to know, for sure." I'd kissed him, long and soft and sweet. "Whatever the outcome, I'll be here for you. For us. This isn't my first rodeo."

The morning after that terrifying night, I packaged the brooch, insured it to the hilt, and sent it off on the FedEx truck, New York bound. Del had assured me she had an excellent jeweler who could disassemble the piece, extract a few hairs, and put it back together.

"It will be good as new," she said. "I promise you, Liv. You won't be able to tell it's ever been messed with."

In a few days, I would know for sure.

Later that afternoon, after a quick trip to and through Birmingham, I drove to the Warren's cottage bearing a huge basket filled with every kind of edible treat imaginable. I had no idea what might make Benjamin happier than having more tasty treats to eat.

"I know these won't be as good as your momma's baking," I said when Ben opened the front door, "but I did visit the three best bakeries in Birmingham."

I sat on the Warren's back porch as Bitsy fluttered

around me, frantic she couldn't do anything more to help.

"Mr. Barrow, he's been so good to us. And to Ben. I'm so glad . . . so glad he could help you last night," she choked out, her eyes filling.

"I as well, Bitsy," I said, taking both of her hands and squeezing them. "And yes, I will take just a wee bit of your special lemonade. I think I earned it last night." I winked at her, and she grinned and whisked into the kitchen.

Ben stood in his baggy overalls, shirtless and barefoot, watching me from a corner of the screened patio. Not *watching* me, I thought, scolding myself. Watching *over* me. I would always think of Benjamin this way, and never feel threatened by him again.

I sipped the spiked lemonade and, wincing, swallowed after toasting Benjamin's heroics with Bitsy.

"Ben, you said you knew where the soldier goes," I said. "Will you show me?"

Heath

Three days after that horrific night, Heath was released from the hospital. No brain tumor. Nothing else wrong with him except the epilepsy. Liv had thrown her arms around his doctor, Carl Worthington, and kissed him full on the mouth when he'd delivered the news.

Heath worried for a moment or two that the shock of the encounter would send Dr. Worthington into heart failure. One thing for sure: he hadn't seen quite as much color in the old man's cheeks since the night he'd come around to introduce himself as Heath's attending physician.

"If you're feeling up to it," Liv said as she climbed behind the wheel of her truck, "I'd like to make a couple of stops on the way home."

Heath raised his eyebrows. "Where?"

"Del called me this morning with the test results. My DNA was an eight-five percent match to the hair in the brooch. Samuel Bernard's brooch. I know his estate went to auction on the assumption there were no heirs. Florence said he had no other kin. I think there's more to the story. There has to be."

Heath stared at her, his mouth agape.

"So, you're . . . a Bernard, then. But, you were born in Boston. How?" he asked.

"That's what I'm hoping Florence Edington can explain."

The found her in her usual spot, at her desk, readers perched halfway down her nose. She looked up and narrowed her eyes when they came through the door. Ruthie, cute as a bug in her librarian's apron, turned from where she was re-shelving books, smiling shyly and waggling her fingers in greeting.

Liv marched straight up to Florence's desk, her chin held high.

"I know you told me Samuel Bernard shared some personal business with you, Florence. And that you promised to keep it private. Mr. Bernard is gone. And now, there's this." Liv slid a piece of paper across the desk. Florence squinted down at it.

The older woman shook her head, a scowl twisting her features as she shoved it back at Liv. "This doesn't mean anything to me, Ms. Larson," she snapped.

"What it means," Liv began in an even, firm tone, "is my DNA is an almost perfect match with the hair inside the brooch I showed you. The one that belonged to Samuel Bernard. One you had already seen."

Florence's eyes rounded and she snatched the paper back up, holding it inches from her nose. "That's impossible," she mumbled.

"No, it's not. My ancestry panel also shows I have familial roots here in the South. One of the surnames on my profile is Bernard." Liv paused until Florence lifted her gaze. "I need to know how, Florence. How might I be related to Samuel Bernard?"

Liv

My mother had been Samuel Bernard's granddaughter, Florence finally revealed. He'd been named to raise her after the death of his daughter, along with her husband, in a fatal crash out on Highway 13. Skye, his granddaughter, was only thirteen years old at the time.

"He said she was a rather difficult child," Florence said, wincing. "Samuel wasn't really equipped to deal with a strong-willed teenage girl. She defied him at every turn. By the time she turned fifteen, she was completely out of control. When she came home pregnant, Samuel had had his fill. He sent her to a reform school in Boston. It's where she gave birth . . . " she paused, awkwardly, sliding her gaze away. "Well, I guess you know the rest."

"He owned the Belle Bride at the time," I said. "And he sold it . . . or deeded it—"

Florence cleared her throat and folded her hands in front of her. "Skye was supposed to inherit the Bride. As well as the brooch. They'd both been in the family for almost a hundred and fifty years. The day the baby . . . *you* were born, and Samuel found out Skye wanted nothing to do with the child . . . *you*, well, he took himself down to the bank and handed over the deed. Said he didn't care what happened to the Belle Bride, as long as it never went to his granddaughter."

I stood there, in shock, feeling as this was all a dream. Not a nightmare, but certainly not reality. Too many coincidences. Too much serendipity.

I swayed a little, and Heath wrapped his arm around my shoulders, pulling me to him. "What happened to Skye, Florence?"

I spun away from him and threw up my hands. "I told you, Heath. I don't want to know. I don't care what happened to a woman who never even wanted to hold her own child." The tears came, and I cursed them, along with the pain inside my heart.

Florence continued in a calm, even tone. "Nobody knows. She slipped away from her guardians before they got her back to the reform school. Neither Samuel, nor anyone I know of, here in Camellia at least, ever saw or heard from her again."

We met Benjamin in front of the Belle Bride an hour later. He'd told me, in his own simple language, that he'd followed the soldier—who I knew now to be the ghost of Daniel Ruffin—more than once.

"He always goes back to the same spot," Benjamin said as he led us across the road and into a small field beyond. "Don't know who owns this land. It ain't never been fenced as I know of. All of this," he paused and swung his arms around him, "All this land was a big fancy farm at one time. That's what Momma told me."

The Belle Bienvenue, I thought. One big, fancy farm. A plantation.

Just a dozen or so feet from the road, near a patch of live oaks bordering the open field, was a jumble of rocks I assumed had been a stone fence at one time. Instead of forming a straight line, though, the stones were grouped together. They seemed to embrace a small square.

"This is where he's buried," I said, my throat thickening with emotion. "Bitsy said the Union soldiers tore up the marker. I'll bet you anything, this is where the body of Daniel Ruffin lies."

The warm breeze rustled the branches over our heads, twirling the Spanish moss into pinwheels. Benjamin hooked his thumbs into the straps of his overalls and kicked at one of the rocks edging the plot.

"He always comes back here. Right here, to this spot. Then he just disappears."

We stood there in an awkward silence until Heath asked, "Where is the rest of the family buried, Ben? Do you know?"

Benjamin nodded. "Sure do. There's a small graveyard, right on my momma and daddy's land. They say we don't really own it, but it's there, just the same."

"Can you show us, Ben?" I asked.

The Bernard family plot lay smack dab in the middle of the pasture where the Warrens' mare, Julia, grazed. Because of the way the land dipped, it was impossible to see from either their house or the Belle Bride. It wasn't much to see anyway. An iron fence, bent and rusted through in several places, encircled a small rectangle bearing three, tilted headstones.

"Oh, my God," I breathed as I stepped over the low rail and dropped to my knees before the stones. The names and the dates echoed those on the biographical note in the plantation records Florence had gotten for me. Only here, the dates of Emma's short life were recorded.

Olivia Kirkland Bernard (1828-1887)

Adam Bernard (1825-1886)

Emma Bernard Ruffin (1842-1869)

That night, I paced back and forth in Heath's kitchen, from the cooktop to the end of the island and back. It seemed to be becoming a habit with me.

"So, why does Daniel Ruffin continue in the same, repetitive pattern he has for the past hundred-odd years? Why doesn't he move on? To the place where Emma is? Where his horse and dog are?" I asked.

Of course, I wasn't really asking Heath. I was thinking

aloud. He sat there, watching me with a perplexed expression. He still hadn't completely accepted the fact that these were ghosts we were talking about. Unsettled spirits. He shook his head and scrubbed his hands down his face.

"Damned if I know, Liv. I don't believe in all of this stuff. At least, I never did before." He blew out a breath and levelled his gaze on me. His eyes grew misty. "Of course, I never believed in miracles either. Until you strolled in to my shop."

I paused in my pacing to wrap my arms around his neck and kiss him deeply. His mouth held the tang of the wine we'd shared with dinner. Before we got too carried away, I pushed back and continued in the track I was wearing in his tile.

"Daniel died in battle during the Civil War. He may have died—most certainly *did* die—suddenly. I've done some research. About spirits that don't move on. It's possible he doesn't know he's dead."

Heath raised his eyebrows. "Okay," he said slowly. "So his bride is buried less than a quarter mile away from where he lays. And her spirit, or something, still cries for him. Inside the Belle Bride." He shook his head. "Why can't they find each other?"

I stopped pacing. Good question, I thought. I wondered if there was something I could do about that.

A week later, the package arrived, FedEx, containing the hair work brooch. Del had been right. The jeweler did an outstanding job. There was no way I could tell the piece had been disassembled and resealed. Only one hair was needed. It was still as perfect as the day Cynthia dropped it into my palm.

Heath

He told her she was out of her mind. But once the woman put her mind to something, well . . .

Liv said she was spending the night at the Belle Bride, and she gave Heath the choice: join her, or not. More than just wanting to reclaim her home, which we both now knew really *was* her home—her family home—she also wanted to try to rejoin the restless spirit of Daniel Ruffin with his bride.

Heath thought she was crazy. Still, he loved her. And so, he packed an overnight bag and carried it, along with hers, to his truck as darkness draped the sky.

"Are we sitting up all night in the foyer to wait for him?" he asked, a little facetiously. "If so, I'll grab my camping gear. I've got a double-sized sleeping bag. The hardwood is . . . well, hard."

She rounded on him. "Don't be a smartass, Heath Barrow. We go to the Bride. We climb the stairs to my bedroom, and curl up together in my Rice bed. If he doesn't come tonight, then maybe tomorrow night, he will."

Heath rolled his eyes and wondered. How many nights before the mysterious night visitor would return? Would he ever? He didn't have too long a wait.

He was spooned behind Liv, his face buried in her hair, when the pounding on the door commenced. Sure, he'd made a joke about it earlier. Yet he couldn't deny the trickle of steely fear that raced up his spine. He felt Liv start to stir.

The bedside clock said two a.m. At least he was a punctual ghost. Two a.m. seemed to be his witching hour.

Liv bolted upright and pulled on a pair of shorts under her tee shirt. Then she grabbed the velvet bag from off her nightstand and headed for the hall.

"Wait," Heath barked, struggling to pull on a pair of

sweat pants. "Don't go down there alone, Liv."

"He won't hurt me, Heath. He can't," she said, her voice rock steady and sure. "Besides, I'm a descendant of his bride's. We're . . . family."

He trotted down the steps after her, stopping on the last riser as she swung the door open. Heath felt the hair stand up on his nape. Standing there, not two feet away from Liv, *his* Liv, was a uniformed, armed, Confederate soldier. Heath took a step forward, instinct screaming to drag her inside and slam the door.

There was no light on in the foyer. There was no need for one. The soldier glowed like a giant, bearded firefly.

"Daniel," Liv said warmly. "You've come home."

The soldier staggered back a step, then blinked and rubbed his eyes.

Emma . . . is it you, Emma?

Heath heard the words, but not with his ears. They resounded inside his head. Another chill slithered up his spine.

Liv was shaking her head. "No, Daniel. I'm not your Emma. I can show you where she is, though." She lifted the velvet bag, opened it, and the hair work brooch tumbled out into her palm. "Here, Daniel. Here's proof I know. I know where Emma waits for you." She held out her hand.

Chapter Twenty-Nine

Liv

The fear was gone. All I felt now was the sadness, the incredible mourning hanging over this house, and tormenting the poor soul standing before me. I wasn't sure if I could get through to him. I'd spoken to him before, and at times, he seemed to hear me.

His form seemed more solid tonight than I'd ever seen it. If I hadn't seen him before, in his more translucent state, I might have assumed he really was a nutcase who like to dress up like a Confederate Soldier. But I had, and I knew more about the history of the Belle Bride now. I knew who this man was—had been—and wanted, more than anything, to free him from his earthly prison.

Daniel stared at the brooch in my hand for a long moment before reaching forward to touch it. Every fiber of my being screamed out to pull away, back off, slam the door. The pin lay warm in the center of my palm, sending its tingling comfort down into my fingers, up into my arm. There was a prickling sensation all over my body now, as if the air around the specter before me emanated some sort of energy.

Of course it did. Life is energy. Energy cannot be created or destroyed, only transformed. Although his body no longer lived and breathed in our dimension, the spirit of Daniel Ruffin still existed. As energy. Restless, untethered energy.

I could relate to that particular state of being. Sort of.

The soldier shifted his musket up onto his shoulder, then reached out toward the brooch. Just before his glowing hand made contact, I heard Heath from behind me shout, "No, Liv. Stop." But it was too late.

Touched by a ghost? I never thought it was possible. Never imagined what it might feel like. Cinematographers did a pretty good job in the final scenes of the 1990 romantic thriller, *Ghost*. Paranormal investigators claim to sense the touch of spirits all the time. I always wondered, though—what does it *feel* like, really?

That night, I found out.

No blast of cold air. No icy needles dancing along the skin. When the spirit of Daniel Ruffin's hand covered the brooch, my hand, my entire body flooded with warmth and emotion. My own consciousness faded away as a kind of movie screen opened up in my mind. I saw, through his eyes, the beautiful face of his bride, Emma Bernard. Adoration shone in her laughing eyes. Her heart—*my heart*—filled suddenly to bursting with an impossible kind of love. A once-in-a-lifetime kind of love.

I squeezed my unseeing eyes shut and concentrated, very hard, on my walk the day before to the Bernard burial plot. I imagined ducking through the fence boards, with Heath helping me through. Following the lumbering steps of Benjamin across a grassy, sunny field. Catching sight of the iron fence, the headstones nearly hidden by tall grass, tucked into the hollow in the pasture. In my mind, the soldier strode beside us.

A sound burst from him, a combination of elation and grief, as he ran ahead to the iron railing, *through* it, and dropped to his knees before the stone of Emma Bernard Ruffin. He covered his face with his hands and wept, the echoes of that torment overtaking every cell of my being.

Why, Emma? Why didn't they bury us together?

A good question, I remembered thinking. It was the last

thought drifting through my hazy consciousness before the world went black.

Heath

Never one to partake of recreational drugs, nothing other than his epilepsy meds, Heath now felt he knew what it might be like to "trip out" on hallucinogens. Standing there in Liv's foyer, he witnessed a scene so unbelievable, so terrifying, he was actually grateful it hadn't triggered another of his seizures. It wasn't a pleasurable experience.

Terror consumed him as he watched Liv confront this . . . vision, this specter of a man who, she believed, lived and died over a century and a half ago. He couldn't believe her courage, or idiocy, to stand there and speak to what appeared to Heath as a wavering, translucent form glowing so bright it almost hurt his eyes. He wanted to look away, yet could not. Every fiber of his being compelled him to protect her, yank her back, drag her away from this place. A house stained with the horrors of the past.

Yet he knew, somehow, Liv saw something more than the grief and the pain infecting these walls. She saw what had existed before the ravages of war had destroyed a young couple's lives. Liv looked through the horror and saw . . . the love.

Heath watched as she stretched out her hand, offering the hair work brooch to a man . . . the ghost of a man . . . containing a remnant from his time on this earth. A miniature frame preserving a lock of his dark hair, lovingly intertwined with the pale blonde they now knew belonged to an ancestor of Liv herself.

She stood tall and brave, although Heath could see her hand shaking violently just before the glowing fingers of Daniel Ruffin touched hers. At the instant of contact, the sudden flash of light engulfing them both blinded him.

For a panicked second, Heath feared Liv would just disappear. That the past would reclaim her. That this desperate, grieving soldier would steal his Liv away from him.

Sweep her away from this world, this dimension, and beyond his reach.

In the next second, the light died, and the doorway stood empty. Time froze as did Heath's heart in his chest. He was oddly relieved to hear Liv's limp body hit the floor.

Liv

Two weeks later, the date I'd set for my housewarming party had arrived. With Heath's help, I finally had the place furnished to some semblance of cozy. Yet with its soaring ceilings and massive rooms, there was no downplaying the Belle Bride's elegance.

My new dining room suite filled the space perfectly, a gleaming, dark wood table with lovely, ivory linen upholstered chairs. After covering the plaster walls with creamy, textured paper, I'd decided on a curved front, Chippendale breakfront to line one long wall. I found it buried in a corner of Heath's Birmingham warehouse, where it had been hiding for years, he told me. Waiting for me. I fell in love with it the minute I saw it.

On the opposite wall, tall windows looked out onto the back yard. I chose a traditional sideboard to line their lower casings. Floor-length, gold brocade draperies framed the view. Cynthia had helped me choose the ornately painted French Rouen vase as a centerpiece for the sideboard. The colors and pattern on its surface coordinated beautifully with the Oriental rug on the floor.

Above it all, a glittering, crystal chandelier hovered, scattering sparks of light over the entire room. Anchored within a sculpted medallion, it matched the one I'd had hung in the foyer almost exactly.

The guest list was small but included all of the people who had come to mean the most to me over the past months. Cynthia, of course, with her life partner, Sarah were there, along with the Edingtons: Florence, Clyde, and Ruthie. Del was supposed to have flown in. Unfortunately, she got tangled up in a paternity case at the last minute. She sent the bouquet of gorgeous, white roses that dressed the Rouen vase perfectly.

Last to arrive were the Warrens. I was impressed to see how well Benjamin cleaned up when I opened my door to find him decked out in a navy sport jacket over clean, pressed jeans.

He flashed me a shy smile as he lifted my hand and kissed it gallantly, and quick tears sprang to my eyes. How I'd misjudged this big, lovable oaf. The events of the last month had taught me a lesson about judging a book by its cover.

I could barely see Bitsy behind a gigantic gift box she clutched before her. It was half-again as tall she was, wrapped in silver paper with an icy blue bow. Grinning, she trundled over to the sideboard, where she placed it carefully, murmuring, "This will go perfect, right here."

Heath and I did most of the cooking. By eight o'clock, the spread of elegant finger foods we'd prepared had all but been consumed, along with several bottles of champagne. We'd flung open the doors and windows to allow the cooler, evening air to blow through the house.

After we toasted my new home and stuffed ourselves with everything from fried green tomato sliders to shrimp boil skewers, I opened the gifts my new friends had so generously brought. Cynthia and Sarah brought me a lovely teapot and warmer, and the Edingtons proudly presented me with a lovely set of embroidered towels.

I left the giant box Bitsy had carried in for last. She helped me unwrap it. She narrowed her eyes at Heath.

"Now told you spoil the surprise and tell her what's in here, Mr. Barrow." Then to me, she added, "It came from his shop. The minute I saw it, I knew it was the perfect thing."

And it was. Bitsy was helping me arrange the milk ware set on the sideboard when I cast a glance out toward their pasture through the window.

"Bitsy, why is it that the Bernards had a separate burial plot for themselves and their daughter?" I wondered. "I mean, Emma's husband is buried in what's now an unmarked grave across the road. We've contacted the historical society, by the way. Daniel Ruffin will be getting a brand-new, marble headstone in a few weeks."

Bitsy looked thoughtful for a moment before offering her answer. "I guess, after them Yankees plundered Daniel's grave, they just didn't feel safe burying Emma out there next to him. So near the road and in plain sight." She gazed out into the fading light toward the burial plot in the center of what was now her pasture and sighed. "The spot they picked, well, you can't really see it unless you cross the field. They owned all this land anyway. They could choose to bury their dead anywhere they pleased."

Still sad, I thought. I could well imagine, once their beloved only daughter passed, how it would just be too painful to dig up her husband and move him to lie next to her. Who would think the small separation of graves could hold the lovers apart?

Different dimensions, I supposed. Just a small level of separation. Like the mysterious veil between the living and the dead.

By ten, we'd said goodnight to the last guest to leave— the Warrens—promising to come by and visit with them again real soon.

When the door clicked shut, Heath wrapped me in his arms and sighed. "Beautiful party, Liv. And not a specter in sight. I guess your theory about reuniting Daniel and Emma hit the mark." He kissed the top of my head. "I just thank God he didn't decide to take you with him."

I tucked my head beneath his chin and hummed. "He's got his own love to go home to. I have mine." I lifted up on tiptoes to steal a deep, passionate kiss. Then I sought his eyes. "I love you, Heath. I never knew what it was like to love another person . . . not like this. Now, I know you are a part of me. We're part of each other. And yes, just like you've been saying all along: We were meant to be."

His hands slid down my back to squeeze my bottom playfully. "I'd like to go upstairs and practice that *part of each other* thing. Right now." He waggled his eyebrows, and I laughed.

"Let's just clear the dining table first. We can tackle the rest of the clean-up in the morning."

We gathered the last of the platters and cups, and Heath had just folded the tablecloth to send out for cleaning. I spun the dimmer switch and watched as the brilliant light spraying from the chandelier ebbed and died.

Then I blinked. The room was still washed with light, yet it was coming from outside. A full moon? I stepped to the window and gazed up into the starry sky. A perfect slice of half-moon was just sliding behind a passing cloud.

Movement on the ground caught my eye. My heart seized, and in a frantic whisper, I called for Heath. He joined me at the window as we watched a scene out of a dream.

A regal, white stallion was prancing about, defying the attempts of its handler to calm it. A woman in a long, white gown was standing by, apparently waiting to mount. Her golden hair was wound atop her head in an elaborate, Victorian style.

The horse's handler was Daniel Ruffin, my Confederate soldier.

Behind me, Heath wrapped his arms around my waist and whispered against my ear, "He was right. She looks just like you. Or you, her."

I brought my hand to my mouth. After the night I'd shown Daniel where Emma was buried, I didn't think I'd ever see them again. The dog, nor the horse had reappeared since. Emma's pitiful sobs no longer oozed from the plaster walls. The bitter miasma of grief and loss no longer fouled the air in my halls. Peace had settled over the Belle Bride.

We watched in silence as, in one graceful sweep, Daniel grasped his bride about her tiny waist and whirled her aboard the steed, who quieted immediately. Emma's trailing skirts left a glowing streak in the dark, like the tail of a comet. The soldier reached up to kiss her hand.

Then he turned toward the barn and whistled. A white walker hound raced from around the corner to dance about their feet, leaving a luminous trail in his wake. Slowly, with the soldier leading his lady on horseback, they headed south, passing clear through the paddock fence and into the bordering woods. Gradually, they faded out of sight.

I hadn't realized I was crying until Heath turned me to face him, brushing the tears off my cheeks with his thumbs. He cupped my face.

"Are you sad to see them go?" he asked, his loving gaze wandering over my face with tenderness and concern.

I shook my head. "No. It's beautiful, that's all. And to think—in my search to find out who I was, I helped bring two, other lost souls together again."

Chapter Thirty

Six months later

Heath

They'd fallen into a comfortable routine, he and Liv. They rose every morning early, early enough to enjoy their first cup of coffee—*hot* coffee—on the gallery outside Liv's bedroom. While she showered, Heath checked his email for online orders, then called in to the Birmingham warehouse to make arrangements for shipping or deliveries.

Once it was his turn in the shower, he settled for a quick one. There was seldom much hot water left after Liv got through.

The only thing Heath Barrow disliked more than cold coffee was a cold shower. They had to do something about that, he thought. It was fine now, during the summer months. But in winter . . . they definitely needed a bigger water heater. He made a note to call Jeremy down at the HVAC shop in town.

It had become Heath's job to fix them a light breakfast, usually pastries or toast. Once in a while, Liv got a baking bug and whipped up one of Florence's special sour cream coffee cakes. Lately, she'd been going off to bed early. By days' end, she'd had little energy to bake.

On their way to the shop, they drove out to the cafe near the highway to grab Liv her favorite morning treat: iced latte —decaf in recent months. They opened the shop at ten, and Liv scurried off to her private corner, now shielded from public view by a beautiful old, teak screen. It's where she ran her web design business nowadays. Heath put in furniture orders, scouted out the next upcoming antiques auction, and fielded the few customers the shop drew in from tourist traffic.

One day, just before noontime, Liv wandered out from her lair and started dropping not-so-subtle hints.

"What time are we breaking for lunch today, Mr. Barrow?"

Heath quirked a half-smile and shot a glance at the grandfather clock. "Why? Is she getting hungry?"

Liv ran a hand over a decidedly growing baby bump and nodded. "And is kicking the tar out of me this morning."

They were just preparing for their stroll up the street to Nan's diner when the front door opened, and a classy looking blonde stepped inside. She was mid-fifties, Heath figured, or maybe a little older, judging by the lines around her mouth. She'd either done a lot of laughing, or a lot of scowling, during her lifetime. Blonde and tall and slender of build, the slick leather biker chaps molded snugly around her lithe form.

Heath didn't know many bikers. Yet something about this woman looked familiar.

Liv huffed out an impatient breath and settled on the cushioned stool Heath had placed for her behind the counter. The woman, though, obviously didn't have any intention to waste time browsing. She headed directly for the reception desk and plunked her Coach purse on its glass top.

"What can I help you with today, Ma'am?" Heath asked, then cringed when the scowl lines on her face deepened. He never did quite know what the dividing line was: when to call them Miss, and when to call them Ma'am. This time he'd obviously gotten it wrong.

"I'm not interested in antiques," the woman said, her nose wrinkling slightly as she gazed about the space. "What I'm looking for is information."

Heath studied her. Something about her looked . . . familiar.

"What kind of information? Are you lost? You know, Highway 13 isn't far from the end of Main Street, right down that way." He pointed west.

"I'm not lost," she shot back. "I was born here. Raised in Camellia. What I want to know is who bought the old plantation house on the other end of town. The Belle Bride. The lady at the museum says you might be able to tell me."

Liv started at the mention of their home's name, then slid a glance toward Heath and settled back. Best to let him field this line of questioning. Probably just a tourist wanting to know about hauntings and local legends—"

"It was supposed to be mine, you know," the woman snapped, stabbing at her chest with an elegantly manicured finger. "My crotchety old grandfather gave it away before I was old enough to claim it."

Heath felt the blood in his veins turn to ice. He stole a quick glance at Liv, who'd gone ghostly pale. He moved closer to her and squeezed her shoulders.

This was Liv's mother.

Heath said, "I'm sure the county office could provide you with that information, Miss . . . "

Liv slid clumsily off the stool to her feet, gripping the counter for balance. Heath *so* didn't want this confrontation. Not now. He didn't want anything to upset Liv in her current, delicate state. Still, he knew better than to intervene. Once the woman set her mind on something . . .

Squaring her shoulders, Liv blurted, "I own the Bride. I bought it almost a year ago. And I love the place. It's the home of my dreams."

The woman blinked, obviously surprised. Scanning her

up and down, she snapped, "You don't sound like a Southerner. You from around here?" There was an indignant snark in her tone.

Liv took a deep breath, then leaned into Heath and smiled up at him. "Yes. I am. My family goes way back in these parts."

"Really." The woman lifted her chin and studied Liv through narrowed eyes. "So, you intend to keep the Belle Bride?"

"Yes. Absolutely," Liv countered. She snugged her arm around Heath's waist. "My husband and I intend to raise our daughter there."

Disappointment clouded the woman's features. Or was it disapproval? Something in her expression changed, and she seemed to visibly deflate. "Well, then. I guess there's no chance I'm ever going to reclaim my rightful inheritance," she grumbled, sliding her designer purse off the counter.

Heath's eyes narrowed. "Why would you think you could? The Belle Bride was deeded over to the bank in 1980. There were no heirs listed on the owner's will. We did a title search—"

"Yeah, well . . . " The woman looked away, wistful sadness darkening her features. "I just hoped maybe I could regain some of what I lost."

After a long, tense pause, Heath asked, "Is that all you lost? The Belle Bride?"

A flash of some emotion Heath couldn't name passed quickly over the woman's face. Blinking, she slid her gaze away, tossing her shoulder-length, heavily streaked blonde hair. "The only thing I could ever reclaim," she murmured, more to herself than anyone else.

At that moment, the shop door swung open and a stocky man wearing full leather biker gear sauntered into the shop.

His hair hung around a weathered face in tawny dreadlocks, and his faded tee shirt read, "Live Free or Die."

He eyed the woman and crossed his arms. "You done here, Skye?"

She slung her bag over one slender shoulder. "I'm done here, Butch. I was just coming out."

After they left, Liv stared after them as if in a trance. Heath waited until the door latched shut, then drew her into his arms.

"I'm sorry, baby. I'm so sorry," he crooned into her hair.

"Why?" Liv drew back and leveled her gaze on his. "I'm not. She's exactly as I imagined her. A strong, free spirit."

Heath studied her, running a finger along her jaw. "I guess you were right not to try to find her."

"I know I was. I realize now I'm truly grateful to her. Skye had the right to decide whether or not to give me life." She pressed a hand to her belly. "Just as I did with our daughter. In the end, Skye did what was best for both of us. My problem was my perception. I've gone through life labeling myself a mistake."

Heath drew back and cupped her face in his hands. "A mistake for Skye, maybe. To your adoptive family, you were a gift from heaven." He kissed her, soft and slow, reveling in the wonder of their love. His misty, chocolate eyes locked on hers. "For me, you are, and always will be, my miracle."

*****

About The Author

Claire Gem

Claire Gem writes contemporary romance & supernatural suspense. You can find all of her books listed on her website: www.thegemwriter.com.